He
Watches
All My Paths

A Novel

Stacey G. C. Jernigan

Copyright © 2019 by Stacey G.C. Jernigan

ISBN: 978-1-79406-707-3

In memory of

all the judges, attorneys, United States Marshals, and law enforcement officers generally who have lost their lives for simply doing their jobs—being guardians of the American justice system and the Rule of Law.

And, of course, for my dear family.

AUTHOR'S NOTE

Because I am a sitting United States judge, and I am also married to a police officer, I feel compelled, at the outset, to clarify certain points regarding this novel.

First, the following is a work of fiction. Some of the characters and events herein are based loosely on actual persons and events, and some of the places (in my home state of Texas and in various other faraway spots) are certainly very real. Moreover, in my capacity as a judge, I have been the recipient of death threats that ultimately required United States Marshal Service protection, like the main character in this novel. But, the human characters in this novel are absolutely fictional. Judge Avery Lassiter, the main character in this novel, is not me and my own situation with threats did not transpire in the same manner as hers.

Second, one should not assume that any statement or opinion expressed or implied by any characters in this novel are necessarily mine or are somehow a reflection on how I might rule on any particular issue in any case in the future.

Third—and perhaps most importantly—the references herein to certain federal judges, public officials, and lawyers (and families) who have been assassinated in this country in the past are, sadly, true—as are certain facts presented regarding the United States Marshals Service. As mentioned earlier, these honorable souls are among those to whom this novel is dedicated.

The author, Stacey G. C. Jernigan, has served as a federal bankruptcy judge, since the year 2006, in Dallas, Texas. Before that, she practiced law many years at a large international law firm, Haynes and Boone, LLP, based in Texas. She is married to a police officer and has a son and a daughter who are both young adults now. She writes and travels extensively in her spare time.

He Watches All My Paths

Prologue: On a Park Bench in Dallas, Texas.

Part I: Meet the Lassiter Family and Their New Guests.

Part II: The Escalation of the Death Threats.

Part III: Six Months and Counting.

Part IV: "Shit Just Turned Real"

Epilogue: He Watches All My Paths—Avery's Post-Note: A Tribute to the U.S. Marshals and Law Enforcement Everywhere.

"Justice, sir, is the greatest interest of man on Earth. It is the ligament which holds civilized beings and civilized nations together."

Daniel Webster

He Watches All My Paths[1]

By Stacey G. C. Jernigan

Prologue

His life had been one of infinite disappointment, largely because of his experiences with the American justice system. Justice for all? What justice? There was no justice. He needed relief. He needed retribution. For 20 years now, there had been no intermission from his pain. He had heard it said once that in our U.S. system of laws, we had a standard of "measure" and knew what to trust: The Rule of Law. Not so. It was time for him to execute his own judgments on those whose actions he could no longer abide.

It was a sunny Saturday afternoon in late November. The Belo Gardens park, situated across the street from the tall, marble Earle Cabell Federal Building in downtown Dallas, Texas, was stirring with its usual activity. Millennials zipping about on scooters. Empty nesters strolling with their dogs. A few homeless campers, gathering up their belongings before the beat officers made their rounds. Oblivious to all of this was a pensive, young man—dressed in a gray hoody, khaki pants, a Texas Rangers baseball cap, and trench boots—

---

[1] Job 33:11.

sitting on a park bench with a Swiss Gear backpack propped up next to him. He was a skinny, pasty white man, wearing stylish aviator reflective sunglasses. The eyewear did nothing to disguise his awkward demeanor or improve upon his plain looks. He was the kind of man who tended to be invisible in a crowd. Generally alienated from humanity. That could be advantageous on occasion, even if it did not lead to much success in the romance department. He was not a man who felt very comfortable in his skin. Always anxious. Frequently sick with one ailment or another. Quietly angry at the world. He had not had an easy life. Very few people knew his story. He thought it was for the best that people not know his story.

The man sat hunched with sloping shoulders in the mid-day sun, with his arms folded, occasionally gnawing on his fingertips and fiddling with his ear buds, watching a group of children who were laughing and playing in the nearby fountains in the park. He observed that the children's parents largely ignored them, and it rather annoyed him. Actually, everything annoyed him. A sign posted near the fountains warned: "Do not discard diapers or urinate in the fountains." People can be so pathetic, he thought to himself. Obviously, there was a reason that the City of Dallas had placed that sign there. The man glanced over towards Murphy's Crosswalk directly in front of the imposing federal building. He seemed to recall hearing that a Dallas Police Officer had been shot and killed there while patrolling in the early 1980's. The man wondered if that fallen officer had been the type of testosterone-fueled hot head that he thought most cops were. He despised cops. He noticed a pair of light blue Converse high top sneakers with red shoe laces draped over the traffic light above Murphy's Crosswalk. The man knew that this was a gang sign that meant drug deals were regularly conducted there by the "Bloods" street gang, and it was also a warning to other gangs that they should stay away from the Bloods' turf. The gang bangers were amazingly brazen, the man thought with a snicker—selling weed, crack and even heroine, right in front of the building that housed federal judges, the FBI, and U.S. Marshals, among other agencies devoted to law and order. He wasn't sure who disgusted him more: the drug dealing gang bangers or the neglectful parents of the brats splashing and squealing in the fountains in front of him right now. Actually, he knew of certain people who bothered him more than either the giggling children and their parents or the thug drug dealers: the lawyers and judges in the corrupt legal system that regularly streamed in and out of the Earle Cabell Federal Building—and in and out of every courthouse in America, for that matter. He hated them worse than the cops. It was all a farce. They played their kabuki theater, pretending to make the world a better place. Pretending to care about equal justice for all. But they were a bunch of frauds. Posers. They were greedy pigs. They had ruined his and his family's lives.

The man simmered and fidgeted and started breathing heavily as he sat on the park bench. He pulled a Dr. Pepper bottle out of his backpack and cracked it opened. He looked up at the Earle Cabell Federal Building again and sighed. He started quietly talking to himself as he often did. "Fourteenth floor. That's where the most corrupt judge of all of them sits—in all her pompous arrogance. And she is married to a cop, too. They both deserve to die. *Now that would be poetic justice. Leave their kids to be orphans*."

As the man lingered on the park bench, he noticed that the area around him was getting crowded with people who appeared to be sightseers. It was probably because of the time of year. The anniversary of the President John F. Kennedy assassination in Dallas was coming up on November 22. This anniversary always brought tourists in pilgrimage-like fashion to the city to commemorate the grim event at nearby Dealey Plaza and at the Texas School Book Depository Building, where Lee Harvey Oswald, at 12:30 p.m. on a clear blue Friday afternoon in 1963, perched his mail-order 6.5 millimeter caliber Carcano rifle out of a sixth floor window and allegedly fired three shots, killing the President and seriously wounding former Texas Governor John Connelly. The pilgrims, like dazed groupies, would be piling onto the so-called grassy knoll in the days ahead, retracing the presidential motorcade path, pointing back and forth at the eerie white "X" painted on Elm Street where the President's limousine was struck, and sharing their conspiracy theories with one another this year, like every other year since 1963. Fools and idiots. Fools that were still obsessing about what happened in 1963. Idiots that believed that the Russians or Cubans killed Kennedy. If the truth be told, Lee Harvey Oswald was just another pawn in our corrupt system—a "patsy" like Oswald had said. Manipulated by people in our own U.S. government, no doubt. In any event, one had to admire the simplicity of Oswald's act—how easy assassinations were to pull off in those days. In the days before Kennedy's arrival into Dallas, several local newspapers had actually described in detail the route of the Presidential motorcade. Oswald—who had only started working at the Texas School Book Depository (conveniently on the route) just 37 days earlier—had brought his rifle into work in a long brown paper bag, telling co-workers it contained curtain rods that he had purchased to take home. No one had thought twice about it. Oswald somehow had managed to settle into his sniper's nest and get his shots off without a single co-worker seeing him, then calmly walked out of the front door of the building, catching a city bus back to his boarding house. The man shook his head in silence and then began talking to himself again. "These days, no way. Video cameras and people with cell phones are always watching. Cops, security, and data monitoring devices are everywhere." Between this and DNA testing kits, he thought, it was becoming nearly impossible to plan the perfect in-and-out assassination. But the heightened challenge tended to make it all the more exhilarating. And he had to do it, no matter what the risk was of being caught. He had a job to do. Certain people needed to be finally held accountable.

The man sat in the warm sunshine motionless, staring blankly at the children, drinking his Dr. Pepper. He was thinking about his plan. He liked to think about his plan. He thought about it all the time lately. The children's shrill and discordant laughter suddenly pierced his concentration. The wretched brats were beginning to irritate him more and more. The man's face was turning red and almost looked wrenched with pain. He was perspiring uncomfortably. Suddenly the man was not so invisible. The children playing in the fountains and their parents started to scurry away from the man, as though they sensed something was not quite right about him. He didn't really care what the people around him thought. He was going forward with his plan. Right then and there he had decided it. It was go time. The decision to proceed almost had a cathartic effect on him—he had been pondering this course of action for a while now, and he was no longer going to let all of them get away with what they had done to him.

He tossed his empty drink bottle into a nearby recycling container. He pulled a pair of gloves out of the front pouch of his backpack. He then pulled two envelopes out of the backpack. He got up and jogged down Commerce Street and then turned around the corner at Ervay Street, just past the Neiman Marcus department store, where wealthy, well-dressed women were dropping off their luxury vehicles at the valet parking stand to start their Christmas shopping ahead of Black Friday next week. He paused near the valet stand, as he saw a petite, blond white woman in her forties get out of a black Audi convertible sedan and turn control of it over to a valet. For a moment he thought it was her—the one who was most responsible for hurling his family down their long, tortured spiral into Hell—but it wasn't. He recomposed himself, then walked a few paces around the corner to a blue U.S. Postal Service mailbox. He looked around to see if there were any people watching him. It was all clear; no one was paying any attention to him. The man had already canvassed this location on an earlier day and made sure that there was not much foot traffic and there were no video cameras in the vicinity.

The man opened the metal clanking lid of the mailbox and tossed in the two envelopes, watching them slide down the chute. The sign on the box indicated that mail pick up on Saturdays occurred at 3:00 p.m. It was 2:45 p.m. Perfect timing. He put his gloves back in his backpack and pulled out his cell phone and made a call as he proceeded north up Ervay Street. There was no answer, so he decided to send a text. "Hey, you awake? Sent them just now. Scare the bitch awhile. Then she'll die. Lol. You know what to do next. Ttyl."

The man grinned icily, then threw his cell phone and cap into his backpack and kept walking. He was feeling rather gleeful— anticipating what would soon be unfolding. He then slipped into The Cathedral Shrine of the Virgin of Guadalupe for the 3:00 p.m. Saturday mass. He nodded a polite greeting to Father Francis as he walked in, reverently faced the altar and made the sign of the cross, and then slipped into his usual spot on the back pew. He didn't think of his plan as killing human beings. It was more like eliminating a scourge. It would not be morally wrong.

Part I:

Meet the Lassiter Family and Their New Guests.

Chapter 1:

A Credible Threat; Invasion of the Feds.

It was the day that everything changed. A day that set off a vertiginous frenzy. A day that Judge Avery Lassiter feared would forever impact her kids, no matter how things ultimately played out. The chaotic events were rushing like a runaway train over them, and there was nothing she could do to foreclose any of it. Her mental state was fractured. But she would have to quickly assume the warrior stance that was her default mode when pressed. The family would just have to live with things—like it or not.

On November 21st, the Monday before Thanksgiving, Judge Lassiter had crawled out of bed in an exceptionally buoyant mood. It was a crisp autumn day—a pleasant contrast to the 90-plus degree weather that North Texas had been experiencing for the first several weeks of fall. A good soaking rain the night before seemed to have cooled the earth down to a place where it should be in late November. The day would be breezy, sunny, and 60 degrees Fahrenheit—good football weather for the upcoming Turkey Day pigskin matchups. Judge Lassiter had decided that she was taking a week respite from her world of law and justice. It was really happening this time. It did not happen very often.

Judge Lassiter worked such long and lonely hours at the courthouse. She always had. And when she did take leave from the courthouse, she usually boarded the family pets while she and the family trekked off to some place exotic like Tanzania, Portugal, or Shanghai. But this particular week, she was staying home. Her police officer husband, Max (or "Officer Max," as she often referred to him), had taken several days off from his crime-fighting in the big city to enjoy the holiday as well. It was time for some leisure and relaxation—concepts that were mostly alien to her. Judge Lassiter was appointed to the federal bench two years earlier. When she was appointed, she told her husband Max that everything would be so different than before—so much more predictable. Avery had previously been a lawyer for seventeen years at a large international law firm—Madison, Spencer & Collins—providing legal services for major corporations. Lawyers and law students refer to mega-firms such as Madison, Spencer & Collins as "Big Law." "Big Law" has the reputation for paying lucrative salaries but demanding very long work days from its attorneys (that is, high "billable hours"), as the *quid pro quo*, and expecting perfect work product for their prestigious blue-chip clients. Big Law tends to have offices all over the world for their international clients. Avery traveled frequently when she was a lawyer. She would "mysteriously vanish" for days back then, as her kids would say. Usually to domestic places on the East or West Coast—Delaware, New York, Washington D.C., or California. She spent long hours at the office and then still longer hours on her laptop computer after her kids, Heath and Julia, went to bed. She always seemed so tired and harried. Being appointed to a federal bench would be good for her and the family. She would finally cease her peripatetic ways—or at least slow things down to a more manageable pace.

But things were not exactly progressing according to plan on this Monday, when Avery had managed to set aside her work at the downtown Dallas federal courthouse to enjoy the Thanksgiving holiday week at her residence in Southlake, Texas. Approximately thirteen members of Judge Lassiter's extended family were due to arrive at the Lassiter house in a couple of days, and there was food to prepare, silver ware and crystal to clean, yard work to tackle, and dozens of other domestic tasks awaiting completion. But instead of attending to all the necessary chores, Judge Lassiter would be spending most of the next few days uncomfortably sitting at her kitchen table, with two somber and stone-faced FBI agents, sifting through her court case files and memory bank, trying to assist the FBI in determining who might want to kill her. Meanwhile, there would be a team of armed and Kevlar-clad Deputy U.S. Marshals swarming around the Lassiter house and surrounding property, apparently looking for places to entrench and wait, in case there was an imminent ambush on Judge Lassiter and her family.

It all started early afternoon, when Judge Lassiter returned home from grocery shopping. Officer Max was opening the family mail in the kitchen as Judge Lassiter unpacked groceries. Suddenly he grimaced and yelled, "Good God! What the Hell am I looking at? Somebody's a little unhappy with you, Avery. You just received some not-so-adoring fan mail." Officer Max put on his reading glasses and squinted at a letter in his hands. "Jesus! This is horrible, Avery. You better come over here and look at this." Officer Max had opened a letter that was actually strangely addressed to "*Mr.* Lassiter," but the letter inside was directed to "***The Honorless Avery Lassiter***." Officer Max's voice became louder and more agitated over the rustling grocery sacks. "Holy shit. This is insane. This goes on for pages and pages, Avery. This is like son of Una-bomber style crazy! A manifesto against you and the American legal system."

"Calm down, Officer Max. Probably just somebody venting. You know, right, that I sometimes get letters at the office from angry people? It's just a hazard of my job. People get upset. In fact, pretty much every day somebody gets upset. Let me finish putting all this stuff away and I will look at it. In fact, feel free to help me. In case you haven't noticed, I have enough groceries here to feed a small village."

Officer Max was not focused on the groceries. "Holy shit. What was I thinking? I need to get some gloves on. I have gotten my own prints all over this thing!"

"Max! Stop! You are overreacting!"

"This is a little more serious than just somebody venting, Avery. And, need I remind you that this letter came to our home—not the courthouse? You need to read this toxic shit! Someone has taken the time to describe in painstaking detail why he despises everything about you, why he is fed up with the 'corrupt American legal system,' and how it is time for him to at long last punish you, by torturing, dismembering, and killing you. I am quoting, 'I will show you no mercy. You are where it all began. I know where you live, I know where you shop, I know everything that you and your family do and when you do it. I am watching you always.' I am leaving out a lot of profanity, by the way, and what I am pretty sure you would refer to as some pretty crude misogyny. Let's see. We have about 10 pages enclosed of nothing but the words 'YOU ARE WHERE IT ALL BEGAN' typed out in all capital letters repeatedly. Oh, and it's got some interesting cut-and-paste artwork enclosed, too. It's cowardly signed 'Anonymous.'" He tossed the letter across the kitchen counter toward Avery. "Don't touch it! I'll go get some gloves."

Avery sighed. "Great way to start off the holiday week, don't you think?"

"Looks like I will be making a trip to GT Distributors to pick up some extra ammo."

Reacting to negative situations was not something that Officer Max did with much tact or tenderness. Perhaps it was just a hazard of *his* job, but Officer Max could be somewhat harsh and abrasive and tended not to suffer fools lightly. Avery suspected that Max was getting upset over nothing, but she knew he had good instincts, so she couldn't be sure. Avery grabbed for an oven mitt from the drawer next to her, decorated with horns of plenty, feeling rather silly. She hovered for a few moments over the pages of the letter, moving them over the counter awkwardly. The letter was surprisingly well written and implied that the anonymous writer had been involved in a court case of some sort with Judge Lassiter (without disclosing *which* case) and that her actions had completely ruined his and his family's lives, that he did not think Judge Lassiter "deserved to live," that he watched her everywhere and always, and that "she would be surprised when she saw him." He vowed that her death would be "spectacularly cruel— just as you were to me and my family." The letter was full of grotesque profanity and screamed multiple times in capital letters "YOU ARE DEAD!" Enclosed within the letter was a page with pictures pasted all over of human eyes, apparently cut out from a glossy print magazine (42 eyes, to be exact, ten of which—or five pairs—had red "X's" marked over them). And, whether coincidental or not, the letter was also dated November 19th–Judge Lassiter's 42nd birthday.

Judge Lassiter dreaded what she had to do next. She phoned into her office to report her receipt of the letter. This was standard protocol. She needed to notify the United States Marshals Service. Judge Lassiter's judicial assistant, Annalise, answered the phone in her chambers and sounded rather shaken, conveying that a similar letter had also been received at their courthouse chambers that afternoon. Annalise had notified the United States Marshals Service already, and they would be showing up at the Lassiter house any moment to visit with Avery and her family about the letter and necessary precautionary measures. "Fantastic," Avery sarcastically uttered.

The whole Lassiter family was somewhat distraught and unsettled after gathering in the kitchen and reviewing and discussing the letter. Avery hated to show it to the kids but chose to be honest with them about why U.S. Marshals would soon be knocking on the door. Heath was 18. Julia was 14. They could handle it. Officer Max's reaction was naturally quite a bit different from everyone else's. After all, he is a police officer whose family's security had just been threatened. To say that this was an affront to his dignity would probably be an understatement. The man's life is all about "law and order" and eliminating threats to society. Officer Max was pacing like a hungry jaguar, and exclaiming things like, "I hope this asshole *does* come to our house. Does he know that you are married to a cop? Does he know that no one needs to call '911' around here? Does he not know that I have a plan to kill anyone who walks in this house wanting to kill my family? He really picked the wrong judge to intimidate, don't you think?" It would not be an exaggeration to say that Officer Max was incensed and annoyed. This was the man whose nickname on the police force was "Mad Max." Mad Max was on a covert task force that investigated and chased some fairly dangerous criminals and also served warrants for peoples' arrests. In an amazing twist of irony, Officer Max's task force had recently been looking for a local man who had murdered and dismembered his wife and cooked her body parts on their home stove. He was certainly no stranger to dealing with deranged, murderous people. He had also just recently received commendations for arresting several high- profile leaders of the so-called "Tango Blast" drug trafficking gang, and additionally participated in a sting that brought down some Colombian jewel thieves that targeted diamond brokers making runs in and out of retail jewelry stores in North Texas. It all seemed remarkably puzzling that Avery was the one that had received a gruesome death threat, when Officer Max was the one who was regularly depriving criminals of their freedom. Avery presides over civil cases—financial disputes—not criminal cases.

But the other members of the family had different reactions than Officer Max's. Heath and Julia, not surprisingly, were afraid that someone might be coming to their house to kill their mother or the whole family. Baba Jo (Officer Max's mother, who lived in the garage apartment behind the Lassiters' house) was, in turn, worried about her grandchildren. And Avery was just quiet. After initially being completely dismissive of the letter, as "someone just blowing off steam," the reality slowly set in with Avery that the letter writer might actually pose a risk to her family. Avery did not tend to hide her emotions. But this was not the case on November 21st. Avery was inscrutable that day. After the family meeting regarding the letter, she scooped up Baxter into her arms and collapsed into her favorite soft leather chair in the living room next to the kitchen. Baxter seemed to sense Avery's frazzled emotions. Avery and Baxter were like connected souls. Baxter is a 24-pound pure bred Cavalier King Charles Spaniel—the "Blenheim" sub-breed type. Baxter is rather beautiful, by the way. He has a silky, wavy coat with chestnut markings against a pearly white background, and a smooth undocked tail. He has an adorable thumb-print sized chestnut spot on the top of his skull (known as the "Blenheim kiss" or the "Duchess thumbprint"), and freckles all around his moist, warm, black nose. His full American Kennel Club-registered name is: Baxter Dakkar Always Faithful of

Heritage. Judge Lassiter had grandiose plans for him when she adopted him–to show him in elite dog tournaments one day, hopefully all the way up to the Westminster Kennel Club Dog Show at Madison Square Garden in New York City where she was sure he would, no doubt, crush the so-called competition in the toy breed category. His canine father, named Dakkar Doug, was a somewhat successful show dog in his day. The death threat letter that had arrived was going to change Baxter's destiny. In that single poisonous act, "greatness" as a famous show dog would forever be denied to Baxter. Judge Lassiter would henceforth be too distracted to focus on all the training and traveling that goes along with showing champion, pedigree dog breeds.

The Lassiters' fat cat, Brimley, on the other hand, seemed completely oblivious and apathetic to everything going on, slinking around in his usual nimbus cloud of narcissism, thinking only of his next meal. Brimley is an 18-pound arrogant, black and white, long-haired, ragdoll cat that began living with the Lassiters long before Baxter, and thinks he is royalty. This is somewhat ironic–since Baxter is the one with a royal blood line. Brimley simply groomed his fur and gazed out of the kitchen window with his green squinty lemon-shaped eyes, intermittently flicking his whiskers. Occasionally, Brimley would throw himself dramatically to the tile floor and lie there in a floppy, contorted mangle of fur—because that's what ragdoll cats do. Their one and only "talent" is lying still and limp, like muscle-less rag toys.

Soon after Judge Avery made the phone call into her office to report the receipt of the death threat, a strange new chapter of the Lassiter family's lives began to unfold. The cavalry (*i.e.,* various Deputy United States Marshals) arrived. Actually, the cavalry, infantry, and projectile warriors all arrived. First, there came only a man and woman in business attire, with small silver pins shaped like stars on their jacket lapels, wearing Oakley bullet-proof sunglasses, and guns on their hips, looking very official and concerned. They studied the threat letter and asked a lot of questions. They took the letter (wearing thin blue latex gloves) and put it in a zip lock bag, like the kind in which Avery put the kids' lunches every day. Then two hours later, four more Deputy Marshals arrived—they were large, muscular, and bearded, and looked more menacing and bounty-hunter'ish than the first two. And on the morning of November 22nd, the Federal Bureau of Investigation arrived to "take over the investigation." Why multiple federal agencies? There was a reason, Avery soon learned. When a federal judge receives a "credible death threat," the FBI undertakes the "threat investigation" (for the most part), and tries to determine who made the threat, so as to make an arrest. A threat to a federal judge—even if never carried out—is punishable with up to a 10-year federal prison sentence. But the U.S. Marshals Service provides a "protective detail" for judges when a credible threat is made (in addition to the Marshals' other more well-known duties of finding and arresting America's "most wanted" fugitives, transporting prisoners, protecting courts, and setting up witness protection, a.k.a. "WITSEC").

What is a "credible threat"? Avery was never quite sure what qualified—but according to the so-called experts at the Behavioral Analysis Unit of the FBI in Quantico, Virginia, who were ultimately consulted, the letter met the standard. It was allegedly written by a seriously disturbed and probably dangerous (not merely angry) individual. So, in FBI-lingo, it was a "credible threat." Avery wondered how the so-called experts determined these things—whether it was from word usage patterns or some sort of high technology predictive algorithms known only to federal law enforcement agencies.

In any event, for the next several months, because of that letter–that so-called "credible threat"–Avery's and her family's lives—and, in particular, Avery's backyard (the one place that she always went to for serenity and solitude) were no longer her own. The "Feds" had arrived and taken over their lives.

The following is the story of how and why the Lassiters had to learn to live with United States Deputy Marshals in their backyard. At least that is how Avery's kids would describe it. Officer Max would call this a story of evil—and the horrible chain of events that evil can cause. But Avery would describe it as a story of guardianship, loyalty, bravery, duty, and service. Avery says that everyone has a "higher calling" during their lives to be guardians to someone or something—to watch out for each other and defend principles that are truly worth defending. She says that this higher calling of guarding and defending people and principles is one of the noblest duties that we can aspire to fulfill on this earth. But the calling can come with a price. Sometimes a heavy price.

Chapter 2:

Howlers and Hunters.

It's not about being brave when things like this happen. You have no choice but to accept things. To be stoic for the sake of your family—if not for yourself. After all, other people endure far worse pain and tragedy in their lives than this inconvenience. If anyone should appreciate that fact, a judge and wife of a cop certainly should. In theory, anyway.

It rained relentlessly all night on November 21st, and into the early dawn of November 22nd. Or as Baba Jo was known to say, it "poured cats and dogs." It was rare to get such a drenching rain in November in Texas. Usually, rain at night was pleasant to Avery—the sound and scent of the rain could soothe her insecurities and fears. Not that night. This was a heavy, oppressive rain, hammering at the window panes, roaring through the house gutters, with gusty winds whipping through the trees. The trees looked black to Avery as she peered through her front window, swaying in the cascading deluge. It all seemed strangely apropos to Avery—as though nature and the letter writer's ominous threats were in synch with one another.

Avery was up half of the night and was already sensing that her circadian rhythm was going to be thrown into serious imbalance by this sudden upheaval in her family's lives and the invasion of the Feds. This might just become intolerable. She needed her rest. She never wanted to become one of those cliché old judges who slept and even snored on the bench while in court. Everyone else besides Avery and

Baxter seemed soundly asleep that night. How was that possible? Well maybe not Officer Max. A few years earlier when Avery became a judge, Officer Max had created a "safe room" in their basement—the "go to" place for the family in the event of trouble—that had every type of survival gear imaginable, in addition to an arsenal with a vast panoply of modern weaponry. Shortly before retiring to bed, Officer Max had visited the safe room arsenal to supplement his upstairs "go to" gun stash. He had put his Sig Sauer P226, a semi-automatic hand gun (15 in the mag, one in the pipe), on the night stand next to where he slept, and Avery also noticed him hiding a Glock pistol, an AR-15, a Mossberg 500 pump action shotgun, and stockpiles of ammunition at strategic spots around the house before lying down and closing his eyes. Officer Max could be so overly dramatic at times. Given his job, he was, naturally, always security conscious with his family, but now, with the "credible death threat," things would be DEFCON 3 in the Lassiter household. Black ops, Soldier of Fortune, Dirty Harry— Officer Max was a walking, talking, breathing stereotype of every macho character ever featured in a Hollywood action film on the night of November 21st and the days thereafter. Avery, on the other hand, was just quiet—strangely quiet, for her. She got up and paced and looked out each and every window of the house, every hour that night. Baxter loyally followed her every step. Through the rain storm outside, Avery could see the shadows of human beings—a couple of the Deputy U.S. Marshals—inside of unmarked vehicles (their "G rides"—as she would learn they refer to their work vehicles) parked at opposite ends of the house. The Deputies were not sleeping. They were wide awake, alert, talking to each other and working on laptop computers, with eyes peeled on the house and on each car that moved down the slushy wet street that night. At one point, around 2:00 in the morning, an unwitting group of teenagers made the mistake of parking the car in which they were riding directly across the street from the

Lassiters' house, where they apparently planned to sit together and listen to music and socialize into the wee hours. The kids soon received the scare of their young lives, when a Deputy Marshal walked like the giant man hunter that he was, through the lightening and sheets of driving rain, and knocked on their car windows. He flashed his badge and asked the teenagers what they were planning to do. Avery never knew for sure if it was that particular event, or "loose lips" of her children on social media, but within 48 hours of November 21st, every teenager in Southlake, Texas seemed to be gossiping about how Federal Agents and snipers were stationed all about Heath's and Julia's house and "something big was about to go down." Anyway, Avery felt so sad and worried for her children. Avery wandered through the house all that night, from front to back, from one kid's room to the other, peeking in on them. She would pick Baxter up off the floor and hold and caress him for a while and then put him down. She would turn on her computer and work a while, then would put her head on her desk in exhaustion. She was not at all herself.

On Tuesday morning November 22nd, the skies had cleared and a bright sun surfaced, and then the youngest FBI agents that Avery had ever seen arrived at the Lassiter home and sat down at the kitchen table for hours with Avery. Avery's vivid blue eyes were swollen and puffy and her skin looked unnaturally pale. Her normally neatly coiffed blond, bobbed hairstyle was disheveled, and she nervously twisted strands of it around her index finger. Avery was not normally the type to be fidgety or anxious. Perhaps it was partially the result of too much coffee. In any event, FBI Special Agents James Handley and Omar Navarrez methodically (and sometimes clumsily) questioned Avery for several hours, as though she were a defendant on trial. Such strange irony–given that Avery had spent her career as a Big Law attorney, honing her cross-examination skills, trying to master the art of verbal intimidation and, as a judge, she now regularly watched witnesses squirm on the witness stand and collapse under pressure. The irony was not lost on Avery, but she endured this spectacle of role reversal quite willingly, since she wanted the letter writer to be quickly identified and apprehended. And it was, indeed, a spectacle.

The young FBI Agents—though polite, serious, and diligent—seemed rather clueless as to what they should be asking Avery. At least, that was Avery's initial impression. Among other things, they asked if Avery could make a list of any parties in her court who *"recently had something bad happen to them."*

"Really?" Avery laughed with discomfort and bewilderment. The FBI Agents sat quietly without responding.

The truth was that every day someone has something bad happen to him or herself in Avery's courtroom—and in all American courtrooms, for that matter. Courtrooms can be rather stressful and unpleasant places—"hotbeds of emotion"—Avery sometimes says. "Law and order" are supposed to be the substitutes for violence and self-help in a civilized society. Handling human disputes and bad behavior in a courtroom, with a set of statutes and rules to guide the process, is obviously far superior to fist fights and anarchy in the streets. But, still, people are generally not happy about being in a courtroom. A court case often is the aftermath of some tragedy that occurred in peoples' lives. Being in the courtroom causes people to re-live things that they would rather forget. And, every day, people lose things that are of importance to them in courtrooms (money, property, freedom). In any event, Judge Lassiter politely regained her composure and cooperated with the meticulous, notetaking young FBI Agents, as did her obsequious staff at work, spending what was supposed to be the festive days leading up to Thanksgiving compiling a list for the Agents of parties who "recently had something bad happen to them" in Judge Lassiter's courtroom. There were, frankly, hundreds of people who "recently had something bad happen to them" in Judge Lassiter's courtroom. The reality of that was quietly disconcerting to Avery. Avery and her staff tried to be discerning and tried to zero in upon litigants whom they perceived to have been especially upset during or after court recently. And the fastidious FBI Agents began cross-referencing Judge Lassiter's staff's very long list with miscellaneous law enforcement data bases, trying to find someone with an especially troubling criminal record, who might really want Judge Lassiter dead. Actually, Avery had no clear idea what the FBI Agents were doing. They seemed to operate under a cloak of complete secrecy. Avery likes transparency. The FBI typically does not. And Avery kept obsessing about how youthful in appearance the FBI Agents were. Avery kept asking Officer Max whether he thought these sprightly, inquisitive agents were "really qualified to swim in the deep end." Avery surmised that, because the FBI has terrorism and other far more serious crimes to investigate, perhaps her measly little death threat had been relegated to Agents-in-training. In any event, Avery just hoped this would all soon come to an uneventful, peaceful conclusion. Could this perhaps be just some harmless letter writer, blowing off some steam, or was it a person truly wicked enough to kill?

The reality is that, while federal judges receive threatening communications somewhat frequently (in fact, more frequently during holiday times, it seems), there are, thankfully, not too many instances of threat-makers carrying out those threats. There have been relatively few instances of assassinations of federal judges or their families (in comparison to other public officials). One of the most notorious assassinations that occurred was that of the late Judge John H. Wood, Jr. in nearby San Antonio, Texas back in 1979. In that case, a hired hitman and card-gambling felon named Charles Harrelson (the father of a Hollywood actor, Woody Harrelson) allegedly used a high-powered rifle fitted with a scope to shoot and kill the judge outside his townhome as he was leaving for work on a Tuesday morning. Charles Harrelson had allegedly been hired by a drug trafficker and gambler named Jimmy Chagra, who was facing an upcoming trial in Judge Wood's court. Jimmy Chagra was concerned that he would not get a fair trial, because of Judge Wood's reputation as "Maximum John" (a nickname that he earned by giving tough sentences to drug traffickers), so he paid Charles Harrelson $250,000 to kill Judge Wood, so he could avoid having Judge Wood try his case. In that high-profile case, it took the FBI almost three years to put all the facts together and obtain indictments against Chagra, Harrelson, and other alleged conspirators. The FBI spent thousands of human hours, conducted 30,000 interviews, collected 500,000 pieces of information, and spent $11 million. Ultimately, to the shock and horror of many, Jimmy Chagra was acquitted on the charges of murder and conspiracy to commit murder but was found guilty of lesser obstruction of justice and drug charges. Chagra later admitted his guilt in hiring Harrelson to kill the judge, in a desperate and unsuccessful attempt to help his wife, who had been less fortunate than her husband, and had been found guilty of conspiracy to commit murder (in a separate trial) for her role in delivering the $250,000 fee to the hitman Harrelson. Harrelson was convicted for his hitman role in the assassination.

Avery was not sure how to feel when the well-meaning FBI Agents reminded her of this tragic, sad story of the late Judge Wood. On the one hand, it was a stark reminder of how evil, desperate people sometimes react to the strong arm of justice. On the other hand, apparently Judge Wood never received a threat letter or a warning of any kind from his killer. In the world of law enforcement threat investigations, there is a special "lingo" that is used. Specifically, investigators distinguish between the concepts of "howlers" and "hunters." Apparently, "howlers" are individuals who "howl" and roar and verbally express their frustrations with "the system" and public officials—perhaps by sending letters or going on social media. But– no matter how angry and bellicose these "howlers" seem–they historically are not likely to commit physical harm on the targets of their anger. On the other hand, a "hunter" will usually not make himself conspicuously known, but will silently simmer with agitation, and will eventually come out of the shadows and strike when least expected. "Hunters" obviously tend to be the ones that cause the most worry to law enforcement officials. Was Avery's letter writer just a "howler"? Some of the investigators apparently seemed to think so. And, it just so happened that there was a major "howler" in Judge Lassiter's life at that precise moment: Jack Panko.

Jack Panko was a convicted felon (arsonist) who had spent ten years of his life in a federal penitentiary before he began frequenting Avery's courtroom as though it were a 24-hour-a-day convenience store. The age of the Internet and the ability to file papers with the court electronically seem to have made courts just that in some respects—24-hour-per-day service centers. Judges and their staffs come in each morning frequently to be greeted with large stacks of papers filed overnight, purporting to need the court's immediate attention. Like a lot of prisoners, Panko apparently spent a lot of time in the prison law library during his incarceration. Panko, in addition to his felony, had other more minor arrests along the way, including several misdemeanor assaults and at least one episode of lewd public behavior in an adult book store. Now Panko enjoyed representing himself on a "*pro se*" basis (that is, without any lawyer's help), in suing everyone he ever dealt with in life: judges; law enforcement officers; attorneys; employers; business associates; media figures. Panko referred to himself as a "businessman" and "political activist" but, in reality, was mostly an unemployed misfit, who lived with his elderly disabled brother and mooched off of his brother's investments and social security. When Judge Lassiter had ruled against Jack Panko and his brother in a civil action in her court recently—labeling him as a "vexatious litigant" and barring him from filing any more pleadings or lawsuits—Panko lashed out in a very noisy manner. He filed unsuccessful appeals and complaints of judicial misconduct against Avery. He accused her of discriminating against and wanting to kill his disabled brother. He even personally sued Avery (along with various other public officials) in civil lawsuits in various districts around the state and country—lawsuits that resulted in large, monetary "bad faith" sanctions against *him*. Panko posted videos on YouTube of him slanderously criticizing Avery. He and certain of his friends created websites with libelous stories of the injustices that Panko and his brother had allegedly suffered in Avery's courtroom (describing themselves as "citizen journalists"). Jack Panko or one of his circle of cohorts (through an anonymous proxy service) even hijacked Avery's name, creating a "judgeaverylassiter.com" web page, where numerous doctored photographs and false articles appeared concerning fabricated "corruption charges" that were allegedly being filed against Avery. Panko frequently protested with cardboard signs across from city hall, proclaiming "Judge Lassiter is a crook." He phoned into extremist talk radio shows complaining about her. He even sat in her courtroom some days and glared at her during other people's cases and then, later, seemingly befriended other *pro se* litigants as they were walking out of her courtroom—helping losing litigants file grievances against Judge Lassiter. Was the death threat letter just his latest venomous way of "howling"? Had Panko's robust exercise of his First Amendment rights finally crossed a forbidden line? This was the "lead" theory early on in the FBI's investigation.

Well, as it turned out, it could not possibly be that simple. The letters (both the one sent to the Lassiter home and the one sent to Judge Lassiter's chambers at the courthouse) were extensively tested by the FBI in Quantico. The letters had no finger prints (other than Avery's and Officer Max's on the letter that arrived at the house) and had no DNA traces of any kind—not on the back of the stamps, not on the gummy part of the envelope seals, not on the bizarre page with all the glued-on pictures of human eyes, nowhere. The letters were typewritten, and the author had utilized very common type-font and ink. There was a cat hair fiber found on the particular letter that went to Avery's home, but it could have been the fur of Brimley the giant ragdoll. The letters were determined to have been mailed from a public mailbox and not from inside a post office, so there were no security cameras to perhaps provide any evidence. The letters had been routed through a central mail collection center in between Dallas and Fort Worth, Texas—thus, the letter writer was obviously someone "local." The FBI analysts at Quantico had developed a profile for the letter writer (from his or her "verbose and loquacious word usage patterns and from computer algorithms"), but they were being very secretive with their information and investigation. Again, no transparency. All that the family really knew was that the threat was for some reason being taken very seriously.

As noted earlier, while actual assassinations are, thankfully, rare, it is not that uncommon for judges to receive periodic threats or otherwise-strange letters. There is the occasional letter filled with baby powder that shows up in the chambers of one or more judges— which ultimately requires notification of the so-called "HazMat teams," to make sure the baby powder is not, in fact, something deadly like anthrax (anthrax is a deadly bacterium that is sometimes used as a bioweapon). There are hoax bomb threats at federal buildings (especially in April each year—likely due to April 15th being Tax Day, and also due to the anniversaries of terrible events falling during that month, such as Ruby Ridge, the Waco/Koresh religious cult fire, and the Oklahoma City federal building bombing). There are bored prisoners incarcerated in detention centers around the country who—utilizing the taxpayer funded computer equipment at their facilities—manage to obtain the courthouse addresses of every federal judge in the country and send them all handwritten letters, venting their frustrations with the justice system. Sometimes these letters are troubling. Sometimes these letters are written by prisoners in *state* penitentiary systems who are hoping to be transferred to a nicer *federal* penitentiary facility (the theory being, if one threatens a *federal* judge, he will get charged with a *federal* crime, and that charge will supersede somehow his *state* conviction and incarceration; this tactic is unlikely to be successful). At least one prisoner who filed a civil rights lawsuit complaining about the quality of the meals in the federal prison system regrettably sent the judge presiding over the civil rights lawsuit an envelope containing a sample of said prison food. This was not a smart move. Finally, there are also occasionally breathy phone calls to judges and their staffs, threatening various types of revenge. Sadly, these types of events are just a normal part of being a public servant. Just a "hazard of the job," as Avery says, "and hardly as serious as what Officer Max and law enforcement and other first responders confront every day." Officer Max jokes that a good day for a cop is getting shot at and missed. But while receiving a threat letter isn't exactly the same as getting shot at and missed, not all threats are created equal. The letter that arrived on November 21st was considered particularly calculated and specific. It contained especially vitriolic and vulgar language. It was lengthy and surprisingly well written, with perfect grammar. It had an element of the bizarre to it — with the pictures of the 42 eyes, 10 with red "X's"—apparently signifying death. And a letter had gone to the Lassiter home (despite Avery's home address being confidential and unlisted in public data bases). So, under all of these circumstances, until further notice, Deputies from the United States Marshals Service would be inhabiting the Lassiters' backyard. The Deputy Marshals would be driving Avery in their G-rides to work and everywhere she went for the time being. And there would be video cameras everywhere–all over the Lassiter property–recording their every step for posterity. Poor Baxter would not even have any privacy when answering the call of nature in his designated spots in the backyard. The poor little guy's dignity was utterly lost. He would be urinating and defecating in front of an audience of armed, badged men and women. In fact, the Deputy Marshals put a tripod stand with a camera in the very spot that he regularly defecated. Avery thought Baxter looked unbelievably humiliated. The Deputy Marshals even had to accompany Avery and Baxter on their walks. Their walks at the nearby lake were sacred. They were Avery's and Baxter's special time together–no one else's. That part (having chaperones on her walks) was probably the most suffocating aspect of any of this to her. Curse the letter writer. Avery was starting to hate the letter writer–whomever he or she was—for what this was doing to her family.

Chapter 3:

The Effort to Blend.

"Oh Lord that lends me a life, lend me a heart replete with thankfulness." So began Avery's thanksgiving prayer with her family that day (a quote from Shakespeare—Avery was still, even as a mature woman in her forties, always trying to impress her well-read, educated father).

Thanksgiving Day at the Lassiter household that year was a little awkward. It was hardly source material for a Norman Rockwell Americana portrait of hearth and family. In fact, it was the first of many awkward days that the family would experience in the coming months. Judge Lassiter's parents arrived Thanksgiving Day and were alarmed, to say the least, about what was suddenly unfolding at the Lassiter home front. The Lassiter house is situated on a quiet secluded street, in an upscale suburban neighborhood between Dallas and Fort Worth, on a roughly one- acre lot, with 40 large and shady trees. The home occupies a wide footprint, set back a bit from the street, and has a separate, quaint apartment behind the house for Baba Jo. A tall brick retaining wall separates the property from neighbors. In roughly 48 hours, the quiet suburban home was transformed into a high security compound. The Marshals positioned cameras everywhere. Some of the tripod stands were visible to anyone, and some cameras were more discretely hidden in shrubbery or inside of windows. A huge gadget-filled RV trailer eventually arrived that would serve as a command center in the backyard, where Deputy Marshals were deployed, fully armed, watching live video feed from the cameras on TV monitors, seemingly ready for a take down. The Deputy Marshals occasionally walked the premises, searching for anything out of the ordinary, and hardly "blended" in the Lassiters' upper middle-class neighborhood. They wore bulky shirts with shirt tails out (known as "5.11" tactical wear–the "5.11" shirts and pants have lots of special pockets for tactical gear, and are designed to be worn shirt tails out, so that one can inconspicuously wear a gun, handcuffs, taser, knife, zip ties, and other crime-fighting paraphernalia on a belt). But one could still always see the Deputy Marshals' firearms, menacingly poking through their clothing. The Deputy Marshals seemed to typically carry semi-automatic Glock handguns (cool weapons, but not as cool as the AR-15s that Avery's kids would sometimes see them remove from their duty lockers in their "G-ride" vehicles). And the Deputy Marshals were all larger than life. One Deputy Marshal, named Bolton Paine, talked with a loud booming voice (thick with a Texas accent) and wore red, white, and blue leather cowboy boots with stars and stripes and "Deputy" stitched down the back of the left boot, and "Marshal" stitched down the back of the right boot. Bolton Paine, with his sandy, crew cut hair, ruddy face, square jaw, thick barrel chest, and broad shoulders paced around the property like he owned the place, listening to country music in the RV command post, and giving fierce looks to anyone who walked by. He leaned his long torso to the side whenever he engaged in conversation and cocked his head back—as though he was skeptical of everything he heard. On the lighter side, Deputy Paine told great stories about his hometown of Abilene, Texas, and rumor was that he supposedly had his own pet armadillo named Rufus back home. Scary and intimidating as he was, Bolton Paine seemed to like the Lassiter kids a lot and they liked him back. He fed Baxter left over barbeque ribs on occasion. This made Avery crazy. Another Deputy Marshal that stood out was Miles Dylan, who usually worked the night shift. He was a former Marine, who cut a striking figure, and was deadly serious—always creeping around the property like some sort of nocturnal jungle cat, ready to spring into action. He had that "I love the smell of Napalm in the morning" type of attitude. He paced around after dark in night-vision or infrared goggles, sometimes crouching behind trees, dressed all in camouflage and acting rather ninja. Unlike the barbeque-eating Bolton Paine, Miles Dylan only snacked (at the precise same times every night) on MRE packets, which are the food rations that soldiers deployed on special combat missions eat. He had numerous high-tech looking surveillance gadgets that he said were "classified" when anyone ever asked what they were. Avery once overheard him lecturing Deputy Paine regarding Paine's outlandishly flashy cowboy boots—telling Paine that, not only were they too attention-grabbing and impractical for a foot chase, but he should wear boots with laces, specifically Kevlar-coated laces so that, in a bad moment, he could resort to using his shoe laces as either a weapon or "jeopardy extraction" device. "Everything on your body needs to do double-duty as a weapon and survival tool!" Yet another Marshal who seemed to hang around the Lassiter house a lot was introduced to the family as simply "Trigger Newsome." Avery never learned or observed much about Deputy Trigger Newsome. She decided it might be nice not to know how he earned his nickname. But she figured Officer Max would be eager to know and would learn. He was probably Officer Max's kind of a guy.

When Judge Lassiter's parents and extended family arrived for Thanksgiving dinner, the Deputy Marshals on the property were fully prepared, with physical descriptions and car makes and models for all of the Lassiters' expected guests; thus, their arrival at the home would be fairly uneventful. The Deputy Marshals stayed discreetly out of sight. But when Judge Lassiter's niece's boyfriend arrived, 22-year-old Brandon (a college fraternity boy—who certainly looked the part), it was an entirely different story. Brandon was a surprise guest that Judge Lassiter had not anticipated that day. When Brandon pulled up and darted out of his Chrysler Ram pickup truck with a 6-pack of Corona beer in a paper brown sack, he apparently looked like a possible threat (despite his khaki pants, Sigma Chi sweatshirt, and top-sider loafers). The Deputy Marshals charged him and told him to put his hands up in the air. Brandon cooperatively dropped his beer and was promptly frisked and otherwise read the riot act. Needless to say, this little episode did not go unnoticed by the Lassiters' neighbors—who were peeking out of their windows and quickly realizing that things were starting to get a little weird on their quiet little street. Brandon was fairly promptly released, after Judge Lassiter darted out of the front door (followed by Baxter, of course) to vouch for Brandon's identity to the Deputy Marshals (and, of course, the act of Avery and Baxter running out of the front door, without being properly flanked by Deputy Marshals, caused a new wave of alarm and consternation on the part of the gun-toting Deputies). But Brandon no doubt had a pretty good story to tell his fraternity brothers the following week back at college. And Baxter got to lap up some of the Corona beer that had spilled from a shattered beer bottle and puddled onto the sidewalk by the house.

Thanksgiving—while strange and unrelaxed—was relatively uneventful for the most part. But Judge Lassiter's extended family was, without a doubt, somewhat traumatized and had never realized that Avery's job had risks like this attached to it. Officer Max's job— sure. He definitely experienced his share of dangerous encounters (practically daily, serving on his covert undercover special task force). Officer Max's and his colleagues' catch phrase was "every day we play the deadly game." But now Avery's and the kids' lives seemed vulnerable to a possibly dangerous predator. This was unsettling and unexpected. Until recently, Avery had been a corporate attorney representing Fortune 500 companies and other wealthy institutional clients for her entire legal career, at a prestigious international law firm. Now she presided over civil and bankruptcy matters in her court. She had no criminal law background or docket whatsoever. She handled financial disputes and ruled in money matters—not murder and mayhem. The most exciting legal matter that she ever encountered was a financial super-web that needed unraveling. Avery's Southern Belle mother, in her pearls and navy, knit St. John suit, and perfectly hair-sprayed bob, kept wringing her hands that Thanksgiving Day and saying, "I thought you didn't handle criminal matters, Honey? Why would somebody want to kill you over money? It's just money! It's only money!" Avery always said that her mother could be incredibly naïve about such things. Strange, considering Avery's mother's appreciation for all things Biblical—and money being "the root of all evil" and such.

In any event, after a very long Thanksgiving prayer led by Avery's father (after Avery's "intro prayer")—in fact, it was longer than any prayer that Avery could remember in recent family history—with more than a few references to "Avery's situation" followed by her mother's sighing and sniffling, Avery's family all managed to pretend like nothing strange was going on for a while. They drank a lot of festive, alcoholic beverages on that bizarre holiday. The Cloudy Bay Sauvignon Blanc, in particular, was flowing rather freely. More than a few red apple martinis were served. And Avery lost track of the number of "dead soldiers" that she heard clatter into the recycling bin that night.

Thank goodness there was a good Cowboys-Redskins football showdown to further distract everyone. Avery and her sister Suzanne later took turkey and dressing and pumpkin pie leftovers out to the

Deputy Marshals in the backyard. The Deputy Marshals seemed very embarrassed by the kindness and said that they were not allowed to accept the food. But Judge Lassiter is not the kind of person who easily takes "no" for an answer. They would quickly learn that about her. So they finally accepted the small feast that she and Suzanne brought them and thanked them. Baxter was especially grateful because, later, the Deputies would give some of the leftovers to him. Beer, turkey, and dressing—all in the same day. Baxter was living like the consort of a king—which, of course, was the true essence of his being.

As Avery went inside that night, one Deputy Marshal told her that some of the Lassiters' neighbors, Paul and Jason, just down the hill from the big retaining wall on their property, were skinny dipping in their swimming pool "in plain view" while listening to loud Lady Gaga music, and asked if that seemed like a normal thing for them to be doing–especially in November. Avery replied that, in fact, this was completely normal for these particular neighbors, adding, "Have y'all heard yet what the nickname is that some people have for Southlake, Texas? They call it 'South Lake Wobegon'—where the women are all strong, the men are all good-looking, and the children are all above average. You get that reference, right? It's from the old Garrison Keillor stories and novels, about Lake Wobegon, the quirky fictional mid-west town founded by Unitarian missionaries and German and Norwegian farmers, that had a pleasant lake and homes with yards with flowers like Las Vegas showgirls?"

The Marshals on duty looked at Avery with vacant expressions. They had no clue to what she was referring.

"Ok. All I am saying is that Southlake has a reputation for being all wholesome and perfect and people have a tendency to overestimate and overstate their status, achievements, and capabilities—and, of course, wealth. The so-called 'Lake Wobegon effect.' But the town is not all that it appears to be on the surface. Quirky, non-conformists abound. Just like Paul and Jason. Just wait until they bring their cellos out on their patio and start playing their show tune duets. Trust me. It's good!"

Avery grinned a little at that moment and turned to go inside. It was the first time Avery had smiled all week.

On the Friday after Thanksgiving it was, of course, "Black Friday." Somehow the phrase "Black Friday" took on a whole new connotation in the Lassiter household that year. Judge Lassiter decided that she was not going to hide in the house. She would brighten her Black Friday by visiting the nail salon and spa that day. She would try to decompress. She used that word a lot–often telling her children she needed to decompress. They never were quite sure what she really meant. Anyway, Avery would not be allowed to drive herself or go anywhere alone anymore. Therefore, the Marshals accompanied her to the nail salon. Avery later announced to Officer Max when she got home that "it is a whole new experience, going to the nail salon with two Deputy U.S. Marshals escorting you." Every woman inside the establishment kept staring back and forth from Avery to the two beefy centurions that held post at the salon door until one elegant woman in her seventies finally asked, "Who are the hot young guys with the guns at the front door? This salon is apparently rising to a whole new level of service!" Another woman sipping on a glass of Moet & Chandon replied, "Which guns are you referring to? The ones that I see poking out of their side holsters or their amazing biceps?" Avery had sat there silently aghast, as women laughed and chimed in with inappropriate comments, not knowing whether to die of embarrassment or enjoy it like some of the desperate housewives of

Southlake seemed to be doing. To be sure, the Deputy Marshals were not that good at "blending" in the tony neighborhoods and retail centers of Southlake, Texas. But the nail salon owner apparently enjoyed the sudden surge of customers that she soon realized, on any particular weekend that Judge Lassiter decided she needed to "decompress" at the salon. The poor Deputy Marshals, no doubt, were pretty desperate themselves–desperate to get back to their "real" and more exciting job of pursuing America's "Most Wanted" fugitives.

Chapter 4:

Profile of the U.S. Marshals.

Things were soon feeling more than a little crowded. Avery wasn't sure how long this would all last or where things would end up. She wondered if she would feel alone when this was all over—assuming she lived through it all. She was a person who richly enjoyed solitude—the glory of being alone, as she sometimes wistfully said. But there would apparently be none of that for a while.

On Monday morning, November 28th, it was time for Judge Lassiter to return to work at the Earle Cabell Federal Building. The kids were going back to school. And Officer Max was returning to work to man a criminal investigator desk (daytime hours) for a few weeks. Officer Max was supposed to do a four-week stint working the graveyard shift starting on the Monday after Thanksgiving. Luckily, because of everything going on at home, a good soul at work offered to trade with him. The brothers and sisters in blue were good comrades, always there for each other. At the house during the day, there would remain just Baba Jo, Baxter, and of course the obese, lazy feline Brimley—the only family member utterly undistracted by the recent home front developments. Plus, all of the family's new Deputy U.S. Marshal buddies. This was the "new normal." Avery decided she was going to have to warm up to and get comfortable with these U.S. Marshal protectors if they were going to be spending so much time around her and her family. Judge Lassiter would be driven into the city that day by Deputy U.S. Marshal Jason Fuentes, the man who would be in charge of her protective detail for a few weeks.

When Avery climbed up into Jason Fuentes' black G ride—a black Ford Explorer with heavily tinted windows—the Bob Dylan song "Chaos is a Friend of Mine" was playing on the car stereo. What were the odds? That song seemed strangely fitting, although an unexpected music genre for a young U.S. Marshal. Deputy Fuentes greeted Avery with a big grin as she settled in and a warm, happy "Hello, Judge." Avery replied, is that what you all are going to be calling me—just 'Judge'? I kind of hoped I would get some cool code name like 'Trailblazer' or 'Tempo.'" Deputy Fuentes looked at her perplexed.

Jason Fuentes was a handsome, stocky man in his mid-thirties with kind brown eyes and the same crew cut hair style that most of the male Deputy Marshals wore. He had a perky, affable personality that seemed somewhat different from what Avery had expected from a Deputy United States Marshal. She sometimes referred to Deputy Fuentes as a "Renaissance Man," because she thought he was so smart, well read, funny, and could talk to her about so many diverse topics on the commute into work. He had a sweet, unassuming manner and, Avery thought, also had a "delicate psyche." Avery frequently put people under a microscope and played amateur psychologist—perhaps another byproduct of her job. Actually, Avery and her daughter Julia both have an unusual, somewhat rare trait called Synesthesia (a.k.a. "sense-fusion"), which is a neurological perceptual phenomenon that causes them both to visualize a color when they see people. In other words, they associate all people they encounter with unique tinges of colors. About 5% of the human population is believed to have some form of Synesthesia (over 60 different types of it have been reported). "Synesthetes," as people like Avery and Julia are known, usually perceive alphabet letters or numbers to be shaded with colors (which is called grapheme-color Synesthesia). Sometimes Synesthetes commingle sounds with scents, or sounds with shapes, or shapes with flavors. It is some sort of automatic, involuntary experience where the stimulation of one sense, or cognitive pathway (*e.g.,* hearing) triggers a second sensory or cognitive pathway (*e.g.,* vision) to be stimulated in some form. But Avery and Julia have a form of sense-fusion that involves colors and visions. Just as people with grapheme-color Synesthesia do, they see tinges of color with all letters and numbers, but—beyond that—they also see tinges of colors with humans. It is a trait that only people who are closest with Avery and Julia know about, because they feel extremely awkward sharing something so relatively rare and misunderstood. Anyway, Avery said she saw Jason Fuentes as a deep cerulean blue color—which was a color she couldn't remember ever seeing in another person, but Julia said she saw him on some days as more of an indigo blue color. The rest of the family had no idea what any of this really meant, since they did not have the trait. In any event, Jason Fuentes, the "cerulean blue Deputy Marshal," was nicknamed "CB" by Avery and Julia (for "cerulean blue") and no one ever knew the real reason they sometimes called him CB. Avery later pretended it stood for "Cool Breeze"—because he was so cool—and Deputy Fuentes seemed to like that. CB had graduated from high school from a small town in South Texas, at the top of his class, and was raised by doting grandparents. He went on to Texas A&M University ("ugh!"—said Avery, who usually favors fellow Texas Longhorns), where he graduated with high honors, joined the U.S. Navy, and eventually gained acceptance into the Navy SEAL program. After a few missions that he "did not feel it was appropriate to discuss," he received his honorable discharge and was accepted into the U.S. Marshals Academy in Glynco, Georgia. He was an over-the-top Type-A personality, adopting an "if you are not first, you're last" mentality in everything he did. He was a world champion in mixed martial arts.

Anyway, Cool Breeze/Cerulean Blue was just the first of what would turn out to be a long series of Marshal-guardians that would rotate in and out of the Lassiters' lives, for over a year, as the FBI invisibly lumbered through reams of data, trying to solve the mystery of who sent Avery the threat letters. Avery patiently waited, hoping that the premier investigative agency in the world (the FBI)—with their motto of "fidelity, bravery, integrity"—would determine who the letter writer was and make a swift arrest, before he or she carried out any harm to Avery's family. Meanwhile, the family put their trust in the oldest and fiercest law enforcement agency in the world (the U.S. Marshals) to protect it.

So who really are the U.S. Marshals? Naturally, the whole situation with Avery really befuddled her and made her wonder and be concerned. Should she really feel safe with these mostly men (and a few women) having unfettered access to her home and life? Were they trustworthy?

Well, she learned, in the coming months, more than she really ever thought she wanted to know about the U.S. Marshals Service. It was partly through her daughter Julia, of all unlikely sources. Julia became absolutely fascinated (as any adolescent might) with the larger-than-life law men and women who occupied her backyard, day in and day out, starting in late November. After all, for better or worse, Julia and Heath were the only teenagers in Southlake, Texas that had men with AR-15s and night vision goggles living in their backyard. Julia had always been a little fascinated with her father's stories of crime-busting police work–kicking in doors of stash houses and whatnot—much more so than her mom's mundane stories about financial disputes in the courtroom. But the Deputy Marshals were more youthful and seemed less cynical and jaded than her father, and they practically enjoyed star quality in Julia's young mind. Julia and her best friend Dara selected the Deputy Marshals who were their favorites and gave them their own secret nicknames like "Marshal McDreamy" and "Usher." Actually, Avery usually gave them all nicknames too, but they were not quite that inappropriate. Wide-eyed Julia wanted to learn everything about the Marshals and soon decided that she might even want to become a Marshal herself one day. When Julia was required to prepare a research project for her middle school's "Talented and Gifted Night Fair," she decided that she would undertake a project entitled: "The U.S. Marshals Service—1789 to Present." She received her usual "A" on the assignment, and this time, it probably did not hurt that she had two real life Deputy U.S. Marshals accompany her (well, accompany her mom really) to the school Fair. There were kids at the Fair who had invented amazing things like electric toy cars and solar-fueled appliances. There was a kid who presented human genome research for his project. Yet another child had presented theories of how mankind could potentially retard the melting Arctic permafrost. These were kids who would invent or discover something that might one day save the world. But Good God, those kids didn't have real life gun-toting, ass-kicking Deputy U.S. Marshals as part of their projects. Little Julia even had "The Peacock" with her on the night of her U.S. Marshal project presentation. "The Peacock" was a Deputy U.S. Marshal who was a former U.S. Air Force officer who was built like a perfectly chiseled, athletic avatar, and had a face as beautiful as a Hollywood celebrity. The Lassiters all affectionately referred to him as "The Peacock," because of his beautiful appearance and confident personality. However, Julia's friend Dara, in a fit of teenaged drama one day, said that his nickname could just as easily have been Adonis (the name of the Greek Goddess Aphrodite's male lover, who was a great and handsome hunter, until a boar killed him and Aphrodite turned him into a rose to remember him). In any event, the Peacock was no dummy either. He had a magnetic, engaging personality. When Julia walked with her mother and The Peacock into the school auditorium that night it was "lights out" and "game over." The U.S. Marshals project was, by far, the best entry of all of the 8th grade entries at the Southlake-Carroll Middle School "Talented and Gifted Night" Project Fair. And, all the while, The Peacock seemed completely oblivious to the fanfare of it all. He was just guarding Judge Avery Lassiter, and monitoring all building perimeters, to make sure nothing and nobody infringed upon his "package" (the term that the Deputy Marshals sometimes use for their human protectee).

The U.S. Marshals Service, it seems, is the oldest law enforcement agency in America, having been formed in the year 1789, consisting of approximately 4,000 deputies throughout the country. It is part of the U.S. Department of Justice (the Executive Branch of the federal government). It is considered the enforcement arm of the federal courts. It is the primary agency for fugitive operations (capturing tens of thousands of fugitives each year; to be exact, more fugitives than any other law enforcement agency). The Deputy Marshals go all over the world in these endeavors—often into foreign countries for extraditions with the cooperation of foreign governments. They arrest high profile law offenders including murderers, drug kingpins, organized crime figures, individuals accused of elaborate financial crimes, escapees from prison, and other persons among America's so-called "Most Wanted." Indeed, as Officer Max says, "Everyday they play the deadly game." But they are also responsible for protection of officers of the court (such as judges) and courthouse integrity and security. They also transport prisoners (such as in the

Hollywood movie *Con Air*). They occasionally perform asset seizures, "till taps," and serve legal process. They track and monitor sex offenders (making sure that they register and comply with procedures required of former offenders, pursuant to the Adam Walsh Act), and sometimes they provide witness relocation and protection ("WITSEC"). Their role has changed over the years. During the settlement of the American West, the U.S. Marshals served as the main day-to-day law enforcement in various territories that had no local government of their own—reminiscent of the legendary Wyatt Earp, Wild Bill Hickok, Bat Masterson, Matt Dillon, and Rooster Cogburn (actually, the latter two are just fictional characters). One of their least attractive duties in years-gone-by was occasionally capturing fugitive slaves in the Old South. The U.S. Marshals have been called upon to perform some extraordinary missions over the years, including registering enemy aliens during war times and swapping spies with the Soviet Union during the Cold War. They also enforced Prohibition during the 1920's. They have had roles in keeping security at abortion clinics, have provided protection to U.S. Olympic athletes, and even have provided law enforcement services with regard to U.S. citizens on the continent of Antarctica. Apparently, there can even be crime and mayhem in the most isolated, snowy corners of the universe where only scientists and penguins typically reside. The U.S. Marshals have performed rather noble duties—providing protection to volunteers on the front lines during the Civil Rights movement of the 1960's, and sometimes accompanying black school children to school during the early, tumultuous days of desegregation.

The U.S. Marshals seemed to have spines of steel and were the closest thing to true heroes that young Julia could ever imagine. But, much to young Julia's disappointment, the U.S. Marshals Service does not have a supernatural crimes section like in the book series *Vampire*

Hunters that Julia loves so much. But Julia is quite unconvinced of that and tells Avery that the information about the *Vampire Hunters* is simply "classified" and known only to a few people at the U.S. Marshals headquarters in Arlington, Virginia. She is holding out hope that one day she can get The Peacock or Trigger Newsome to "crack" and tell her all the details.

The U.S. Marshals are an unusual lot. Many of them have prior military experience and college degrees in any number of fields. A significant number have worked first for local, state, or other federal law enforcement agencies. One of Avery's guardians, John Louis, shortly after serving on her protective detail, retired from the Marshals Service and went to Afghanistan to work in military intelligence, finding locations of improvised explosive devices (sort of like the character from the movie *The Hurt Locker*, Avery said). He had been a Marine officer and DEA agent before working for the Marshals Service. Another one of her guardians, Ginny Oliphante, had been a Navy cryptologist and an art history major in college. Still another, Tom Green (whom she referred to as "Montana Tom"—since he was from Montana), was with the U.S. Secret Service before joining the U.S. Marshals. He had guarded former Presidents, Vice Presidents, and First Ladies. Avery told Montana Tom that "she was the most unimportant person that he had ever guarded, and—for that matter— the most unimportant mission that the U.S. Marshals Service had ever undertaken, and that all of her dear guardians must be so terribly frustrated and bored with having to provide protection to her." Montana Tom simply replied, "Ma'am, don't you worry. We'd definitely all take a bullet for you."

Avery did not get it. Why would anyone, except Officer Max, take a bullet for her? She was not the President. She was a fairly low-level judge, in the federal judge hierarchy. She, of course, knew that our judicial institutions and the people who play a role in these institutions were worth defending. When she pondered her own soul deeply, she knew that she would be willing to die for certain people and things that were important to her—even abstract principles. But Avery still could not fully understand the mindset of the U.S. Marshals—at least not in the beginning. She would later get it. The U.S. Marshals live by their own Code. The world would be a better place if more humans lived by such a Code.

Chapter 5:

Life Goes on—Friday Night Lights with the U.S. Marshals.

In any event, life went on. Judge Lassiter and the Lassiter family reluctantly had to grow accustomed to being shadowed everywhere they went with guardians. Before this phase of her life, Avery used to say that she loved going to the grocery store on Saturday afternoons and feeling like a normal suburban house wife when she did. It was one of those special rituals in life in which Avery could put on a ball cap and some casual clothes, and no one around her knew who she was or what she did for a living. She could get lost in the produce section, smelling and feeling the melons and whatnot. She loved going through the bakery, smelling the warm bread, visiting with the butchers, and relaxing in the wine section—picking the sommeliers' brains at the Central Market for interesting new labels. But apparently the Deputy United States Marshals thought that grocery shopping was a very dangerous activity. Perhaps the prime suspect— that *pro se* litigant Jack Panko—might jump out from underneath a stack of produce at any time, wielding a sharp knife or improvised explosive device. It is hard to grocery shop with Deputy U.S. Marshals in tow. Were they secretly questioning Avery's product choices? Did she eat healthy enough? Too much junk food? Too much wine purchased? And then there was the quandary of how to buy personal toiletries with two hulky, young Deputy Marshals flanking you as your wing men. Judge Avery said that one day she was going to go to the pharmacy and purchase every embarrassing product in the store, just to see if she could rattle her stone-faced Marshals. After a while, it became something like a personal challenge, just to make them crack from their seriousness.

Anyway, it was not just trips to the grocery store that became a "family affair" with the Deputy Marshals. The Deputy Marshals accompanied Avery to church ("Good morning, Pastor Carlson. Who's this? Oh, it's my U.S. Marshal bodyguard. No big deal. Somebody just wants to kill me. In any event, the sermon today was so lovely."). The Deputy Marshals also accompanied Judge Avery to her monthly hair salon appointments. This was an experience–to be sure. Visiting "The Salon Viva" with the U.S. Marshals in tow was a bit like living through a scene from *La Cage aux Folles*. There was Rex, Judge Lassiter's gregarious, handsome hair stylist, who whirled around the salon excitedly singing "It's Raining Men, Hallelujah" every time Avery came in with her U.S. Marshals entourage. When Avery told Rex to please "ratchet it down a level," and jokingly asked, "Hadn't he ever had a client with bodyguards before?" Rex replied yes, twice. Once, when Rex styled the hair of a member of the 1980's rock group the *B-52's* and another time when he styled the hair of a high-priced call girl who was dating a drug cartel king pin. Avery did not feel too special about being a part of this small club.

And then there was Friday night football. Like a lot of folks in Texas, the Lassiters could be considered enthusiastic high school football fans—actually, more like rabid high school football fans. The last "pure" sport left—Avery was known to say. It was always "time for some football" in the Lassiter household. Officer Max, long before he was Mad Max busting heroin dealers and methamphetamine lab operators, happened to have a first career as a high school football coach—having no tolerance in that role for the weak or faint-of-heart player (quotable: "the *asthma* field is that way, son; this here is the *playing* field").[2] "Coach Max" led many young athletes to that "promised land" of state high school football championships and NCAA "signing day" glory, before later leading other young people to hard time in prison. In any event, most people are aware that, in Texas generally, high school football is big. Strike that. It is enormous. But, make no mistake, Southlake, Texas is not just any small suburban Texas town that loves and celebrates its home town grid irons. Southlake is the cradle for arguably one of the most storied high school football dynasties in Texas and the nation.

In Southlake, Texas, everyone in town goes to *every* Friday night football game–rain or shine (although, without a doubt, most of the games are played in sweltering 104-degree weather). Southlake has won more State high school championships than any town in Texas—although some would definitely challenge that claim. Southlake calls itself the "Dragon Nation"—stubbornly sticking to one high school in town, so that everyone is a "Dragon," no matter how populated the municipality becomes. Kids start learning the no-huddle, fast paced offense at the peewee football league level (with all teams in every peewee league using the mascot "Dragons—it's "Dragons v. Dragons" in every game). By the time the youngsters are 15-years-old, every football play in the official playbook is engrained in their brains, and hard work in the gym all summer long (unsupervised by coaches, of course—U.I.L. rules and all) is the norm. "Hard work beats talent when talent doesn't work hard" is the locker room mantra. The football uniform is emerald green and black, with a menacing-looking, fire-breathing dragon against a background of the Lone Star State map. The Dragon football stadium is nicer than most

---

[2] Coach Max *possibly* borrowed that phrase from former Dallas Cowboys NFL football coach Jimmy Johnson.

college stadiums throughout the country. When the football team departs the high school campus on Friday afternoons in the fall in its long, school bus caravan, heading toward the stadium for its pregame warmups, it is accompanied by a police escort that is befitting of the President of the United States. Only, instead of "Hail to the Chief," the loud speakers on the buses blast "Green Day" rock band songs. Vehicles pull over to the side of the road along their route, to pay homage and respect to the team—letting the school buses pass by as though they are part of a royal procession. And tailgating for the games, if it is a particularly good opponent, starts at 8:30 am on Friday mornings. Games are always selling out—standing room only—and an absolute spectacle. There are pregame activities such as paratroopers jumping onto the football field during player warmups, fighter jets passing by, pets in costumes, fireworks, and vendors selling sushi and other gourmet food. The 500-member school band blares "Dr. Who" and "We are the Champions" and the usual big game playlist of tunes to rev up the crowd. Big blond hair, pink cowboy hats, diamonds, furs, glitter, bling, and boots are the proper attire for the women. And for Homecoming, the girls' mums are as big as picnic tables. The half time shows are a cross between a Broadway show and a Rose Bowl Parade. And during the all-important playoffs, all football team players, as well as boys as young as preschoolers, bleach their hair bright blond in a show of solidarity to winning. "PROTECT THE TRADITION" is the motto emblazoned everywhere. But, with all the fanfare and hoopla—with all the extravagance, curiosities, and pageantry—perhaps no one, until Heath, Julia, and the Lassiters, had ever attended Southlake Dragon football games with bodyguards—Deputy U.S. Marshals—in tow. At one game, a friend of Avery's whose son ran cross country with Heath said to her, "Oh my gosh! Those guys with you look like your bodyguards." Avery smiled. "Yea. They are." Actually, Avery was just relieved that her friend did not think that they looked like a hit squad (sadly, Southlake, on a recent occasion, had a drug cartel "hit" occur on a defense lawyer in the middle of the town square).

The Southlake Carroll Dragons won the State Class 5-A High School Football Championship in mid-December—four weeks after the U.S. Marshals started protecting Avery. The game was played at the Dallas Cowboys' AT&T Football Stadium, otherwise known as "Jerry World." The Deputy Marshals' top concern that night seemed to be making sure that they and the Lassiters did not randomly end up on the world's largest Jumbotron screen, sprawling 50 yards in length, above the Jerry World football field. No such luck. Fun-loving, giggly Julia found her way onto the big screen twice that night, to the Marshals' chagrin.

There were other fun victories that "Fall of the U.S. Marshals"—as it would later become known in the Lassiter household. Heath Lassiter's cross-country team also won the State 5-A High School Cross Country Championship in Roundrock, Texas that Fall. Perhaps the U.S. Marshals were the secret good luck charm that year.

In any event, time lagged on. Nothing bad happened, thanks to the Deputy U.S. Marshals, and Avery slowly regained her confidence and peace about the whole situation. This chapter of her life would eventually pass, and it would probably be fine in the end. But unbeknownst to Avery, the letter writer remained nearby. Time would reveal that the letter writer was never very far away from Avery. *He watched her paths always*. He would make his move when he was ready. It would not be too long until he was ready. As far as he was concerned, Avery's life expectancy was not very long at this point. And there would be others who would be brought down, too. There would be a massacre if he made everything fall together just right.

Part II:

The Escalation of the Death Threats.

Chapter 6:

The Next Communication.

One of the many changes to the Lassiters' daily routines after November 21st was that the family members were not allowed to go to the mailbox in front of the house anymore. The Deputy Marshals who were stationed at their residence assumed the chore of receiving and inspecting the daily mail, as one of their many official home-front duties. They insisted that they would be the only humans to possibly handle additional threatening letters or to intercept any dreaded, hazardous packages such as bombs that might arrive. Never mind that Avery and certainly Officer Max had plenty of expertise regarding what a suspicious package often looks like: a missing or nonsensical return address; a bulky or lumpy appearance; spots, stains, smudges or powders; careless wrapping; protruding wires.

As mentioned earlier, thankfully, there have not been too many cases of federal judge assassinations over the years. However, one rather notorious assassination involved a shrapnel-sheathed pipe bomb that was mailed to an Eleventh Circuit judge's home in Mountain Brook, Alabama—the late Judge Robert S. Vance—on December 16, 1989. The pipe bomb killed the judge and injured his wife. Walter Leroy Moody, Jr. (who had attended law school) was eventually convicted and sentenced to death for that crime. Moody had earlier declared a "war on the federal judiciary" and also targeted the NAACP, sending a smoke bomb to the NAACP's Atlanta office, and sending a letter to an Atlanta television station threatening more attacks. Moody was both a "howler" and a "hunter"—to use the U.S.

Marshals' terminology. In the same month that he killed Judge Vance, he sent the same type of pipe bomb to a respected civil rights attorney, Robert E. Robinson in Savannah, Georgia, killing him as well. Two other bombs, one directed to the Eleventh Circuit Court of Appeals building in Atlanta, and another to the NAACP building in Jacksonville, Florida, were intercepted. In any event, Avery—while acknowledging the necessity—vented about how awkward it was to have the Marshals retrieve and inspect her daily mail. "Guess I won't plan to order anything from the Victoria's Secret website anytime soon." That was sarcasm. University of Texas Longhorn running apparel was more often her lounge-around-the-house style. Avery also joked about how this was yet another intrusion into poor Baxter's personal space and his daily habits. Despite Baxter's pure blood lineage and superior pedigree, he was like the most ordinary and common of cross-bred mutts, when it came to the subject of the daily mail delivery. Avery surmised that it must be fundamentally at the canine core to bark ferociously and jump up and down wildly whenever a U.S. Postal Service truck winds its way down a quiet street. No amount of royal breeding or obedience training in the world can wrench this primal instinct away from any dog. The postal delivery woman who delivered the Lassiters' mail is named Marcy, and she always winked and smiled at Baxter whenever Avery and Baxter retrieved the mail, no matter how much toughness Baxter would feign on any particular day. It was a daily, late-afternoon ritual. Marcy would occasionally even give Baxter a treat and pat his pretty little dome head (that's what Marcy called it). In any event, the Deputy U.S. Marshals had no respect for this dog-postal carrier tradition and every afternoon, Baxter would look out the front window crestfallen as the mail truck came and went, without him being let anywhere near it. The stern-faced Deputy Marshals would daily strut to the curbside before Marcy even made her way to the next-door neighbor's box and hold out their big bear-like hands and take the Lassiters' mail without letting Marcy get out of the truck. Marcy looked horrified and confused. Avery wanted so very much to tell Marcy what was going on in the Lassiters' lives. Day after day, she prayed that Marcy would come early or that the Deputy Marshals would be on a bathroom break during mail delivery time. But it was as though the Deputy Marshals had bladders of gods. Perhaps they wore adult diapers like the spurned female NASA astronaut who, according to news media reports, one day drove across country from Houston to Florida, to surprise and murder her former boyfriend's new astronaut paramour. "Probably a silly thought," Avery sighed to herself.

In mid-December, such silliness and fretting over the daily mail retrieval procedures seemed unimportant. The letter writer suddenly resurfaced—once again choosing the Lassiters' home mailbox. After almost four weeks of radio silence, Avery had almost started to relax and wondered if the Lassiters would spend the Christmas holidays without their Marshal guardians. But that thought was a mere fleeting fancy. Unlike the first letter, the new one did not contain profanity, nor repeated, hate-filled threats. It was not a bloodthirsty rant. It was not a lengthy manifesto. The new letter was, once again, directed to the "Honorless Judge Lassiter." But this letter was cryptic and strange and full of riddles and bizarre language (actually, it was all literary references, although the Deputy Marshals and data-analyzing, algorithm-running young FBI Agents did not at first recognize that). The new letter read as follows:

"I have not moved on. I
have not forgotten or forgiven you. I
am definitely not scared of your

Marshal protectors. In fact, I mock their seriousness and their apparent belief that they can disrupt my mission. THIS WILL BE A TRILOGY IN FIVE PARTS. My plan to punish the elitist judiciary and its cronies will give a whole new meaning to the term trilogy. Here are some clues about me and my mission. He drove a Ford Prefect. And now I know the ultimate meaning of life, the universe, and everything. The answer is 42. And the universe is in the safe hands of a simple man living on a remote planet in a wooden shack with his cat. I've always said that there was something fundamentally wrong with the universe. You are part of the problem. You judges, the lawyers, the rich who rule the universe—you are all part of the problem. Soon you will die like the Paranoid Android."

Judicial Inspector Mark Eason was the Deputy Marshal who came to Avery's chambers, the next day, and broke the news that a new letter had been received at the Lassiters' house the previous day. Avery was not sure why the Marshals had delayed a bit in telling her.

It was very close to the Christmas holidays—maybe they were trying to spare the family more bad news during what should have been a happy, joyous time. Sweet of them, if that was the case. Julia was at the courthouse that day with Avery—the kids were already off from school for their Winter Break. Julia was standing next to the large aquarium tank full of colorful tropical fish in Avery's chambers as Mark Eason read the new letter to them both. Julia pulled away from the fish tank and appeared visibly shaken. She walked over toward her mom and Deputy Eason. Avery and Julia had, by this point, developed a fond admiration of and friendship with Judicial Inspector Mark Eason. They nicknamed him "Big Easy" because of his last name "Eason" and because he had gone to college at Loyola in New Orleans. Avery and Julia both saw Mark Eason in a green hue—a peaceful shade of emerald green. Judge Lassiter and Big Easy had coincidentally gone to the same large Texas high school (different years) and felt a unique bond because of this connection, but they also somehow seemed to be kindred spirits who shared similar philosophies, faiths, and interests. They had, in a short time, shared much of their views on life.

"Weird shit, huh?" stated the serious Mark Eason, asking apologies for his coarse language in front of Julia. "But please don't start to panic all over again, Judge. The FBI has put Quantico onto this. This is strange, specific wording that will hopefully mean something to the profiling geniuses at Quantico. But do any of these bizarre references mean anything to you, Judge Lassiter?"

"Uh, yeah. This is crazy. It's mostly references to the *Hitchhiker's Guide to the Galaxy* set of books. You know what I'm talking about, right? The geeky British science fiction set of books that were made into radio and television shows. I think there are even comic books and computer games based on the books. Anyway, there are weird references in the books to the number 42 being the secret to the meaning of life. And Ford Prefect is actually the name of a character in the books, although I understand it is actually also an old British car that was made."

Big Easy sighed and rolled his eyes. "OK. So I guess our letter writer is a real geek. Maybe it's that dark web porn freak that you had in your court recently?"

"Or, maybe it is someone who just gets my quirky sense of humor, Big Easy. I'm frequently, at random times, using the number 42 in court when I use examples and hypotheticals. You know like, 'Defendant, I've given you 42 chances to get this right' or, 'I'm taking a recess and we will reconvene in 42 minutes,' *etc*. It's my own bizarre inside joke to geeks. The book series references the number 42 as being 'the answer to the meaning of life.' It's just a bizarre cult type of thing. 42 is my favorite number—if such a thing is possible—because of my inner geek. I suppose a lot of lawyers know that I am nerdy that way and that I sometimes throw out veiled references to those *Hitchhiker* books in court."

"Judge, I guess I should ask you what *color* is the number 42 in your and Julia's unusual brains. I'm not sure I am ever going to understand this whole Synesthesia thing that you both have going on." Deputy Eason quipped.

Avery and Julia both chimed "it's orange" in unison. "Actually, "4" is red when it stands alone and "2" is yellow, so "42" looks kind of orange."

Deputy Eason shook his head. "Anyway, do you think the letter writer was in court one day and happened to hear you make those veiled references to 42 and those books? What could it mean? Do you know what all those references mean?"

"No. I don't know. I really have no idea." Avery sighed. "I confess that I am a little freaked out right now, Big Easy. I was starting to think this was all about to end—after four weeks of silence. In the past few weeks, I've gone from being a little bit afraid—mostly for my kids' sake—to thinking that this is a big nothing. Now this. Now he is wanting to play some stupid sort of game with me? Why is he doing this? Why is he putting me and my family and the Marshals through such insanity? Actually, I guess I am starting to feel more mad than scared. In fact, I am furious about what he is putting so many people through. I am actually embarrassed and humiliated by all of this. Did I do something to deserve this? I actually feel that way sometimes. Maybe my judicial temperament caused this or something."

Julia suddenly stood up. "Mom and Deputy Eason, do you think it is strange that the first letter last November had that page enclosed, that had the pictures of the 42 eyes (21 pairs) and it was also sent on Mom's 42nd birthday? And now there are all these references to 42 in the new letter?"

"From the mouths of babes," Avery whispered. "I think she could be on to something, Big Easy. But what—I have no idea."

Again, the FBI Agents subsequently studied the letter. They asked Avery's staff to search through every court audio recording or transcript of hearings in her court for the last few years, to find instances where Judge Lassiter had made a veiled reference to the *Hitchhiker's Guide to the Galaxy* during court (an unbelievably time-consuming and arduous task). They asked Avery's staff to search court records of any person in her court who might have owned a Ford

Prefect automobile (an equally arduous task). They would simultaneously search Department of Motor Vehicle records for any persons in the U.S. who owned this type of car. There could not be that many—the old British vehicle had not been in production since the year 1961 and had only been sold at selected Ford dealerships in the U.S. from 1958 through 1961. But, as for the newest letter, there was once again no forensic evidence left. No immediate clues regarding who may have written the letter, except that it was someone who, for some reason, wanted to reference *The Hitchhiker's Guide to the Galaxy.*

It felt as though, after approximately four weeks, there had been absolutely no progress in identifying the letter writer. And now the letter writer was at it again. Avery was at an absolute loss for making any sense of any of this. She thought things might be winding down. She thought that the letter writer had possibly done a little howling and then had moved on with his life. This was the fantasy of the uninitiated. This apparently was not the case. In any event, at least Avery and her family remained unharmed. She tried to keep the right frame of mind about all of this. This was just another tricky day in their lives. The new letter was so extremely specific, with what appeared to be "clues" sprinkled in. Maybe he wanted to be caught at this point. Surely this new letter would lead to identification of the author and an arrest.

Chapter 7:

Just Like the Game "Clue," Everyone is a Suspect.

After the second death threat letter was sent to Avery, there was more inexplicable silence. The letter writer did not appear in the Lassiters' lives in any way—either with another letter or other action. And the FBI likewise was uncommunicative. Christmas approached, and no one seemed to have any hint about how the FBI investigation was going, or if the invisible, reclusive Special Agents had even made the slightest progress in identifying the letter writer. Avery did not receive updates of any kind. There were no weekly status conferences or memos. She constantly bemoaned the fact that she was on a "need to know basis" and apparently was not perceived as needing to know anything. And, yet, someone in the inner circle of knowledge (whomever was in that "inner circle") deemed it necessary to keep Avery under 24-hour-a-day Marshal protection. Why was that?

Avery's frustration grew exponentially with each passing day. Avery kept a running tabulation, of sorts, on a white, dry erase board in her kitchen of how many days had elapsed since the death threat letters had first arrived: Day 1, Day 2, Day 3, Day 42, *etc.* She joked that it was like her own private, hellish version of the Iran Hostage/Ted Kopel *Night Line* day-count. No one in the family knew what that meant. Avery had a tendency to launch into monologues—attempts at conversations as to which no one in the household had the first clue as to what she was referring. Kind of like when she referred to people as emanating certain colors. In any event, one of Avery's friends must have "gotten" the *Night Line* joke, because she gave Avery a digital clock for her desk, that worked similar to the digital clock that lurks high above New York City's Times Square and counts the ever-growing U.S. National Debt, and joked that they should wager a bet as to how long this clock would keep counting and this would all go on. Avery decided to keep the digital clock up on a shelf in the kitchen, next to the white dry erase board, to replace her daily ritual of marking the days by hand on the board. The day after she did that, Officer Max wrote one of his favorite quotes on Avery's white board: "There are hunters and there are victims. By your discipline, cunning, obedience and alertness, you will decide if you are a hunter or a victim." General James "Mad Dog" Mattis. What a lovely, inspiring thought, Avery smirked. Avery looked down and sighed at Baxter and patted his pretty domed head, "That cop we live with has such a way with words, doesn't he Buddy?"

Not knowing what is going on–not having information–is a particularly bad feeling when one is a victim of a crime and possibly a target of a wolf—a predator—wanting to harm you or your family. It can create paranoia. It can create enormous stress. It can create grumpiness. And–in Avery's case in particular–it created a lot of amateur detectives. Everyone had a theory. Everyone felt under an obligation to report anything suspicious to Avery and the Deputy Marshals. And every strange occurrence led to agitation and distrust. Every person who acted bizarrely in court or any place else became a suspect. The paranoia and suspects surfaced at the strangest times in the strangest ways.

Case in point: during the week of Christmas, Avery had a trial in her courtroom. The courthouse was largely empty, dark, and quiet that week. Avery's chambers smelled heavenly with the aroma of

Christmas tamales and warm salsa—dropped off by one of Avery's favorite judge friends who had drawn the short straw to be "duty judge" during that week (the "duty judge" is the magistrate judge who signs warrants when necessary and presides over initial appearances and bond setting hearings that are required for any criminal arrests that occur; such hearings are required to be held within 72 hours of an arrest). Many employees had taken leave from work. Most lawyers had asked for continuances or settled their matters the week of Christmas. It always amazed Avery how the holidays could engender goodwill and cheer among even the most uncharitable and recalcitrant members of the bar and their clients. But not the litigants in *Huang v. Swan*. They were ready for trial.

The trial would be a bench trial—as was usually the case with Avery's financial disputes—so Avery at least did not need to feel guilty about bringing in a jury the week of Christmas. And two good lawyers would be involved in *Huang v. Swan*, which was always a treat for Avery and her staff. It would be the "Robot" versus the "Whale." These were nicknames that Avery's staff had given the lawyers privately back in chambers. The Robot was a lawyer who had a voice like a master thespian—always taking dramatic pauses at the right time and always using the perfect metaphors, quotes and phrases. The Robot was perfectly groomed, perfectly dressed (with an American flag pin on his lapel), had a blond crew cut, piercing green eyes, and could recite verbatim every Rule of Evidence and statute ever enacted. He had memorized every case ever decided. Avery's law clerk and intern said he was a cyborg; he absolutely had to be part man and part machine. They joked that they expected the Robot to one day turn into liquid metal, like the T-1000 shape-shifting android-assassin in the movie *Terminator 2: Judgment Day*. The Robot's perfection in the courtroom was absolutely frightening (intriguing and entertaining, but frightening). The Robot would be representing Mr. Swan in the trial. Meanwhile, the Whale would be representing the plaintiff, Mr. Huang. The Whale was a very tall and quite heavy attorney who was like a junk yard dog. He had long black hair, a gray and black beard, and had droopy brown eyes. While disheveled and always reeking of cigarette smoke, he had no quit in him and could eke out a win or settlement in the most hopeless of situations. He wore his Harvard college ring on his right middle finger—no doubt a subliminal gesture of sorts to his adversaries. He once sat on the corner of counsel table in the middle of a trial and it broke in two (he paid for it). He was well known to have been married four times—each time to a much younger woman. His lavish weddings and spectacular divorces were often the subject of headlines. One of the Whale's classic *modus operandi* was to constantly mispronounce everyone's name (except his client's and the judge's), as if to subtly signal "you mean nothing to me—I cannot even remember your name." The Whale was a little obnoxious—to say the least. But he had street smarts. And, boy, was he good in the courtroom.

Huang v. Swan involved a romantic relationship between two men that had grown sour, to say the least. The defendant, a man named Peter Swan, was quite handsome, gray-haired, sophisticated, and suave—the kind of guy who wears an ascot tie (Hermes, of course) and $1,000 cuff links. He had filed a personal bankruptcy case shortly after he had jilted a naïve younger boyfriend who had loaned or given Swan $750,000. A bankruptcy case—for shame! The "Scarlett B." The jilted boyfriend, Mike Huang, was the plaintiff. He was a small, skinny tech wizard who had made lots of money during the early days of Google, but now was unemployed and had squandered much of his fortune. Mr. Huang filed a lawsuit within Mr. Swan's bankruptcy case, asking Judge Lassiter to treat the $750,000 he gave to

Mr. Swan as a loan, rather than a gift, and bar his former paramour from wiping the debt out in his bankruptcy case.

The trial testimony became quite salacious and Mr. Huang became quite emotional throughout the trial. The trial was like a soap opera on steroids. Among other things, Swan had many other romantic entanglements–both male and female and young and old— many of whom were sitting in the courtroom, as though this would be a day of reckoning for Mr. Swan. Swan had, only two years earlier, become divorced from his second wife, who was enraged at him for now being delinquent in paying child support. He also had a pregnant secretary, dutifully sitting by his side during trial. He had a much older female friend that referred to herself as Swan's "sugar momma" that he had met at Alcoholics' Anonymous, who testified that she had also loaned Swan more than $500,000 herself. He had a stripper girlfriend nicknamed Brown Sugar. And then there was an endless list of young men whom he had met at the "Dragon Fly Night Club," including Mr. Huang. If all of this were not enough, Swan kept winking at Avery throughout the trial. Frankly, just another tricky day in Avery's court—as she would later say. But on the second morning of the trial, Mr. Huang looked rather distressed and ashen sitting at the table next to the Whale. He was called as the first witness of the day. As he oddly sashayed across the courtroom from his seat to the witness stand to be sworn in, he turned to Avery and said in his thick Vietnamese accent, "I brought everyone here today a Christmas present." Avery was somewhat confused and could not fully understand what he was saying. She looked around at others in the courtroom to gauge their expressions. Mr. Swan creepily winked at Avery for about the fourteenth or so time during the trial. Then Mr. Huang said it again, "I brought everyone here today a Christmas present." At that point, Avery sent Annalise, her judicial assistant, an

Instant Message, asking if she was listening-in, back on the chamber's intercom, to the court proceedings. Moments later, for a third time, Mr. Huang stated that he brought everyone in the courtroom a Christmas present. Seconds after he said it for the third time, two Deputy U.S. Marshals bolted into the courtroom with guns drawn. They didn't know what Mr. Huang was about to do, but it could not be good and–maybe, just maybe–this was the letter writer. After all, Mr. Huang had been in court a few times before on discovery disputes and other pretrial motions. Maybe Mr. Huang was so upset about this lawsuit and something Judge Lassiter had done already that he was the one who had sent the letters.

But as it turned out, this was not the case. Mr. Huang was a sweet and meek young man. He was devastated about what Mr. Swan had done to him and to so many others. He was exhausted with his lawsuit. The Deputy Marshals questioned him, and he simply wept. He said he was simply going to drop his lawsuit and forget about Mr. Swan and his mistake in ever getting involved with him. And this (*i.e.,* dropping the lawsuit) was his "Christmas present." And, although his lawyer the Whale did not know of this strategy, they took a break and talked, and that is precisely what Mr. Huang decided to do. Mr. Huang had no weapon, no criminal history, no mental illness, and–happily for him–he had found a new job in the last 24 hours. While it all seemed rather strange, Mr. Huang apparently meant no harm and was not the letter writer. He had just used the strangest choice of words at the strangest time and scared everyone in the courtroom to death.

But this was not the only scare and "false alarm" that Christmas week. Later that same day of the Swan-Huang trial, Avery was in her court chambers quietly working, signing some orders. She had holiday music playing softly in the background and was thinking about heading out soon, to maybe work in some last-minute Christmas shopping at the Galleria. The Deputy Marshals were going to love that—hitting a crowded mall with her during Christmas. Maybe she should not stress them out in that way. Suddenly Avery's thoughts were interrupted by a scream from Annalise outside of her office. Avery rushed over to Annalise's desk and Annalise was trembling, holding the mail. Annalise said, "Judge Lassiter, it has just gotten so much worse; now someone has threatened to slash and kill your son Heath! I've got to call the Marshals and ask if they can go check on him! Do you know where he should be right now?"

What had come in the mail? Well, unbeknownst to Annalise, it was not a threat to Avery's son. It was actually just an autographed picture of the rock musician Slash (of *Guns 'N Roses*, fame). It seems that one of Judge Lassiter's friends was in a romantic relationship with a Los Angeles fashion designer "Sean," who happened to be working on a reality television show that would feature the famous rock star Slash and his then-wife Pearla. "Sean" was working on Pearla's wardrobe for the show. When Judge Lassiter had heard about this, she told her friend that her son Heath was a huge fan of Slash. Judge Lassiter's friend then decided it would be a special, fun thing to ask "Sean" to see if Slash could send Heath an autographed picture–which he did. The picture was of Slash with his wild, long, black messy hair, in his trademarked black top hat, playing his famous Les Paul electric guitar. Slash had written on the picture, in messy cursive writing: *"To Heath–Rock 'n Fuck 'n Roll, SLASH."* Annalise had no idea who this wild black-haired tall thin man in a top hat was, and she could only make out the words *"Heath"* and *"SLASH."* She naturally jumped to the conclusion that some strange, menacing, wild black-haired tall, thin man in a top hat was threatening to "slash" young Heath. Judge Lassiter quickly recognized that it was, in fact, a picture of the rock star Slash, and Avery's friend had sent her a very sweet (except for the profanity) Christmas gift to give to her son Heath.

Actually, the paranoia and crazy stories proliferated on an almost daily basis. Judge Lassiter had been one of three judges who had handled certain aspects of a high-profile bankruptcy case of a professional sports team and her name appeared in media reports during that case. A lot of the public were unhappy about things that happened during that case. Was some disgruntled sports fan the letter writer? People in Texas are outrageously passionate when it comes to their sports teams. Judge Lassiter also presided over a case involving a Bitcoin exchange site where millions of dollars' worth of the cryptocurrency had gone mysteriously missing, despite the allegedly impenetrable exchange site and secure online wallets in which the Bitcoin was traded and stored. Actors ranging from Russian hackers to rogue government agents-gone-bad were suspected of misappropriating the missing cryptocurrency. Judge Lassiter was pressing for answers in that case. Was someone worried about what she was going to find? Was there some dastardly evil actor behind it all? And then there were the many *pro se* litigants, so-called "Constitutionalists" or "sovereign citizens" who hated the U.S. government generally. Currently there was a fellow in Avery's court who referred to himself interchangeably as an Aboriginal Native American, a Moroccan sheik, and the High Priest of the Fahme Nation Church. He would submit paperwork to the court that, instead of being signed, contained a red thumb print that looked like it was blood stained. Was this the letter writer? When he would come to court, he came with an entourage, and he wore long black and gray dreadlocks, a black pinstriped suit, and a giant cross around his neck. He relied on an international treaty from the year 1789 between the governments of the United States and Morocco as a defense to everything. Sometimes he would inexplicably attach to his court paperwork documents that were purportedly signed by former Secretary of State Condaleezza Rice and former Texas Governor Ann Richards. He accused Judge Lassiter, in an evangelical-like fervor, of imposing slavery upon him and violating the U.S. Constitution. His modus operandi was to sue big corporations for millions of dollars for reasons hard to ascertain. Judge Lassiter had recently come down pretty hard on him— designating him as a "vexatious litigant," awarding monetary sanctions to a large corporation that he had sued and enjoining the fellow from filing future lawsuits.

Another litigant in Judge Lassiter's court, Dilbert Franz, a bankrupt internet website designer who had connections to child-porn websites and illegal "dark web" activity, came under suspicion. This individual believed Judge Lassiter had ruined his life by exposing some of his illegal activity. Strangely, the FBI investigators had discovered that Franz happened to be friends with Jack Panko—the earlier described "howler" whose life mission seemed to be complaining in public regarding "all of the terrible things Judge Lassiter had done to him and his disabled brother." Was Franz the letter writer—or perhaps Franz and Panko working together in tandem? And then there was the Nigerian wholesale diamond and "gold dust" dealer who stole millions of dollars from elderly investors for a fraudulent enterprise. Judge Lassiter had approved a bankruptcy trustee's confiscation of a rare 6.32 carat pink diamond from him that he had secreted and ordered the diamond to be sold by Sotheby's Auction house in New York to pay the investors whom the man had defrauded. She had also referred him to the U.S. Attorney for securities fraud violations. Was it this unscrupulous, conniving Nigerian that wanted to kill her?

The truth is that, when you make rulings that adversely affect a person's money and livelihood, it can motivate people to do strange things. When you have the ability to take a person's freedom, that's one thing. But when you have a measure of control over a person's pocket book, it can inflame passions just as much. Judge Lassiter presided over thousands of bankruptcy cases and hundreds of civil lawsuits (adversary proceedings) related to those cases. Someone became upset with Avery almost on a daily basis. When Judge Lassiter was a young attorney–on a hot July day in the 1990's–one of her former "Big Law" colleagues went into a Texas state courthouse to make an oral argument to the court of appeals in a business dispute. Just another day in his life. But it would be the last day of his life. A disgruntled civil lawyer named George L., with no criminal record whatsoever, walked into the same courtroom that day, with a gun, and fired randomly into the courtroom at three judges and several lawyers whom he did not know. This was in the days before metal detectors were a normal way of life in Texas courthouses. The disgruntled lawyer was upset about a recent divorce that he had personally endured. When George L. was finished with his shooting spree, two lawyers whom he did not even know were dead, including Judge Lassiter's law firm colleague, and a Texas state assistant district attorney. Various others including a judge were shot but lived. George L. later pleaded guilty to capital murder and asked to be put to death. George L. eventually died by lethal injection. In Texas, there is no hesitation to punish murderers with the death penalty. In fact, some folks would prefer it if death sentences were carried out by firing squads and would not hesitate to volunteer to be on those firing squads.

Judge Lassiter had never forgotten this painful memory from her early law practice days—the memory of a hardworking decent family man, who worked hard as a lawyer every day of his life, always trying to do the right thing, who was senselessly gunned down by a stranger who was simply angry at his own ex-wife and the legal system. It served as a constant reminder that Avery's current situation was not a simple matter to unravel. People get emotional, indignant, apoplectic. It is not always the felons or people with terrible, troubled histories that lash out. Courtrooms are crucibles where emotions catch fire. Judge Lassiter often said that her courtroom was a lot like a playground for upset adults. Identifying the letter writer was going to be like finding a needle in a haystack. Judge Lassiter felt like the proverbial sitting duck who would just have to wait for the letter writer to strike or make a mistake. He would. Sadly, the letter writer would strike and strike hard when he did. She had no idea how bad it would soon become.

Chapter 8:

The Sword of Damocles.

It was December 31st. The 42nd day since November 19—the day that the letter writer had penned his very first angry missive to Avery. It was a frigid New Year's Eve. The air outside had a whitish-purplish hue and felt thick with moisture. Visibility was low. Avery was working at home in her study—surrounded by a sea of paper and law books—on an opinion involving the legality of a medical doctor's offshore asset transfers, that she hoped to get out before the end of the year. She was drawing all over a couple of white dry erase boards like a mad scientist, creating flow charts mapping out the doctor's opaque bank accounts and shell companies that he had scattered about in exotic locations. Avery was also planning to take on the dreaded task of taking down the Christmas tree later, since Brimley the cat was getting ever-more brazen in his attacks on its low-hanging ornaments. He was currently waging war on a Grinch ornament—having obviously recognized a kindred spirit in that character. The kids were, of course, still out of school for Winter Break. Like all kids, Avery's were hoping for snow on a day like this. But it wouldn't happen. Baba Jo and Julia were in the kitchen making cookies for the poor Deputy Marshals that had the unlucky job of working on New Year's Eve, out in their gadget-filled RV in the Lassiters' backyard. Officer Max was at work himself, sitting in the cold for hours in an old beige Oldsmobile undercover police car in a parking lot in front of the Wa-Wa Spa, next to North Dallas Bank, trying to catch a band of "juggers" that had been targeting Korean business owners recently at a couple of banks in Northwest Dallas.

Meanwhile, despite the chilly temperature, Heath Lassiter had dutifully gone out for a long afternoon run. It was Heath's senior year of high school and his cross-country career had just finished in the fall, but he still ran at least 50 miles per week. He would run the 3,200-meter event during the spring track season. Maybe the 1,600-meter, too—although he was much better at long distances. He liked running during cold weather. There was only about a month or two of really crisp cold temperatures in North Texas. It was a rare treat to run in the frosty air, Heath thought. A different kind of adrenaline rush took hold when he did. Heath's running was especially good right now. No problems with his plantar fasciitis or other aches and pains. He was wondering how close he could come to his personal record best of a 4:24 minute mile today if he really pushed himself. Maybe he would run up to the senior high school track in a bit and test his time. Or maybe not—he didn't have his cleats because he only planned on a long endurance run that day. Heath wore only running shorts and a sleeveless tank as he barreled down Southlake Boulevard in the below-freezing temperature. He had his ear buds in that day, even though his coach had told the team never to run with head phones. He had gotten the new ear buds for Christmas and he wanted to test them out.

As Heath decided to turn the corner into the nearby Southridge Lakes neighborhood, he slowed up his pace. He saw three girls from his team running together up ahead. A nice unexpected development. Maybe he would catch up with them and just clock in the rest of his mileage with the girls that day. He definitely would not be trying to break his personal best up at the track. They were some of the cutest girls on the team. As he pondered the situation, he noticed he had an untied shoe and bent down to tie his right Nike. He took a few sips of water from his camel back tube and checked his watch. Then he refocused on the girls and decided to plow ahead toward them.

Suddenly Heath noticed an old beat up maroon Chevy van slowing down near the girls. The girls had stopped and were apparently visiting with whomever was inside. He had a bad feeling about the van. It looked like it did not belong in the neighborhood. Heath suddenly thought to himself that he sounded like his dad, profiling people. But in all seriousness, the van didn't look like a work van of any sort—no ladders or signage or anything like that. And he noticed the van had paper license tags—Heath's dad had always said that about half of the paper tags out there were fake and whenever he saw a vehicle engaged in suspicious maneuvers with paper tags on it, his antennae went up. Heath was afraid the van driver might be some creep trying to pick up the girls. Even a predator possibly. He sped up his pace. As he was closing in, he saw the girls turn around and look in Heath's direction. Perhaps that was a signal to him that something wasn't right, and they were looking toward Heath for help. But why didn't they just scream and run away if something was wrong? Heath saw someone inside the van hand a piece of paper to the girls. The van then sped away as though it were being chased.

As Heath caught up to the girls, the van was well out of sight— leaving only a faint trail of exhaust fumes in its wake. The girls turned to Heath, each with a funny expression. One of them, Sarah, said, "Hey, Heath. That was really, really weird. I'm not sure what just happened."

Heath looked at her strangely, "Who was in that van? Did y'all know him? Was it some creep trying to pick y'all up?"

"There was a guy in the van who seemed pretty weird, alright, but he asked about you, Heath. He stopped and yelled out at us, 'Hey, do y'all know Heath Lassiter?' When we said yes, he asked was that you back there a few yards behind us. We turned and saw you and said yes, and then he handed us this piece of paper and said to give it to you. Then he sped off."

Heath took the piece of paper. On it was a handwritten message. It read:

> *"Heath, you take Latin in school, right? Translate this for your mother. METUS EST PLENUS TYRANNIS (literally, 'fear is plentiful for tyrants').*
>
> *Tell your mother that the Sword of Damocles is hanging over her head, and that someday soon, I'll be cutting down the thread."*

Heath looked up at the girls. "Did you get his name, a description, his license tag number, anything?"

They looked back at him blankly. "Sorry. It all happened so fast. What is it?"

Heath didn't say a word. He abruptly turned and bolted home at a breakneck pace. The girls looked at each other in confusion. They didn't know if they should run after him or not. Heath was definitely on a pace to break 4:24. He ran recklessly through red lights and stop signs and angled through a Tom Thumb grocery store parking lot, at last reaching home. He stumbled into the backyard and found an Oak tree to crouch behind and vomited next to it, lingering there for a few moments as if he didn't know what he should do next. After his wave of nausea passed, he stood up and went and beat on the Marshals' RV door. The Marshals on duty opened the door and looked at Heath who was still panting almost uncontrollably. Bolton Paine was one of the deputies in the RV and he greeted Heath. "Hey, what's wrong, buddy? You look terrible. Why are you running dressed like it's summer time?"

"Some creep in a maroon Chevy van was stalking me and my friends just now on my run. He gave my friends this note to give to me. Please, don't tell my mom." Heath ran inside looking white as a sheet, hurried to the freezer in the kitchen, and—consistent with his usual ritual after a long run—scooped up a bucket full of ice, to go dump into his bath tub, where he would sit in ice water for a few minutes before following it up with a hot shower.

Meanwhile, Avery, oblivious to anything that had just happened, was on the phone with Officer Max who had just called in to check on things. Avery could hear the faint sound of ABBA music playing in the background.

"Honey, why do I hear the song *Dancing Queen* playing in the background?"

"Oh. That's our newest playlist for when we arrest someone and are hauling them in one of our squad cars to the jail. Why? Do you think that's 'cruel and unusual punishment' or something, Judge Lassiter?"

"Oh geez! Don't do that, Max! Y'all are just going to set someone over the edge, don't you think? I think the CIA used to do that to terrorists in Gitmo. That's probably where y'all got the idea. Anyway, you said you were trying to catch "juggers" today. Remind me again what 'juggers' are? That term sounds so post-apocalyptic somehow."

"Juggers are crooks that wait in bank parking lots, hoping to prey on people that they profile as always carrying, depositing, or withdrawing a lot of cash. Especially immigrant business owners. The term comes from old days, when merchants would bring jugs of coins into banks. The juggers scout banks where they know a lot of small business owners come and go every day. They see the patterns, when they come and go, they follow them, figure out where they work and live. They eventually mug or rob them. And while the juggers are spying on the innocent business owners, we are spying on the juggers. They probably think we are their competition some days—guys there to do the same thing. Anyway, we made two arrests today. Got eyes on several more. I'll be home in a bit. Anything going on at home?"

"Nope. Absolutely quiet today. Almost finished with my opinion."

"Good. Maybe tomorrow will be a good day for marathon college bowl game-watching. Get the popcorn ready."

"Longhorns, baby. Sugar Bowl at 7:45 tomorrow night. That's my main focus."

"Avery, actually, there is one sort of serious thing I want to discuss with you."

"Go on."

"Today I obviously had a lot of down time. When I was sitting in my car, I decided to just randomly do some google searches of your name and see what popped up. Were you aware that there are tons of websites where crackpots go and complain about judges? There's a website called "rogues in robes," another called "justice for sale," another called "the corrupt judiciary," and so on and so on. I found one where someone has nicknamed you "J-Lass" and they rant and rant about you. Have the FBI or any of the Marshals ever told you about this?"

"Really? Do you think they tell me anything, Officer Max?"

"Well, I'm going to mention it to Big Easy. Maybe it's completely unrelated to your threats. But some of this shit that is posted is pretty bad. It's arguably inciting violence—subtly suggesting that people should terrorize the judges and maybe do harm to them. You know, things like "confront them wherever they can." Maybe they can figure out who is behind them and shut them down at least."

"Well, good luck with that. There's this little thing called the First Amendment. See you in a bit."

"Copy that, J-Lass."

"Not funny."

Avery and Max were completely oblivious that on this "day 42" since the original threat, that all was not calm and quiet. The threat-maker had just reached out to rattle them once again. Only Heath and the Marshals knew.

The number 42.

Chapter 9:

Jury Duty.

It was a cold, gray January day. The nondescript, thin, pasty white male—the one who had mailed the letters to Judge Lassiter—walked into the Central Jury Room at Dallas's George Allen County Court House, situated several blocks west of the Earle Cabell Federal Building. Today, he was dressed in a gray business suit, plain blue striped tie, and black well-shined shoes. He carried his Swiss Gear lap top backpack with him, as always. He was neatly put together but did not appear to be comfortable or relaxed in his surroundings—despite his professional appearance. He nervously checked in with the jury room clerk, accepted a juror number card, and took a seat in one of the least crowded areas of the room, and waited with the rest of the citizens of Dallas County who had been summoned to jury duty that day.

The room was stuffy and cramped. Eventually a rotund elderly woman, with clown-like thick makeup and bright red lips, emanating the scent of a cheap lavender perfume, sat down next to the man and started coughing uncontrollably. "Great," he thought, "fuck my luck." She eventually stopped and reached for some breath mints out of her large over-stuffed purse and offered one to him. He declined. She then started chattering incessantly about how hard it was going to be to get through the day without smoking a cigarette. He curtly replied to her, "It will be good for you. Those things will kill you." She gave him a sullen look and turned the other direction. "Good," the man thought. "That comment had the intended result—she won't talk to me anymore today." There was an escalating buzz of awkward conversation among the strangers in the room—most of the people could be overheard complaining about being there, but some of them were idealistic and excited. Fools, he thought. The man was surprised that such a large number of people actually opened their mail and complied with their civic duty to appear. People were such losers, he thought. He figured that half of the people in the room couldn't even read or understand a jury summons, and the other half wouldn't care about the consequences of not showing up. The man pulled out his cell phone and began texting someone.

"Wake up! Want to hear an example of irony? Been called to jury duty. Lol. At the county court right now."

"Yep, that's irony for sure. Lol. But shouldn't have updated ur driver's license and shit—bread crumbs!"

"Too late now. I probably know more than any of the fucking lawyers and judges in this building, given my history. I could school them. Maybe I should put the lawyers in their place during *voir dire*. Lol."

"*Voir dire?*"

"It's when the lawyers question the people in the jury pool, trying to figure out who might have biases or prejudices and might not make a good juror."

"Biases or prejudices? Lol. Oh, nah, you don't have any of those. LMAO. Do you hope you get picked?"

"Hell no. Well, I don't know. Depends, I guess. You know how I feel about lawyers and judges—and people generally, lol. I may blow a gasket if I have to sit and listen to loser lawyers for days and days, talking down to me like I'm an idiot. But maybe I could use this opportunity to add a few more names to our list of corrupt assholes who do not deserve to live. I'm sure the lawyers and judges are as bad and corrupt over here in this courthouse as everywhere else. Speaking of this courthouse, the security here is way more lax compared to federal. Metal detectors, yes, but only on the first floor, and there are not that many security guards, and it seems like they only scan about half the people who come through. Too bad it's not this easy at Earle Cabell. Lol."

"Oh, you'd get bored if they made things too easy for you. You like a challenge. It's only satisfying if you have to be creative and show your genius to them all. Lol. Gtg. Ttyl."

The man looked around the jury room. What a bunch of fucking pawns. They all would probably fall for anything a lawyer told them. They all probably had no clue about how the system works and would follow like lemmings into any ridiculous place the lawyers led them. At least he hadn't been summoned to criminal court. The trials over there were just a bunch of asshole DAs putting asshole cops on the witness stand. The idiot jurors always believed the cops. And the cops always lied. The only defendants who were ever found not guilty were the ones who got the priciest defense lawyers who could trick the jurors into believing anything. No doubt money payoffs were a regular part of the process. He hated them all. They were all scum.

The man's thoughts were suddenly distracted when the clerk told the jury panel to listen and turn their attention to the overhead monitors where they would be shown a 15-minute video about the importance of jury service. After that, folks would be told where to go next. The man shifted in his chair uncomfortably and glared up at the nearest screen. Good God. The video featured some of the pillars of the Dallas community, telling him how special jury duty was and how important they all were. He'd go through the motions today. But what a joke.

About an hour later, the clerk finally started calling people for jury panels. The man had a low number, so he suspected his chances were pretty high of being put on a jury panel. He was right. He was in the second group called. He was told to report to a courtroom on the 5th floor. He followed the line of people moving like sheep toward the outrageously slow elevators. He avoided eye contact and speaking with the masses. He didn't want to be there with them.

Finally, about thirty minutes after being forced to sit shoulder-to-shoulder with strangers on the cold, hard pews in the courtroom of the Honorable Wayne T. Barnes, there was some activity. Approximately a half-dozen lawyers came into the front of the courtroom, exiting from the chamber doors of Judge Barnes, and started settling into places at the counsel table. There were dozens of banker boxes piled up around the walls of the courtroom, and lawyers began pulling files and notepads and laptop computers out of them. It was obvious that one group of lawyers (four of them) represented a deep pocket corporation, and the other two lawyers were likely representing a humbler client. One group of lawyers (all men) wore slicked back perfect hair and expensive dark wool suits with tailor made shirts, silk red ties, cufflinks, and Italian loafers. They each had a polished, fraternal, athletic look. They had similarly well-dressed clients who were sipping Starbucks lattes, constantly checking cell phones, and looking incensed about being in a courtroom. They no doubt had billion-dollar companies that they needed to be running, or a golf game or three-martini lunch at the Dallas Country Club that they would be missing. Or maybe they were hedge fund managers—they had that air of hubris about them that was so characteristic of those

Wall Street assholes. The two other lawyers had bad haircuts and cheap, ill-fitting suits (one wearing Seersucker in January), with brown, smudged loafers, and looked as though they had been up all night. They had an elderly man and three blue collar looking adults in their 30's or 40's sitting next to them. A courtroom deputy suddenly jerked to attention and yelled "all rise; the 199th Judicial District Court of Dallas County, Texas is now in session. The Honorable Wayne T. Barnes presiding." A tall, lanky African American, bald man in a black robe said hello and kindly smiled, telling the jury panel members and lawyers to take a seat.

The man found the next thirty minutes to be absolutely excruciating. During this phase of jury duty, the lawyers informed the jury panel a bit about the trial for which they were seeking jurors. The lawyer in the Seersucker suit starting things off, standing up and wandering toward the jury panel with a lumbering gait and an exposed large girth. He began speaking in a velvety Baritone voice with a very Southern drawl: "May it please the court. And ladies and gentlemen. Let me share with you fine citizens of Dallas County some of the salient facts of the case at bar."

"Why did fucking lawyers have to talk that way?" the man thought. "*Salient* facts. Why can't they just say 'hey, here's what happened."

The lawyer soon shared that the plaintiffs were the surviving widower (age 74) and three adult offspring of Mrs. Dottie Wilson. The plaintiffs alleged that they had suffered damages due to the death of Mrs. Wilson, on August 6, 2015, allegedly caused by Mrs. Wilson's exposure to asbestos dust and fibers when she handled and laundered the allegedly asbestos-laden clothing of her husband, Myron Wilson. Mr. Wilson had been employed for 30 years at a large natural gas field and processing facility in East Texas, known as the Chandler Lake Refinery. In the course of performing his work, Mr. Wilson allegedly was occupationally exposed to large quantities of asbestos-containing insulation products that were utilized and/or handled by, or in the close proximity of, Mr. Wilson. Mr. Wilson's initial job for Chandler was a switcher. When he was a switcher, he worked with steam coils on certain flow lines and each of them was covered with insulation containing asbestos. Also, certain heaters within the work area had insulation in them. Mr. Wilson later became a compressor operator and then a chief operator. When he was a compressor operator, he worked with turbochargers, engines, and compressors that had insulation on them. Mr. Wilson later became a member of a maintenance crew (fixing anything that broke throughout the plant). Mr. Wilson also believed that he was exposed to asbestos at the Chandler Lake Refinery through certain pipe insulation—specifically "hot oil piping" used in the process of "drying" natural gas—that is, getting propane and pentanes out of the hydrocarbon gas. Mr. Wilson believed, in particular, that he may have been exposed to asbestos dust in the compressor building at the Chandler Lake Refinery where, once a year or so, he would have to pull out, repair, or rip off pipe insulation. Upon completion of Mr. Wilson's daily work, he would leave the worksite and return home with asbestos dust and fibers on his clothing and person. Mrs. Dottie Wilson was allegedly then exposed to the asbestos dust and fibers when she gathered, handled, and laundered Mr. Wilson's dust-laden clothing and ultimately sustained a very serious injury to her body. In 2015, Mrs. Wilson suddenly developed pain and trouble breathing. Shortly thereafter, Mrs. Wilson was diagnosed with the asbestos-related lung cancer known as mesothelioma. Mrs. Wilson's contraction of mesothelioma resulted in immediate disability, physical pain and suffering, and severe mental stress, and she soon passed away, on August 6, 2015.

The plaintiffs soon filed their petition for survival and wrongful death damages in Dallas County, Texas, where the behemoth Chandler Corporation was headquartered. Chandler Corporation somehow had avoided mass tort litigation from the plaintiffs' bar until the Wilson lawsuit, and they were not going to go down without a fight. If they lost this suit, it would be the tip of the iceberg and they would soon be fighting hundreds or thousands of copycat lawsuits just like this one. They had to stop the floodgates.

It was soon time to question the jury panel and find those with biases or other propensities toward one side or the other. The man smirked and raised his hand. He had a free ticket out of this place. When the man was called upon, he confirmed his name, and quietly announced that, in the year 2002, he had lost a grandfather (his guardian at the time) to mesothelioma. He had been a plaintiff with other family members in a subsequent lawsuit against the grandfather's employer. But his grandfather's employer had later retreated into a bankruptcy case under the weight of massive litigation. He and his family members had been funneled into an asbestos claim trust process, set up for exposure victims and their families, but that trust (like his grandfather's bankrupt employer) had also run out of money and he and his family never received one dime of recovery. Before he said anything else, the Chandler Corporation asked to have an immediate sidebar with Judge Barnes. A few minutes later, Judge Barnes excused the man, thanking him for his time and service.

The man happily exited the courtroom, took the elevator down to the ground floor and left the courthouse. What were the odds? He didn't even have to make up anything to get excused! Maybe he should have kept his mouth shut to see what might have become of the jury duty experience. That thought quickly evaporated. He decided that there was no need to go back to work at this point in the day. The man looked up at the gray January sky. He went over and grabbed a rental bike at the rack in front of the courthouse. He hopped on it and rode down past the Earle Cabell Building glancing up toward the 14th Floor as he did and smirking. Suddenly he had to swerve to avoid missing a man wearing a T-shirt that read "REPENT" who was holding a Bible and preaching to a nonexistent crowd on the sidewalk across from the courthouse. A man with an acoustic guitar stood next to him, strangely playing what sounded like a bad rendition of "Michael Rowed the Boat Ashore," if the man remembered his childhood Sunday School songs correctly. "IDIOTS!" The man kept peddling down to Klyde Warren Park and grabbed lunch from a taco truck. He then headed into the Cathedral Shrine of the Virgin of Guadalupe. He would catch the afternoon Mass there. He didn't know why he found peace there. It really made no sense, given all that had happened to him.

Chapter 10:

Guns and Ammo.

Avery sat at the kitchen table on a Saturday afternoon, sorting through recent mail (all properly vetted by the Marshals first, of course). She pulled out a card from her mom. The envelope was pink and puffy and smelled of Chanel No. 5. It was addressed with perfect, cursive handwriting. It had a Florentine Madonna and Child forever postage stamp on it. It was as if every detail had been carefully considered. Inside was a pretty bookmark with the following words: "I shall not fear anyone on Earth. I shall fear only God." Avery smiled and sighed. "Easier said than done, Mom." She got up and put it in the drawer of other book marks and motivational trinkets that her mother had regularly been sending her.

There are obviously many ways to conquer one's fears. Quotes and prayers are helpful, to be sure. But guns and ammo can also go a long way toward helping one triumph over fear—or at least making you look and feel like a total badass. Packing heat can be immensely empowering. Make no mistake, any time a person (especially a public official) receives a death threat *anywhere*, there is probably going to be an obligatory discussion initiated by law enforcement regarding "prudent self-protection mechanisms." And guns, naturally, are going to be one of those possible protection mechanisms that are considered. But, again, Judge Lassiter and her family live in Texas. It is no accident that the state's motto is "Don't Mess with Texas." Most everyone in the Lone Star State (well, most everyone in the rural areas anyway) owns a gun–or certainly is not averse to the full and robust exercise of one's Second Amendment rights. Officer Max, of course, already owned several guns before the death threat (some department-issued guns and some of his own, accumulated through the years). But, Good God, the multiple death threats surely meant it was time to obtain more weaponry for the Lassiter household! The longer the situation lingered, the more heated the discussion got. "We could not possibly have too many firearms!" This was the statement often uttered by Officer Max. God Bless him.

So, in January, it was time to acquire more guns and ammo and also time to start making more frequent trips to the gun range for target practice. It seems as though there are few greater ways for human beings to have fun in Texas on the weekends than by strapping on a few firearms, heading to a store called "Cheaper than Dirt" to buy some ammunition and zombie targets, and then driving to Bubba's Target Masters and shooting off a few rounds. Bubba's Target Masters is located across from the Texas Motor Speedway, on Dale Earnhardt Boulevard—just past the Triple XXX adult bookstore. Just north of Fort Worth. If one has an especially good day, he can head back down highway I-35W and hit Joe T. Garcia's restaurant, in the stockyard district, for some spicy Tex-Mex food and margaritas afterwards (with lots of Jose Cuervo tequila and Cointreau).

Judge Avery had decided fairly quickly after her death threats started that she was not going to be solely dependent on Officer Max or the U.S. Marshals Service for her ongoing safety. That's just not the way she is. She's slight, but still gritty and tough. Soon after the initial death threat letters, Avery acquired a Ruger .38 caliber revolver (light and small for her diminutive hands) and, later, a Colt 1911 semi-automatic .380 caliber steel handgun. She loved this one, in particular. It had a pretty horse insignia on it. Avery is quite the shooter and taps into her "more aggressive side" when handling these weapons.

However, her favorite weapon of choice soon became a Glock 19x coyote color pistol. Avery spent more weekend time than ever, after the death threats, going to the gun range–feeling pretty empowered and awesome, since she was accompanied by Deputy U.S. Marshals when she went there. No ne'er-do-well at the gun range would *ever* consider confronting a preppy blond female with a big bag full of ammo, three guns, and two Deputy U.S. Marshals standing on either side of her. She felt like a modern-day Annie Oakley.

Of course, preparation for the unknown requires more than simply brushing up on one's shooting skills. Avery carried a Beretta Storm Tactical Knife with Tanto Blade in her robe pocket and everywhere she went. She soon insisted that each of her staff members (her judicial assistant, Annalise; her permanent law clerk, Millicent; her courtroom deputy, Kasi; and her court reporter, Sheila) carry and keep handy at their desks Grizzly spray for any unexpected assaults. Normal pepper spray would not suffice. Grizzly spray will bring a predator to his knees. And a few self-defense classes and active shooter classes followed as well. Judge Lassiter learned to think of everything as a weapon. The flagpole in her courtroom could be a spear if necessary. The fire extinguisher provided a good way, if necessary, to knock a predator to the floor. Even a ballpoint pen could do lethal harm when necessary. It was all about self-defense and situational awareness, although she worried that she was starting to look and sound a little like Officer Max's hero Mad Dog Mattis ("Be polite, be professional, but have a plan to kill everybody you meet") or a doomsday prepper. If the end-times were coming, she was actually in pretty good shape. All she needed now was some freeze-dried food and stockpiles of antibiotics. She also wouldn't mind getting some of those Kevlar-coated shoelaces that one of the Deputy Marshals had. And speaking of shoes . . . well that's another subject altogether.

Chapter 11:

The Fashion Quandary.

Being the subject of a death threat presents many quandaries. With a female target, there is, in particular, a fashion quandary that, according to Avery, a male target simply cannot begin to comprehend or appreciate. Case in point. Judge Lassiter likes her shoes. She prefers to wear high heel pumps, to compensate for being "vertically challenged." Officer Max, from the moment Avery received the death threats, chastised her to start wearing "tactical practical" footwear, to make a quick getaway if ever required. The problem is that shoe designers such as Jimmy Choo and Christian Louboutin do not make anything that fits into the category of "tactical practical." And Judge Lassiter likes her designer shoes. She also likes her designer handbags: Kate Spade, Coach, Fendi, Louis Vuitton, Juicy Couture, Burberry. Unfortunately, none of these designer brands easily accommodates even a small handgun like a .38 caliber Ruger Revolver, the sleek steel Colt .380 caliber semi-automatic, or the Glock 19x. While the shoe conundrum was never resolved to Officer Max's satisfaction—Avery stubbornly insisted that a tall spiked heel can nicely double as a deadly weapon—Avery eventually learned that a woman can actually "pack heat" in the 21st century in style. Long before Judge Lassiter had ever thought of the problem of how to carry a concealed weapon and still look fabulous, there was "Gun Tote'N Mamas"; the "Well Armed Woman" ("where firearms and feminine meet"); "GunGoddess.com"; "CarryChic"; *etc.* They have the fashion dilemma wonderfully solved! Suddenly Louis Vuitton and Burberry seemed boring and impractical.

And then there was the J-Dar. How does one incorporate the J-Dar into a female wardrobe? What is a J-Dar? Well, many people are probably familiar with the television commercial that aired many years ago, featuring an elderly lady lying on a bathroom floor named Mrs. Fletcher, writhing in pain, who said, "Help! I have fallen and I can't get up." Luckily, for Mrs. Fletcher, she was wearing a pendant around her neck that had a button that she could easily push, activating an audio receiver device into which she could speak to a kind dispatcher who would send help to her immediately. The "Life Call" device turned a medical emergency—that could have been dire or even tragic—into a happy ending! It was a life saver to a person who was immobile and could not reach for a telephone. The commercials–with their drama and bad acting–became the subject of silly jokes in pop culture.

Well, as it turns out, the U.S. Marshals have their own version of this device. It's called the J-Dar. Avery was "not at liberty to speak" about the technology or capabilities of the J-Dar device, but it appeared to be a lot like what that old Mrs. Fletcher had in those television commercials. It was apparently a little more sophisticated and could pinpoint Avery by satellite technology, even when she was on safari in Tanzania. But Avery grew to hate the J-Dar. She constantly feared setting it off on accident. And when she did not charge the battery in it, some well-meaning U.S. Marshal employee in Washington, D.C. was always calling her to make sure she was okay and knew that it needed charging. Avery threatened to bury the J-Dar in a hole in the ground in the Serengeti Plains when she went there on safari to watch giraffes, zebras, and elephants. But she did not. She actually appreciated that the J-Dar was there to protect her from the letter writer. Just one more thing to protect her from the letter writer. And the letter writer had not gone away. As Avery would soon learn, the letter writer had not moved on or forgotten about his bad experience with the legal system. His quest for revenge had barely gotten started.

Chapter 12:

From the Lone Star State to the Garden State: The Tale of the Two New Jersey Judges.

The Honorable Helen M. Lupinaci and the Honorable Ronald P. Murphy were long time judicial colleagues in the District of New Jersey, and they and their families had been social friends for many years as well. Judge Lupinaci was in her seventies, and Judge Murphy was in his early nineties, and the two had served as federal judges in Camden, New Jersey for almost three decades—she as a federal bankruptcy judge and he as, first, a magistrate judge and then later as a district judge. Coincidentally, they had both lost their spouses to cancer a couple of years ago and, since then, had faithfully gone to mass together every Saturday evening up at the beautiful gray stone St. Paul's Roman Catholic Church in Princeton, just in front of the centuries-old cemetery where U.S. Presidents, Vice Presidents, scholars, and famous patriots were buried, and just down the street from the University—which was both their alma mater. The pair would dine together after mass at the Vecchia Roma restaurant in the township of Cherry Hill near both of their homes. The judges drank Chianti when they dined together and reminisced for hours about the grueling cases that they had collaborated on over the years. Cases involving some of the Atlantic City casinos. Litigation involving some of the many pharmaceutical companies based in the area. Cases involving manufacturers of asbestos-containing products and the mass tort victims that lined up to have their mesothelioma claims redressed. And, most memorable and painful for them both, a bankruptcy case of a south New Jersey Catholic Diocese that had dragged on for many years and involved dozens of claims that a priest at Our Lady of Perpetual Help, Father Ignatius, had molested altar boys and other young victims. The Diocese had filed for Chapter 11 bankruptcy— joining the ranks of more than a dozen others around the U.S. that had taken such a step—to ensure the financial health of its assets and those of its parishes and schools (or to thwart victims' efforts to obtain redress—depending upon which set of lawyers one believed). Judge Lupinaci had presided over the Chapter 11 case of the Diocese, and Judge Murphy had presided over an alternative dispute resolution procedure for the abuse victims who were seeking damage recoveries from either insurance policies or the assets of the Diocese. The case had received national attention and was brutal for them both. There were not enough funds or insurance to adequately compensate all of the victims, by any reasonable measure. The personal injury lawyers for the abuse victims had wanted to go after the assets of the Holy See itself. The case had been emotionally devastating for the two judges, because of the horrible facts that they had learned about the abuse, and also since they were both devout Catholics. In many ways, it had shaken their faiths to the core. Father Ignatius was full of charisma and had been adored by his parishioners. He was one of the most popular priests in the region and on a fast track to becoming a Bishop until—pursuant to a search warrant issued by Judge Murphy—a treasure trove of child pornography DVDs, sex toys, children's underwear, and vials of pubic hair, meticulous labeled, were found in Father Ignatius's presbytery. The priest had somehow hidden his crimes well for decades. Perhaps others in the Catholic church had hidden his crimes well, too. It was all heart-wrenching. There were dozens of alleged victims. The kind of thing that haunts a judge for years, seeing things that you can never un-see, and hearing things that you can never un-hear. However, this "judge trauma" certainly pales in comparison to what the actual humans involved endure.

In happier conversations, the judges bragged about their many wonderful children and grandchildren. The judges had a sweet caring relationship. Judge Lupinaci was still quite youthful and spunky for her age and tended to dote on her older colleague. Judge Murphy had recently become wheelchair bound, but Judge Lupinaci made sure it did not limit his life. In February, Judge Lupinaci bought season tickets for the pair to the Philadelphia Opera. She was still more-than-able to drive them into Philly in her Lincoln Town Car. In early February, the judges attended the season opener, *Aida*, and shared a night cap afterwards at the Violet Room lounge, two blocks down Locust Street from the opera house.

At 11:00 p.m., a man strolled into the Violet Room lounge and took a seat at the bar alone. No one really noticed him. It was late and most people in the bar had imbibed a few too many drinks by that point. The man was a young adult, white, thin, bearded and had dreadlocks. He wore denim jeans and a Jimi Hendrix T-Shirt under a black leather jacket. He didn't really blend with the older, after-opera crowd, but the Violet Room draws an eclectic crowd most nights, so the man did not conspicuously stand out. The man ordered a Crown Royal and Coke and pulled out his cell phone, pretending to read from it as he surveyed the room. He spotted Judges Lupinaci and Murphy in the back corner of the lounge, each sipping on cocktails and deep in conversation. They were entirely oblivious to their surroundings. They certainly had not noticed him.

The man sat at the bar for more than an hour. As the crowd at the lounge eventually began to thin, the judges continued to chat like two millennials with no cares or weariness. But the man with the dreadlocks could tell that they were tipsy and would have no ability to fight off danger.

The man looked at his cell phone as he sipped his third drink. He typed a message: "In Philly at Violet Room. Got eyes on targets. No Marshals. No driver. Will be fucking EASY. Lol."

The stark difference in security perplexed the dreadlock-wearing man for a moment. Why did the Texas judge have so much security around her? He chalked it up to stupid, macho Texans, just being fucking assholes. "All hat and no cattle"—as the saying went. Philly, on the other hand, would be just a walk in the park. It was like they didn't even care up here at all. He laughed to himself as he sipped his drink.

Chapter 13:

The Stuff that Dreams are Made of: Is this Becoming Some Strange Variation of "Stockholm Syndrome"?

"Stockholm Syndrome" is a term that has long been used to describe a psychological phenomenon that sometimes develops when hostages in a kidnapping or other criminal situation develop sympathy for, or empathize with, their captors. These feelings are generally considered irrational, obviously, because of the context and danger in which the hostage is involved. It has also been referred to as a type of traumatic bonding, in that the hostage or other victim develops strong emotional ties to a person who might be inflicting something negative her way, such as beating, intimidation or other forms of abuse. It is based on a Freudian theory, the notion being that the bonding is the individual's own unique coping response to the trauma of becoming a victim. Identifying with the aggressor is one way that the ego defends itself. The theory originates and gets its name from the Normmalmstorg bank robbery of Kreditbanken at Normmalmstorg in Stockholm, Sweden, back in August 1973. In that incident, several bank employees were held hostage in a bank vault for about five days, while the robbers were in ongoing negotiations with the police. Supposedly, the hostages became attached to and somewhat sympathetic toward their captors during the standoff, rejecting assistance at one point, and defending the captors to some extent after the episode had ended. The term was originally coined by criminologist and psychologist Nils Bejerot as "Normmalmstorgsyndromet" (in Swedish) and later became known as "Stockholm Syndrome." It has been used on occasion by law enforcement officials to interpret developments or otherwise aid and manage hostage situations. So-called experts have traced the syndrome back to very early times in civilization. For example, sadly, the phenomenon of women and children being captured in early times of human history by neighboring, rival bands or tribes was very common, and women who resisted in such situations risked being killed. Adaptive traits such as capture-bonding became a survival instinct. This phenomenon has been observed recently with some of the young women kidnapped in year 2014 from a Nigerian school in Chibok, Nigeria by Boko Haram terrorists (some of the young women were rescued and returned home but showed signs of missing their captors). Some experts think that this bonding mechanism may explain, to some extent, the so-called battered wife syndrome, the ability to endure certain types of difficult military training, and even fraternity hazing. There are variations on the phenomenon, including Lima Syndrome (when abductors develop sympathy for their hostages) and Oslo Syndrome (when an entire people under siege can allegedly be afflicted).

As the weeks and months went on, the Deputy Marshals continued to stay and stay with the Lassiters. Old Deputy Marshals were relieved from duty and new ones stepped in line. To use Avery's words, they became like family members to the Lassiters. Baba Jo made baked goods for them constantly and placed them in their command post RV trailer in the backyard and refused to take "no" for an answer when they tried to refuse them (like Judge Lassiter, Baba Jo has a hard time accepting "no" for an answer). Judge Lassiter went shopping with them and target shooting with them. They accompanied the Lassiters to restaurants and church. There were the long daily commutes in the G-rides from Southlake into work, day after day. One day, Julia and Avery were watching the A&E channel on television and there was a crime show discussing "Stockholm Syndrome." Avery thought to herself, "Do I have some sort of odd variation of this? Are the Deputy Marshals akin to my 'captors'?" She was fond of them. She knew their kids' names and their spouses' names and their hobbies and favorite foods and book interests and music. It was hardly the same as "Stockholm Syndrome"–the Deputy Marshals were not bad-guy captors. But it still seemed somewhat irrational to her.

One day while Avery, Julia, and Baxter were watching an old Whitney Houston movie called *The Bodyguard*, the conversation suddenly turned awkward when Julia said, "Mom, you aren't going to fall for one of your Marshal protectors like Whitney Houston did for Kevin Costner, are you?" Then Julia started picking out suitable candidates for Avery (noting the tinges of color she associated with each one, as she named them) and taunted Avery to play along. This had officially gotten ridiculous.

Then Avery started making confessions to little Julia about strange dream patterns that Avery had developed—on the nights she could sleep soundly, that is. Avery elaborated, "Julia, you know that this is all highly inappropriate for you to suggest, but last night I did have the strangest dream." She went on to describe that she kept having recurring dreams about Deputy Marshal Miles Dylan peering through their windows. Miles Dylan was the MRE-eating former Marine who walked around at night with infrared goggles, camouflage outer-wear, Kevlar-coated shoe laces, and was ferociously intense. Deputy Marshal Dylan was, in all candor, a beautiful and beguiling man. Both Julia and Avery associated Deputy Marshal Dylan with the color black and Avery always started humming the Rolling Stones' song *Painted Black* whenever they talked of him or saw him on duty. "Mom, OMG! Stop it, you are embarrassing me!" Julia screamed. Avery said, "Oh my God, is right. This is crazy. But you started it! Maybe we have some warped version of Stockholm Syndrome playing out here, Julia. We are bonding in a warped way with the Marshal protectors. Julia, the FBI has **got** to identify and arrest the letter writer soon. Or maybe we just need to stop this protective detail and I will take my chances!"

"Mom, you can't! I don't want the letter writer to kill you! What if he comes and kills you and all of us? Daddy has other people out there to protect. He can't always be here. And you are not as good with a gun as you think you are!" Julia began sobbing.

Avery held Julia in her arms until Julia eventually stopped weeping. Poor Julia. When one is a child of a cop, she has it engrained in her head from an early age to "trust no one." And there are always more security layers and procedures in your house than at all your friends' houses. You overhear stories that are horrific, and you learn to work past the stun and shock. You periodically hear about someone's dad or mom getting killed in the line of duty. You hear people saying terrible things about cops and it hurts horribly, but you shake it off. But things were now starting to take a hard toll on Avery's steel-fibered, Teflon-coated kids. Perhaps they had always thought that at least one of their parents had a somewhat normal job, but not so much anymore. Avery hated the letter writer for what he had done to her kids' sense of security. Avery desperately wanted to end the Marshal protective detail. But her concern and love for her kids would not allow that. They were—as most any mother would tell you—the most important thing in Avery's universe.

As Avery lay her head on her pillow that night, she closed her eyes and tried not to dream. At least not dream one of her *new* dreams. She would gladly go back to having her old, normal "lawyer" and "judge" dreams. As every lawyer knows, for years after one becomes a lawyer, he or she has recurring dreams that he or she is still in law school. Avery calls it "terminal law school." She says she is pretty sure that this is a universal curse on all lawyers—the life-long aftermath of having gone through three years of law school—not just her own psychological disorder. You dream that you are running late for an exam for which you have not prepared. You dream of being unprepared for class and getting called upon and humiliated in front of your classmates by an arrogant, egotistical, Socratic-style law professor. You dream of not being able to find your most important case book, horn book, outlines, or not being able to get into your locker to retrieve them. And, likewise, every judge will tell you that, for years after becoming a judge, a judge has recurring dreams of his or her earlier career of being a lawyer—and these involve such things as having an important brief due imminently and not having enough time to finish it. Or an anxious client calling at ten o'clock at night. Or an unreasonable law partner making unreasonable demands. Or forgetting to keep time sheets for days and days and having no ability to recreate your tasks and times. Or a looming discovery deadline that you cannot possible meet, *etc.* Avery dreams of sitting in a law office at Big Law surrounded by thousands of boxes of documents that need to be Bates-labeled and reviewed. She dreams of being at the California Capitol Building in Sacramento in early 2001, where she once worked on a project for the Speaker of the California Assembly, where late one night, an enraged tanker truck driver committed suicide in spectacular fashion by driving his big rig up the Capitol steps and into the Senate chambers, just as the Senate was adjourning, where the tanker exploded, nearly taking out hundreds of law makers–she dreams of trying to run through the smoke and people and noise, but being unable to run. Avery's absolute worst recurring dream of law practice is a dream about a former client of hers who was a wealthy Texas businessman who had to file bankruptcy when his ex-wife caught him philandering and divorced him and "took him to the cleaners." The client looked like an older, scarier version of the Hollywood actor Christopher Walken. Avery saw this client as tinged with the color dark red—blood red. In the middle of their frequent 11:00 a.m. meetings, in the fancy Madison, Spencer & Collins oak paneled conference room, sitting in their leather high back chairs at a 25-foot-long Italian marble table, overlooking the skyscrapers of Dallas, the pompous client would pull out from his briefcase a can opener and can of Wolf Brand Chili for his lunch, pour it into a bag of Lay's potato chips, and eat like he was starving, staring at Avery with a crazed look on his face, as she tried to give serious legal advice. Avery's colleagues used to leave on her desk, as a joke, cans of Wolf Brand Chili and Lay's potato chips, next to a cowbell—an apparent reference to an old *Saturday Night Live* skit involving the rock group Blue Oyster Cult and Christopher Walken.

Avery was experiencing a new kind of dream now. The dream of a judge, post-death threat. She was dreaming of Deputy Marshals popping out from behind trees or shrubberies and peeking into her windows. She was dreaming of Deputy Marshals surrounding her. It was comforting, but suffocating. She was dreaming of a mad man coming to attack her. She was dreaming of running scared. She was dreaming of the Deputy Marshals not being able to protect her, of guns jamming and not being able to shoot, of doors and gates being left unlocked, of no one hearing her scream. She wanted to go back to dreaming about the anxiety of law school and Madison, Spencer & Collins. Except for the dreams about the Wolf-Brand-Chili-potato-chip-eating client who looked like Christopher Walken. She did not want to dream about him ever again.

Chapter 14:

A Different Dream Sequence.

The man with the dreadlocks anxiously paced back and forth in his tiny, dank apartment on the top floor of a rundown building overlooking the Camden, New Jersey Waterfront, south of the Ben Franklin Bridge. It was 3:00 am. He flipped on a pot of coffee. May as well stay up now—the chances of him getting anymore sleep at this point were shot. He powered up his Sony Play Station. It would be two hours before he needed to head into work. He could play a couple of hours of *God of War*. He wondered if his brother or any of his friends were up and online playing. Probably. Like him, they really had no lives.

The twinkling lights of the Philadelphia skyline could be seen in the distance out of his foggy bay window. Police sirens and car alarms broke the quiet stillness every few minutes—as was typical for this area. The crime was still terrible in his neighborhood, although the corrupt politicians bragged about how much better it was these days. But it was not the sirens that had awoken him early this morning. He had been awoken two hours earlier with another one of his dreams. It was the dream that he had most often. It was the dream where he walks into Father Iggy's rectory and hears Puccini opera music blasting from the priest's old vinyl record player. The thick red curtains in the rectory are drawn and it is dark and shadowy, except for candle light. Through the darkness, he sees in the right corner of the room the almost life-sized marble reproduction of Michelangelo's statue Pieta, along with various religious artwork and a large wooden crucifix. There are numerous wine bottles and stained, dirty glasses on a coffee table in the middle of the room, along with some crack pipes, some candy, suppositories, a power drill, and a Polaroid camera. There is a soiled sofa. And on the floor next to the coffee table lies his brother, curled up in a fetal position, naked and whimpering in pain. His brother has welts on his back this time. Father Iggy must have beaten him again. Or maybe the welts were from him being strapped him into a chair while Father Iggy raped him. Probably told him again that this was "how we show God love." Father Iggy is yelling at his brother, telling him to stop sniveling and get dressed. Father Iggy has women's makeup on. He looks like a clown in clerical clothing. He sees that the boy's brother has entered the room. Suddenly Father Iggy's demeanor turns strangely cheery. Father Iggy comes at him with a twisted grin, thick with red lipstick. In a whispery, raspy voice he says, "Go help your brother, my child. He needs your help. And remember, *don't tell*. I am watching you always. Don't tell." Father Iggy kisses him on the mouth, smearing his red lipstick on his face, and then hands him some candy. He tells him to meet him next door in the chapel in fifteen minutes to prepare for the Eucharist. "Don't be late."

Don't tell. Don't tell. Really? Who was he ever going to fucking tell? Who would have ever believed him? He had no family, except for his brothers—one of whom was curled up in the floor in a fetal position sobbing, and the other of whom had the good sense to pick up and run the Hell away from this house of horrors. No one would believe him anyway. The one time he had said anything to anyone, he was ordered to a psychiatric hospital to have a mental health evaluation and then required to endure several weeks of "therapeutic counseling" to address his "insecurities" and "low self-esteem." When he had told one of the counselors that he was depressed and suicidal, he was told to "Pray to St. Jude, the patron of the impossible."

Father Iggy was ultimately revealed for the monster he was—a prolific priest pedophile—and had eventually been laicized, or defrocked, by the Vatican for his sexual abuse of children. He had never been arrested, though, and whether he had ever reoffended was unknown. Since being defrocked, he had supposedly been a hermit and counselor at the Hermitage de Paz in Guadalajara, Mexico. Another rumor traced him to the St. Paolo Church and Priory in Valetta, Malta. But Father Iggy wasn't even the only one at the parish who had been engaged in atrocities against little boys. Another priest visiting from another parish sometimes joined Father Iggy in having parties with the children, filming them in orchestrated sex acts. That visiting priest had suddenly disappeared to attend to "personal matters." It was all an abhorrent cover up to protect the church and the archdiocese coffers. It was a sickening culture of secrecy. Rather than investigating and punishing offenders, these pedophiles were usually just sent away, to either reoffend or never to be seen again.

The man was startled from his dark thoughts by the sound of the rattling engine and back up beeping of a garbage truck making its morning rounds outside of his apartment. His game had booted up now. He noticed that his brother was up playing.

"Hey, bro. You up, too?"

"Yup. Couldn't sleep. Text me offline. Have some updates. Oh, and check your Bitcoin wallet at the Malta exchange. Should like what you see."

Chapter 15:

Officer Max's Mishap, a.k.a. the Attack by Giant Metal Decorative Wall Spoon.

During the many weeks and months that passed during Avery's judicial protection, it was not "all about" the U.S. Marshals and Avery. Life goes on when the awkward unpleasantry of a judicial death threat happens. Well, life mostly goes on. As the saying goes, "we plan, God laughs."

For Avery's beloved Baxter, despite Avery's strongest intentions, there would be no Westminster Dog Show training any time soon—or perhaps ever. Elite show dogs–like fashion super models–hit their prime fairly early in life. February (the month of the Westminster Dog Show–the most epic of all dog competitions) came and went that year of Avery's judicial protection. Approximately 3,000 pure bred dogs made the annual trek to Piers 92 and 94, and then Madison Square Garden in New York City that year, to compete with the best of the best, in this glorious Super Bowl of canine competitions, which dates back to 1877, and is so steeped in rich history and tradition. But, sadly, Avery and Baxter would simply watch the competition from afar on television at home that year. In horror, Avery and Baxter witnessed a so-called "indomitable" little Pekingese dog named Malachy win "Best in Show." Really? A Pekingese? Has a Pekingese ever shown up in a Van Dyck, Gainsborough, or Landseer painting, as has the Cavalier King Charles

Spaniel? Has the Pekingese breed been a European court favorite for
centuries like the Cavalier King Charles Spaniel? Is a Pekingese as
intelligent, agile, adroit, nimble, and eager to please as the Cavalier
King Charles Spaniel? Poor Baxter, Avery thought. *"**You could have
been a contender, sweet boy.**"* A Cavalier King Charles Spaniel first
entered the Westminster Dog Show (toy breed category) in 1997. The
breed has not had too much attention or success yet. Well, actually,
there have been a few examples of near-glory. There was Avery's
hero "Rocky" from 2007 and 2008 (otherwise known as "Ch. Pinecrest
Rock the Boat") who, like Baxter, was bred and born in Texas. Rocky
won many honors at Madison Square Garden. And then there was
more recently the sweet, Cavalier King Charles Spaniel named Halli
Galli–originally from Denmark but shown by the same handler as
Rocky–a Texas oilman who had once been a client of Avery's at Big
Law. Like these two remarkable Cavaliers, little Baxter had the
ambition, the talent, the will, and the beauty to do it. Baxter was like
the dog-version of Marlon Brando. He could have been a contender.
Baxter could have been a contender.

In late February, Avery received one of those phone calls that
family members of police officers hate to receive. She was in court
when the phone call came in. She was dealing with a nasty dispute
involving two feuding hedge fund managers. There were several SMU
law students in her courtroom observing the court proceedings. The
students had wanted to learn something about what hedge funds were
and how they made their money. Avery had been explaining to the
students before court about how hedge funds work—describing how
they are a less-regulated side of capital finance. Avery had further
lectured to the students that hedge funders raise money from wealthy
"accredited" individuals and institutions, such as government pension
funds or university endowments, and the hedge funders deploy (that is,

invest) that money as they see fit. These high-flying hedge fund managers essentially suck up money ("fresh powder" they call it) like an i-Robot vacuum cleaner from every corner of the universe and invest it, generally earning compensation of 20% of the assets they invest and another 2% of the profits that the assets earn. They make money no matter what—whether their investments are successful or not—because of their 20% cut. Avery explained, to the law students' surprise, that lawyers, physicians, and investment bankers were now yesteryear's rich, esteemed professions. The law students were probably starting to re-think their decision to attend law school (that had not been Avery's intention). Avery had been quietly daydreaming about whether one of these hedge fund manager guys (they are mostly men—in a stereotypically competitive "bro culture") could somehow have been connected to her death threats—she was recalling the comment in the second threat letter about the "rich who rule the universe." Hedge fund managers were certainly worthy of that description. The hedge fund managers in her courtroom right now were rich alright—they were centimillionaires. They probably thought of anyone making $1-$5 million per year as middle class. Some of these managers were intelligent with impressive academic credentials. They all were bombastic talkers imbued with an outrageous amount of hubris. They vacationed in places like Lake Como and Bora Bora and consulted meditation gurus in places like the Bay of Bengal. They sailed catamarans around the world and bought airplanes and race horses like it was candy. Everything in their life was about winning. In the current lawsuit Avery had before her, the hedgies were accusing each other of being greedy sociopaths. As Avery's mind drifted deeper toward wondering if perhaps someone in her court involving one of these hedgies had perhaps sent her the death threats, Annalise quietly slipped into the courtroom and handed her a note, telling her that she needed to take a recess. That was never a good sign. Avery had a call holding from one of Mad Max's police department colleagues, saying that Officer Max was at a local hospital emergency room, because he had been injured in a mishap while on duty, but it appeared that he was going to be alright. Avery would probably want to come to the hospital—but he thought Mad Max would be fine.

A mishap? There is such ambiguity in that term–especially when it relates to a big city police officer. Remember, "every day they play the deadly game." But here, the term mishap was "code" for "you're not going to believe this crazy shit storm of a story when you hear it."

Officer Max had responded to a "911" call around 1:00 p.m. that day, which had been reported as a home invasion burglary in progress (a "41/11" in police lingo), in a posh, gated North Dallas neighborhood. The "911" call was made by an elderly man hiding inside his house in a bathroom. The old man stated that a wild eyed, erratically-behaving burglar had broken into his house while he and his caretaker were in the kitchen making lunch, and the burglar currently remained in the kitchen, attacking the old man's caretaker. There had been other recent daytime home invasion burglaries in the area. Mad Max had actually been tracking down leads, looking for the burglar, when the call came out. Mad Max was just around the corner and went to the house—expecting backup help to arrive momentarily. As Mad Max drove up to the house, the caretaker (a 40-year-old man) came running out of the front door. The caretaker said that the burglar was inside, still in the kitchen, pulling out knives and cooking utensils and waving them around and "acting psycho." The caretaker had blood streaming from his left breast. When Mad Max asked him if he was badly hurt, the caretaker responded that the burglar had bitten his nipple off, and that he was going out to his car to get his own gun (remember, lots of regular well-meaning people in Texas own guns;

God Bless them, each and every one). Mad Max told the well-meaning, bleeding caretaker to "stay the Hell outside," while Mad Max ran inside to the maelstrom. Once in the kitchen, a fight ensued. The burglar was a sinewy man, wielding a butcher knife and was wearing a body vest made of adult magazines and duct tape. Yes, porn magazines and duct tape. The burglar had apparently recently smoked some PCP-laced marijuana and thought he was Superman. It turns out that the man was a 28-year-old convicted felon, whose most recent felony was assault on a public servant. Irony. He had actually recently attacked another police officer—a police chief in a small town in Oklahoma—after stealing the chief's police car and shooting at the police chief with the chief's own rifle. When Mad Max gave the burglar all the usual police commands, there was no cooperation. The porn magazine-and-duct-tape-clad Superman was not going down without a fight. After approximately two minutes of hard core mixed martial arts kicking, punching, crashing pots and pans, and a few broken dishes, the well-meaning caretaker came back inside into the kitchen (thankfully without his gun) and decided to play Good Samaritan. The caretaker grabbed a giant, metal, decorative wall spoon off of the kitchen wall (yes, an objet d'Art), and started trying to break up the fight by swinging. As Mad Max shouted at him to stop and to get out of the kitchen, the caretaker tripped and accidently plunged the giant decorative metal wall spoon into Mad Max's forehead, causing a gash that resulted in a large amount of blood loss and required several stitches. Around this time, another policeman (good naturedly nicknamed "Sam the Terrorist" on the force–because his real name is "Osama" and because of the remarkably high number of people who have died in Osama's custody over the course of his career for one reason or another) showed up and ran into the house and, together, they subdued the porn magazine-clad burglar and cuffed him.

Mad Max spent five hours in the hospital emergency room that February day, with a crowd of colleagues by his side, giving him the moral support that the brothers and sisters in blue are always eager to give. The nipple-bitten caretaker was being treated at the same facility and came down at one point to apologize for his misfire with the wall spoon, and to thank Officer Max for his heroics. Luckily, the caretaker's nipple was going to be just fine, and, likewise, the CT scans and other medical tests showed that Officer Max suffered no concussion or brain injuries. Just head and scalp lacerations requiring several stitches. When Mad Max came home, Heath and Julia told him he looked like the monster Frankenstein and they wished, if this had to happen, it could have happened around Halloween. Officer Max also had some broken fingers, a dislocated thumb, and a fractured wrist and later would have to have surgery (bone grafting and metal staples) to fix the "dead" lunate bone (Keinbock's Disease) that had already plagued his wrist from his altercation with the Columbian jewel thieves a few months earlier. Mad Max was also put on prophylactic drugs for HIV and hepatitis, since the arrestee was a drug user, and there had been lots of bodily fluids exchanged and open wounds. Just another tricky day in the life of a law enforcement officer. Every day they play the deadly game.

The home invasion burglar would later go to a state prison for various felonies. In any event, the story served as a sober reminder to Avery that anything can happen, any time. A frightening letter is one thing. A person who writes a vile, hate-filled letter may or may not ultimately resort to violence. But public servants like Mad Max, and the Deputy U.S. Marshals, deal with unexpected violent actors all the time. No warnings. You walk into danger. You walk into the cesspool. Things happen, and you just deal with it.

The large metal decorative wall spoon that became a deadly weapon was described as a "shovel" by Mad Max's colleague (Sam the Terrorist) in the police report—perhaps by mistake or perhaps in deference to Mad Max's tough reputation. It did look somewhat like a shovel. But Mad Max, in good humor, said "Make no mistake, it was really a giant metal decorative wall spoon that became a deadly weapon." Actually, it is being generous to suggest that Mad Max was in good humor. He was on "dreaded light duty" for the next few weeks. And when he arrived at his desk the next week at the police station, it was covered in hundreds of red, white and blue plastic spoons with a note "Remember, Mad Max, everything can double as a weapon"—some office humor from his trusted colleagues. Officer Max being on light duty was not a good thing. Every cop hates "light duty."

The last time Mad Max had been on "light duty" was after he had gotten into an altercation with "Fake Dick Cheney." "Fake Dick Cheney" was part of a group protesting "Guantanamo Bay and torture as a war crime." Specifically, a few years back, Mad Max served on the police department's riot response and crowd control team that is called into action whenever a parade or protest occurs in town. One day, a protest erupted near the George W. Bush Presidential Library and Museum, when dignitaries including former Vice President Dick Cheney, were attending an event there. At the protest, Fake Dick Cheney (that is, a man wearing a paper mache head piece in the likeness of Dick Cheney) charged a police barricade, screaming "stop water boarding, stop water boarding." When Officer Max grabbed Fake Dick Cheney, he fought back and eventually pulled out a lighter and tried to self-immolate. Officer Max was on the 6:00 p.m. news cast that night, taking down and putting out the flames of Fake Dick Cheney. In fact, there was a You Tube video of said event that eventually received 450,000 clicks. Avery's mother, whose standards of propriety were very high, was mortified over the whole episode, and would not leave the house for several days—telling everyone she was suffering from one of her migraines. Avery's kids thought the whole thing was awesome.

In any event, after the Fake Dick Cheney self-immolation episode, Mad Max was on three weeks of light duty, with some minor burns to his forearms. During that phase of light duty, Mad Max had been assigned to handle low level crime investigations—the highlight of which was bringing down a prostitution ring of "proportional dwarves" that was advertising on the Craigslist back page and whose "MO" was to taser and rob their "Johns"–not exactly the most fulfilling of all police work. Avery had pleaded with Mad Max not to use the term "proportional dwarves"—she thought it was "politically incorrect" and terribly insensitive. "But that's how the prostitutes advertised themselves!" Mad Max retorted back. "And, they even exploit the fact that they charge half price because of it." Avery also pleaded with Mad Max not to relay the story of the "proportional dwarves" at Julia's upcoming "parent career day" at her middle school. "No promises," Mad Max said with a wink. Anyway, the next several weeks would be impossible with Mad Max being on light duty. Never mind the death threat. Never mind the chaos of Deputy U.S. Marshals swarming around the backyard. That now seemed trivial. Mad Max was not going to be in a good place.

Part III:

Six Months and Counting.

Chapter 16:

"It's Got to be Raining Somewhere" (Strange Days).

Winter turned to spring, and Texas was soon dotted with its famous bluebonnets. There had not been much rain during the winter (and no snow at all—there rarely was), so the bluebonnets were not quite as thick and vibrant this year. And by Easter, the humid, warm days had begun. Tornado season and spring storms would soon arrive, with their usual wild vengeance. But as the seasons changed, and as all of the festive Texas holidays came and went—Texas Independence Day, San Jacinto Day, Cinco de Mayo—Avery did not feel very celebratory and refrained from some of her usual, annual social activities. She felt more and more reclusive all the time. Her outward personality had noticeably changed, and her inner self was in turmoil. There was still no progress in the investigation of the death threats. And there was a long lapse of time with no more letters.

What to do, what to do. More and more, Avery was wanting to just pretend like nothing had happened and go back to her old life. Even if there was still someone out there who wanted to kill her, she had developed new self-defense skills (and acquired new weapons). She considered herself a fairly hard target now. But there was the issue of her children. Avery could not possibly take risks with her children's lives. She would have to embrace the Marshal protection for the kids' sake and have patience with the FBI investigation for a while longer—as frustrating as it was. The subject of Avery's children was especially troublesome. Avery naturally cared more about her children than anything else in the world. She sensed that the Marshal protection was taking a hard and emotional toll on them. Julia was more verbal than Heath. She sometimes cried on her mother's shoulder. She was not too old for that. She expressed how she sometimes could not sleep at night and how she still, after all of these months, woke up in the middle of the night afraid of the letter writer—that he would come and kill her mom and all of them. Heath, like any 18-year-old boy, was not as prone to sharing his feelings. He was quiet and stoic, but Avery sensed anxiety in Heath like she had never observed before the death threats. Avery sometimes convinced herself that Heath's anxiety was rooted in the fact that he was a senior in high school about to go off to college soon. But there seemed to be more to his anxiety. He was embarrassed when friends came over and saw the Deputy Marshals camped out behind the house, and he was worried about his mom. Avery was so sad that the children of a police officer—who always bear the stress of knowing that their dad might not come home from work on any given day—were now also feeling a new stress about their mom. They were no doubt worried about their own safety as well.

Some days were definitely harder than others. Luckily, Avery had good friends and colleagues that helped her forget about things every once in a while. There was her good judge friend, Maria Ramos, who took her out for drinks and on "retail therapy" excursions to upscale clothing and shoe stores occasionally. There was another judge friend (Judge Franklin) who was a jovial amateur artist and painted her a picture to cheer her up. The painting was of Baxter and Judge Franklin's dog Geno, on a desert island surrounded by palm trees and sand and "Baxter and Geno—island dogs" was written in the corner. Judge Franklin was known for giving out paintings of his dog Geno to people in the courthouse. Avery thought he loved Geno as much as Avery loved Baxter. Judge Franklin loved Geno so much that he had drained his home swimming pool and had a mural of Geno painted on the bottom of the pool. Avery received cards and visits and lots of support during this whole awful phase of the death threats. And her own staff and law interns and externs were the greatest. They were her court family.

There is an old legend that has been handed down among judges for generations that the fourth Chief Justice of the United States Supreme Court, Justice John Marshall, was fond of spirits, and would allegedly permit the drinking of wine and other alcoholic beverages during Supreme Court deliberations on rainy days. But only on rainy days—the excuse being that it was for medicinal reasons. This happened to be in the days before the Justices met at the hallowed halls of the United States Supreme Court building (it wasn't built and completed until the year 1935; the Court met in boarding houses in Washington, D.C. and in a stuffy room in the Capitol building back in the days of Justice Marshall). The story goes on that, on sunny days— if Chief Justice Marshall was having a particularly bad time–perhaps struggling with a mentally taxing legal conundrum, or on a day when the Court brethren were quarreling, or on a day when political actors in the other Branches of Government were threatening to insert themselves into the Court's business–Chief Justice Marshall would gaze wistfully out of the windows, and eventually say, "It's got to be raining somewhere." At that point, he would supposedly grab for his favorite bottle of Madeira wine infused with brandy (imported from the Portuguese island off the coast of Morocco) and imbibe generously. On some days, he might even throw together his famous "Quoit Club Punch" consisting of 14 lemons, 2 and ½ cups of raw white sugar, a bottle of dark Jamaican rum, a bottle of Madeira, and a bottle of cognac VSOP.[3] On a Friday in early April—five months after her death threats and Marshal protection phase of her life commenced—Judge Avery was having one of those mentally taxing days and wished she had a bottle of her favorite Cloudy Bay Sauvignon Blanc nearby, to follow in the grand tradition of the great Chief Justice John Marshall. Or, still better, she wished she had the ingredients to throw together some of that crazy "Quoit Club Punch."

Judge Lassiter had snuck Baxter into court with her on that particular Friday, in his dog kennel, like she sometimes did. Avery joked with her kids that Baxter seemed to love the big white, majestic, marble courthouse. Baxter sat quietly behind Avery's bench that day, dozing in and out of lawyer appearances–no doubt sometimes dreaming of "Halli Galli," the pretty Cavalier King Charles Spaniel who had been shown a while back at the Westminster Dog Show. The first docket that Judge Lassiter had set on that day was a docket involving "serial bankruptcy filers." These are individuals (some are sad and desperate, and, at the other extreme, some are scam artists) that file bankruptcy cases for themselves again and again and again, and eventually must appear before the court and explain why they keep doing this. More specifically, these individuals are required to come forward and prove their good faith. They are frequently *pro se* (that is, they have no lawyers, so they represent themselves—because in noncriminal matters the court will not appoint a lawyer for those who cannot afford one). On this day, there were a lot of serial filers in court to testify.

In the first case up, a large man wearing a green "Teenaged Mutant Ninja Turtle" tee shirt and with tear drop tattoos coming down

---

[3] C. Cushman, Table for 9: Supreme Court Food Traditions & Recipes at 9 (Sup. Ct. Historical Society 2018).

from his right eye was sworn in by Avery to testify. The man gave the following excuse for his problems with money that necessitated repeated bankruptcy case filings: During his last court case, he had to make a visit to the nearby VA hospital, and while walking through the parking lot there, a strange lady charged at him with an ice pick, and "he had to hit her upside the head." Not surprisingly, the man (actually, apparently both of them) had been arrested for assault and had to go to jail for a while. This caused the man to miss work and default in making his bankruptcy plan payments in the last case. Now he had his life back on track, but needed a little help from the court. When Judge Lassiter looked at him for a few moments rather blankly, he said he could get an "Act of David" from someone at the VA hospital to prove what happened, if she wanted him to do that. She assumed he meant affidavit? Anyway, Avery wondered the rest of the day what the teardrop tattoos on this man's face meant. When Officer Max called in later that afternoon and she asked if he knew, he said it was typically a tattoo that gang members choose to get, to indicate how many murders they have committed. But not always—it sometimes symbolizes loved ones that a person has lost. Or still further, it could mean that you were raped in prison. Officer Max was always such a fount of knowledge when it came to this type of important societal information.

The next case up involved a very large lady who brought a bullet-ridden car door in as an exhibit to show her good faith. She testified to Avery that she was falling behind in her personal finances because she was having transportation issues getting to work (and, thus, was missing getting paychecks). Pointing to her car door, she accurately stated that one cannot drive a car to work with a missing driver's side door. She went on to say that the FBI was monitoring her and her son because of certain whistle blowing that she had undertaken against them, and the FBI had shot up her car door, late one night in retaliation against her. When Judge Lassiter asked her if she had consulted with a lawyer regarding all of this alleged activity, she said yes, but the lawyer was downstairs in the lobby of the courthouse, scared to come upstairs. The lawyer allegedly had vertigo and could not take an elevator past the 6th floor of any tall building without becoming nauseous. The lawyer's vertigo was allegedly caused by a June bug that had gotten stuck in her ear (as it was only April, perhaps the June bugs were out early this year—global warming and all).

A third case involved a handsome fellow with wavy black long hair, wearing tight white polyester pants, red shiny shoes, a red silky shirt, and a turquoise squash blossom necklace. Avery's Southern-belle mother would have called this wardrobe selection a bit of a fashion faux paus (at a minimum, because of the white pants before Easter). The flashy gentleman was the sole director of an allegedly faith-based charitable organization. He had used charitable donations from mostly elderly people to fund a lavish lifestyle—including purchasing an Aston Martin vehicle (the type of vehicle that the movie character James Bond 007 drives). The flashy handsome gentleman stated that he did not understand why Judge Lassiter would think that this was a problem. Just because he was an executive of a nonprofit organization, he said, did not mean that he needed to take a vow of poverty. He had been blessed with these charitable donations. They were "love offerings." Judge Lassiter swiftly ordered the Deputy Marshals to seize the Aston Martin vehicle. Avery also directed the Deputy Marshals to escort the flashy fellow away, when he started repeatedly screaming in his preacher-like voice, "Abandon all hope, all ye who enter here. She is going to unleash all Hell on you. She is defiling this temple of justice! May God have mercy upon your souls! She is the Devil's mistress. She is the Devil's mistress!"

When the fourth matter was called, a young female lawyer began to question her witness and then suddenly passed out at the courtroom podium and dropped still on the floor, nose bleeding. Before anyone could react, one of the most abrasive and disliked lawyers in town, Manuel Slim (with a misleading last name, by the way), whom Avery's staff affectionately nicknamed "Unibrow," and who happened to be waiting in the courtroom for his matter to be called, rushed forward, leaping over the pews in the courtroom, as if he was about to administer first aid. Everyone in the courtroom was shocked–an heroic and kind gesture, from an unlikely source. But first impressions can be deceiving. Mr. Slim (a.k.a. Unibrow) stepped over the young attorney's body and asked if Judge Lassiter could quickly hear his matter (*i.e.,* the next one on her docket), while everyone waited on the paramedics to arrive, because he had somewhere else that he needed to be soon. At that point, it was as if Baxter heard what was going on and could not restrain himself. Sweet little Baxter bolted out from behind Avery's bench and charged the despicable Manuel Slim. Manuel Slim embodied every quality that makes the public dislike lawyers. Baxter chewed on Manuel Slim's leg for a good 30 seconds before the courtroom deputy, Kasi, and Millicent, Avery's law clerk, bolted out into the courtroom to subdue him. In a moment of lost self-control, Baxter even urinated on Manuel Slim's leg. Apparently, Baxter just could not control himself. Millicent scooped him up in embarrassment and handed him over to Avery, who quickly hid him under her robe and headed to her exit behind the courtroom bench. As they fled out of the courtroom, Baxter peeked out from Avery's robe and seemed to be giving Manuel Slim the stink eye.

At that point, the paramedics rushed in and Judge Lassiter's court was in recess. The good news was that the young female lawyer who fainted was fine—just a little nervous and dehydrated. Avery went back to her chambers, took off her robe and sighed. She petted Baxter and reached into her desk drawer and gave him a roasted sweet potato treat from the stash that she usually saved for Nico, the Department of Homeland Security dog that sometimes came by to sniff for explosives in the courthouse. "This treat is for putting Unibrow in his rightful place, better than I or any other judge has ever managed to do. You absolutely earned this treat today, buddy."

Avery turned and sighed and looked out of her chambers window. "I could use a treat myself. It's got to be raining somewhere."

Avery always said that her dockets were a regular reminder that everyone is just one day away from a disaster. Sad but true. People are riding high one day, and then tragedy hits. People lose their jobs. A spouse cheats and an ugly divorce ensues. Someone gets diagnosed with cancer or has a stroke. A hurricane or other natural disaster destroys a lifetime of achievements, possessions, and memories. Someone gets chased through a VA parking lot by a woman carrying an ice pick. A mother trying to raise kids in a blighted neighborhood gets her car door shot up and cannot get to work. This was the drama over which Avery presided every day.

A wise lawyer who once practiced in the world of financial distress and insolvency, when Avery was a young lawyer, was known to say of the federal bankruptcy courts that "Bankruptcy is where society ultimately decides what's important."[4] This is true. Life is hard. Are we going to throw people into debtors' prisons, like in medieval times, or give them a second chance? Maybe the second time around these people will accomplish something that will change

---

[4] This was said by the late and great attorney Harvey Miller of the Weil, Gotshal & Manges law firm.

the world. Even Abraham Lincoln once resorted to filing bankruptcy before he went on to achieve more monumental things. And Davy Crockett, "King of the Wild Frontier," traveled across country to live in Texas, allegedly fleeing from angry creditors back home. Remember the Alamo?

It is very difficult to hear people's sad stories laid bare before the bench and then be faced with determining how to apply the law and fix the broken places. As the famous jurist Benjamin Cardozo once said, "Legal opinions often antiseptically leave out the human experience." There is a "back story" that does not always make its way into the law books. Avery tells her law clerks that law students imagine that the courtroom will be exciting—even glamourous. They imagine cross-examining witnesses who will spew acrid lies and will be caught in exciting, dramatic fashion. Injustice will be exposed. They will save people and companies from calamity. They will forge litigation that will change society. They will handle cutting edge complex legal issues and will make millions of dollars in the process. This is the fantasy of the uninitiated. Reality check: it is not all roses and sunshine. And it is not all *To Kill a Mockingbird* or *Inherit the Wind*. The sea of humanity that has legal problems and that passes into and out of the typical United States courthouse can sometimes make one feel terribly sad and emotionally spent. Some have said that despair is one of the greatest sins against the Holy Ghost. If so, then Avery daily witnessed that sin, sometimes feeling rather powerless to do much to change it.

But one thing Avery knew well was that—no matter how strange or sad any particular day of hers was in court—life was usually so much stranger (not to mention more risk-filled) for law enforcement officers. Stranger than her day of hearing testimony about a woman chasing a man with an ice pick through a VA hospital parking lot.

Stranger than her day of listening to a woman with a bullet riddled car door testify about how the FBI was retaliating against her (while her attorney, by the way, was downstairs unable to ride the elevator, because of vertigo caused by a June bug in her ear). Stranger than Baxter running out from behind Avery's bench and biting and urinating on the Unibrow's leg. Mad Max proved on a regular basis that the life of a law enforcement officer could be amazingly strange (his previous bust of the half-price charging proportional dwarves' prostitution ring was one of Avery's all-time favorite strange stories). And the Deputy Marshals guarding Avery proved the theory to Avery as well. Avery loved to hear the Deputy Marshals' stories—whenever Avery could coax one out of them. At the end of Avery's weird day described above, Deputy Marshal Ginny Oliphante was assigned to drive Avery home from court. Avery was glad. Ginny was usually good for an interesting story or two.

Ginny Oliphante was a little rough around the edges but was perky and adorable and an all-around great Deputy Marshal. She was 35-years-old, and Avery and her kids found her enormously fun to have around. She was a tall, thin, brown-haired beauty. Avery and Julia both said that they saw Ginny as emanating a pretty violet color. Avery and Julia nicknamed her "Ginny from the Block" or just "Violet Ginny." Ginny from the Block mostly spent her time hunting down fugitives on a regional task force but was sometimes assigned to Avery's protective detail for a couple of weeks at a time. She had grown up in the Bronx, New York, the daughter of a single mother who was a baker. Ginny never knew her father and had no siblings. Her mother died when Ginny was just 19 years old. All alone in the world, Ginny joined the United States Navy after that and eventually worked as a cryptologist in the bowels of a ship. After a few years sailing around the world decrypting and decoding messages, Ginny received her honorable discharge, earned a couple of college degrees on her G.I. bill (one of which was in art history), and eventually was recruited by the U.S. Marshals Service. Ginny had, like Avery, traveled a lot (both while in the Navy and on her own) and shared really good tales of her travels. Avery jokingly referred to Ginny as her kids' "Vodka aunt" because her language was rough, she shared gripping, scary stories and sometimes inappropriate jokes, and she told the kids that she would go out and drink with them one day "when they were old enough and mom was not around."

On that particular Friday, Ginny from the Block shared an interesting work story with Avery while driving her and Baxter home. Ginny was very frustrated. Ginny had received an assignment two years ago to find and arrest a certain fugitive—a high profile rising leader within the La Familia drug cartel—who was likely dead, but she could not close her case until she had reliable proof that he was, indeed, dead. The fugitive—named Antonio Castillo—who was wanted on federal drug trafficking charges in several U.S. jurisdictions, was reported by three somewhat reliable sources to have been killed down in a small village in Mexico three years ago (that is, one year before Ginny had been assigned to track him down and bring him to justice). There was no death certificate for Castillo or other official proof of death, so Ginny had to somehow collect reliable evidence that he was really dead and not just hiding. It was difficult because of the circumstances in which Castillo allegedly died. Castillo had allegedly been kidnapped out of a pool hall in a small village in Mexico, along with several other La Familia cartel members, and taken into the desert where he was forced to watch each of the other cartel members have their arms and legs chopped off, and then each was eventually shot to death. After watching all of this carnage, Castillo supposedly suffered the same gruesome death.

The alleged killer was someone only known as "Paco," and Paco was allegedly a rising leader in the competing Knights Templar drug cartel. Paco also happened to be an actor in B movies in Mexico. Allegedly, with the killing of Castillo, Paco was not only trying to score an intimidation victory against a rival drug cartel, but was also avenging his older brother's murder at the hands of La Familia (and likely pursuant to the orders of Castillo). Ginny had heard this same story regarding Castillo's death from three sources: Castillo's wife in Texas, from a DEA informant, and most recently from another La Familia cartel member who had been arrested and pleaded guilty to certain charges, in exchange for sharing some of the secrets of the cartel. Ginny had at long last gotten a break in her case. She had learned Paco's real name and learned that he was serving time in a prison in El Reno, Oklahoma. Ginny was hoping to go interview Paco at the prison this weekend and was frustrated because she was hearing from Paco's lawyer that he was wanting legal "favors" before he would confirm the rumors about how Castillo died or otherwise provide verifiable information. The U.S. Attorney was not likely going to be in the mood to do any "favors" for this hardened criminal.

Suddenly a thought crept into Avery's mind. *What if her letter writer was now dead?* It had been over three months since the last threatening letter had been received, with all the *Hitchhiker's Guide to the Galaxy* references. Nothing had happened since. Could that be why he had not written further, and had not carried out his threat, or otherwise been caught? Avery hoped he was dead. She felt guilty that she hoped that another human being was dead. But she definitely hoped he was dead.

Chapter 17:
The Third and Darkest Communication; The Voicemail Regarding Blood, Incineration, and an Acid Bath.

Well, as it turned out, the letter writer was not dead. In fact, he now seemed angrier and perhaps more depraved than Avery had ever before imagined. The next Monday, after the previous Friday's strange day of courtroom shenanigans, Avery walked into her chambers. She was actually feeling fairly positive and happy on this particular day. She had made plans over the weekend for a summer vacation to Portugal in late June—one of her favorite travel destinations. She was going on a vacation no matter what. June was two months from now. Surely this would all be deemed "over" by late June. But as Avery walked into her chambers that Monday morning, Annalise immediately caught Avery's eye. Annalise stood at her desk looking pale as a ghost.

"What is it, Annalise? Is something wrong?"

"Judge, you have just entered the turn styles to crazy town."

"I beg your pardon?"

"I'm sorry. I should not joke. I don't know if this has become crazy town or a horror chambers at this point. There is a new threat. A horrific voice mail was left on the chambers' phone number over the weekend. At 11:42 p.m. Saturday night, to be exact. Sit down and I will play it for you, if you are ready. I want to warn you. It is very, very bad."

Avery put down her things, took off her jacket, and grabbed a cup of coffee at the new Keurig coffee machine that she had just purchased the preceding week. When Avery had first started working at the courthouse a few years earlier, she had inherited a coffee maker from the previous judge that she was pretty sure was a vestige from the Ronald Reagan administration. She was pretty excited about the prospect of decent, gourmet coffee now. At the rate she and her staff drank coffee, this more modern gadget would be broken from overuse in a few short months.

As Avery sat down, Annalise queued up the voicemail. The caller had spoken in a breathy but clear voice, leaving the following message:

"Greetings, Honorless Lassiter. It's been awhile. You have heard from me before. But only in writing. Have you figured out who I am or what I am going to do to you? Did you recognize the reference to '42'? Or the reference to the Ford Prefect? Oh, I know you did. When I am in your courtroom, I imagine that I see a forest of crucifixes between me and your bench, which gradually turns to trees. At first, there appears to be dew or rain, dripping from the branches. But as I approach your bench, I realize it is blood. Dripping from your bench. The whole courtroom seems to writhe and your bench, dark and erect, seems to ooze blood. I try to catch the blood with a cup. I want to drink it. I want to drink your blood. But I am unable to move.

Anyway. I think I know how I am going to kill you now. First, I think I will kill your cronies. Your partners in crime. I am thinking about incineration. That would be especially satisfying—considering how you all burned me, metaphorically speaking. I am also thinking about dumping one of you in a 45-gallon drum full of sulfuric acid and two days later the body will be sludge. I will pour the sludge down a man hole and they will never find it—a fitting death—just dissolving away in anonymity, never to ruin anyone's life again. But remember I said there would be a trilogy of five. Hmmm. Maybe I will try something more cataclysmic. . . Well, more to follow. Remember . . . It all began with you, you horrible bitch!"

That was the end of the message. Avery was trembling. "OK. Maybe he wins. I think I am officially afraid of this guy now."

There was the usual activity after the discovery of this voicemail, of Deputy Marshals rushing in. The FBI Special Agents were notified. But something was different this time. The Deputy Marshals and FBI seemed to go disturbingly silent after this communication. There was not just a lack of transparency like before. It was as if they were saying nothing at all. The silence was so deafening that it made Avery both worried and suspicious. If they had a reason to suspect someone in particular, they were sharing nothing at this point. Did they have someone in mind now? Did they have a reason to think something was about to happen imminently? All Avery and her family and staff knew was that things seemed to have ratcheted up a couple of notches. And it didn't feel good. The saga went on. And on and on. But there was silence. Hushed, muffled, deadened quiet. All questions asked by Avery were met with blank sullen stares. She was being told nothing. How could she trust the process if she was not being told anything? This was mental torture. Was this exactly what the letter writer wanted?

Chapter 18:

The Support of Colleagues.

While living under a death threat, it helps to have the support of close friends. And there was no better friend to Avery than her close colleague Judge Maria Ramos, a magistrate judge. Nothing seemed as scary to Avery when she was around Maria. Judge Ramos handles an arguably more exciting docket than Judge Lassiter. She handles criminal matters, and Avery jokes that she handles a disproportionate number of bank robbery matters because the bank robbers "time" their robberies so that, if arrested, it will be during a week when beautiful Judge Ramos is on criminal duty and will be the one handling their initial appearances and bond setting hearings. Maria is beautiful, spunky and Avery swears that the criminals adore Judge Ramos, even when she comes down hard on them–which is frequently the case.

Judges Lassiter and Ramos work out together, shoe-shop together (Maria calls this "retail therapy"), and generally share their lives. Avery prefers working out with Maria in the Federal Building gym, as opposed to going to her neighborhood health club. At the neighborhood health club, Avery has had a long string of personal fitness trainers who never seem to last very long term. There was first "Evil Bruce Lee." He tortured Avery with weight-lifting and cardio regimes that did nothing but make her feel old. She terminated him as a trainer after he one day asked Avery (whom he knew loves old rock and roll music) if she had, by chance, attended Woodstock. Woodstock was in the year 1969. August 1969, to be exact. Avery was not old enough to have attended Woodstock. That foot-in-mouth question spelled the end of the "Evil Bruce Lee" torture fitness sessions. Then there was the female trainer who looked like the ghost of Amy Winehouse. Avery could not handle having a female trainer who looked like a dead, anorexic blues singer.

But, in contrast, workouts in the Federal Building gym were nice and private, and Avery could input whatever personal data that she wanted into the treadmill (for example: age 25; height 68 inches; weight 118 pounds), without getting incredulous and disdainful looks from some millennial, Barbie doll-like fitness trainer with fake Chinese words tattooed onto her arms and ankles. Avery's workouts in the Federal Building gym were also accompanied with nice, long conversations with Avery's kindred spirit. On the day of the horrible voice mail that mentioned acid bath sludge and blood dripping from Avery's bench, she needed some decompression time with Maria.

When Avery walked into the downstairs gym, Maria smiled and asked how Avery's day had been, adding, "Bet you can't top this, Avery. I had a guy take the witness stand and, five minutes into his testimony, asked if I minded if he dipped snuff while testifying. Top that, friend."

"Did you let him? Well, someone left me a breathy voice mail message, saying that he imagined crucifixes and blood dripping from my bench when he was in my courtroom, and he wants to kill me and put me in a drum full of sulfuric acid where I will dissolve into sludge and die in anonymity."

"Holy shit! God, I'm sorry. To heck with the gym . . . maybe we should skip our workout today and go have some tequila shots."

And that's exactly what they did. Actually, they went out and drank margaritas instead, on the patio of a nearby dog-friendly Tex-Mex bar and grill. The Deputy Marshals hated it when Avery wanted to do anything outside. And they hated it even more when she wanted to bring Baxter along to create a further distraction for them. On this particular day, Avery persuaded the Deputy Marshals to run by the house and pick Baxter up to go out with her and Judge Ramos.

Judge Lassiter repeated in a whispered hush to Judge Ramos, over margaritas, the content of the breathy voice mail message, as best she could remember it–feeling somewhat guilty because the Deputy Marshals and FBI had given her strict instructions, now that the multiple threats kept coming, not to share details with anyone. Maria naturally expressed horror over the gruesomeness of the latest communication. "To say this is twisted and disturbing doesn't begin to be adequate. I know you were going down a trail of thinking this might be some geek–because of the references in the earlier letter to *The Hitchhiker's Guide to the Galaxy,* and because you have had a multitude of high-tech nerds and internet types in your court lately that were sort of socially awkward. But this sounds Edgar Allen Poe'ish or maybe Edgar Allen Poe mixed with a serial killer or something. Sorry. I hate to make you feel worse than you already do. This is just sick and awful."

Avery replied, "Well, he's referring to a serial killer alright. Have you heard of the so called 'Acid Bath murderer'?"

"Don't think so."

"There was a serial killer named John George Haigh who lived in London during the early part of the twentieth century, and he was nicknamed the "Acid Bath Murderer." He eventually was executed by hanging, for the killing of at least six people. He would actually use acid, not as a method of killing his victims, but simply to dispose of the victims' bodies after he killed them by some other means, because he misunderstood the term "corpus delicti" and thought that, if he could destroy his murder victims' bodies, he could never be convicted for murder if there was never a body found. So, to kill them, he would do very uncreative things like hit the victims over the head or shoot them. But then he would put the victim in a drum full of sulfuric acid to hide the evidence. His motive was always financial. He would kill a victim (usually a wealthy victim) and forge papers to assume the victim's identity and sell his possessions and collect a lot of money. He once did it to a friend of his with money. He also did it to a married couple that he met under the pretext of being interested in property that they were selling. He also did it to a widow that he lured to his house. He ended up pleading insanity, but that did not sway the jury, who sentenced him to death. What is most interesting is that there are some historical accounts of things that John George Haigh said to policemen and doctors who interviewed him in jail, pending his trial, and he said a lot of things very similar to what was left on my voice mail today. So the guy who left the voice mail, I guess, is borrowing some lines and ideas from the 'Acid Bath Murderer' for some reason."

"Avery, do you know this kind of stuff off of the top of your head, or did the Marshals and FBI already piece this together or what? Because if you know this type of stuff off of the top of your head, you are really seriously scaring me!"

"Well it doesn't take a genius in Quantico to figure out all of this information. I don't know if my crazy-guy threat maker thinks he is smart or what, but the truth is that it only took a few Google searches to make the connection to the 'Acid Bath Murderer.' My law intern Matt actually did it in about fifteen minutes with some word searches. But that still doesn't answer the question of why or what exactly he is threatening–much less who this crazy-guy is."

"Avery, I just don't know how to process all of this. I have had some bizarre things happen on occasion since I have been on the bench—things that were at least initially thought to be threats—but nothing has ever come close to any of this."

"Like what kinds of bizarre things? I don't think you have ever told me about any threats?"

"Didn't I ever tell you about the time that I started finding crosses marked on my windows and doors in my chambers that were made with some sort of clear oil—like they were marked in the dust with someone's finger?"

"No. I think I would remember that. What happened with that?"

"There was an innocent but really weird explanation. It turns out that a cleaning lady did it. She saw on my desk a voodoo doll that I had gotten on a trip to New Orleans, at some little souvenir shop, when I was at a judges conference, and she thought that the voodoo doll would bring evil spirits into my office and the whole courthouse, so she was spiritually cleansing my office or something like that—with some sort of oil and making the sign of the crucifix everywhere. The cleaning lady cried when confronted about it and said she was trying to save my soul and the souls of everyone who came into the courthouse."

"Sweet of her, I suppose."

"Yes, well you know that there have been rumors forever about our courthouse being haunted. I suppose my office wasn't the only place in the courthouse that will benefit from the exorcism or whatever it was. Avery, in all seriousness, do you think that, after close to five months, the Feds are any closer to figuring this all out than they were on Day 1? Is the voice mail going to make it easier? I mean I am assuming that they can figure out where the call came from, from Caller ID or subpoenaing phone records from the phone company or something? And I assume that they will compare the voice qualities to different people who have testified in your court from the audio recordings your court reporter keeps, right? And did you recognize the voice at all? Did your law clerk? Court reporter? Courtroom Deputy? Anyone?"

"The answer is 'no, no and no.' I mean, the Deputy Marshals and FBI seem to be telling me less and less—especially after this latest phone call. It's like I am on a "need to know" basis. You know how I am, Maria. I want transparency—the unvarnished truth. But that's just not the way they operate. Everything about their investigation is shrouded. Anyway, they did at least tell me after a couple of hours this morning that this phone call was made from a throw-away burner phone. I mean I think they might be able to pinpoint the geographical location of the caller, for whatever that is worth, but I am not sure. I am sure he was not foolish enough to call from his house or anywhere where he could be easily tracked down. And none of us has the first clue who this voice sounds like. But I suppose someone may eventually listen to audio recordings of some of the court room testimony of our 'prime suspects' that we have compiled. Not sure if that will be a good use of time or not. This is crazy. I don't think we have any good ideas at this point, to be honest."

"All I can say is 'drink up, friend. Drink up.'"

"Yes. It's got to be raining somewhere, right?"

Chapter 19:
QM2.

In late April, Judge Lupinaci surprised Judge Murphy with a birthday present for his 92nd birthday: a cruise on the Queen Mary 2 ocean liner—otherwise known as the QM2. She knew her dear friend would love the elegant and regal idea of traveling on the largest ocean liner ever built. It would be lovely. She booked a suite on a 13-day cruise from New York to the Caribbean. Everyone at the Camden courthouse was thrilled to hear of the judges' plans. Colleagues giggled and gossiped, wondering if the two were secretly eloping.

The cruise was scheduled to leave on a Friday afternoon. Both judges took the full day off from work. Judge Lupinaci had errands to run and packing still to do. A young sweet maintenance worker at the courthouse, Buddy, who often did handy work at Judge Lupinaci's house for extra spending money had agreed to take both of the judges to the ship. Buddy would be at Judge Lupinaci's house at 1:00 p.m. She and Buddy would pick up Judge Murphy after leaving Judge Lupinaci's house. Judge Murphy lived very close by. As Judge Lupinaci was going through her mail before she left, she noticed a strange letter addressed to the "Honorless Helen Lupinaci." She had gotten a letter a month or two ago that was similarly addressed. The earlier letter had contained a vile death threat and was generally a long angry rant against the justice system. She had decided to ignore that earlier letter and threw it in the trash without ever reporting it to the Marshal Service. She had decided that she was too old and had been a public servant way too long to let herself worry about that kind of thing. Judge Lupinaci almost decided to throw this newest envelope away without even opening it. Why spoil her trip with something potentially negative? She started opening the letter. She read a few lines, started shaking her head in disgust, and then threw the letter into the recycling trash. She cinched up the trash and then left it out on the curb for tomorrow morning's trash pickup. As she turned to head back up to the house, the young man from the courthouse drove up to her curb, rolled down his window, and asked if she was ready to leave. She smiled and waved and asked Buddy to park and come inside for a few minutes. She had a few more things to pack and then she would be ready. She asked Buddy to call Judge Murphy and tell him that they'd be at his house within the next thirty minutes.

Chapter 20:
Money, Money, Money. Follow the Money.

So many times in this world, a crime all boils down to money—and someone being angry about money. This is not a revelation. Most people probably realize this. In the immortal words of the Notorious B.I.G., "Mo' money, mo' problems." So maybe the letter writer—despite his creepiness, and despite his cryptic wording—was simply mad about money. The root of all evil. Maybe there was nothing clever or mysterious about him. Maybe he was just a sad, sick nerd who was festering about lost money. Maybe he was involved with one of the two more high profile cases in Avery's court that involved disastrous losses of money—and, in both cases—a somewhat atypical constituency of people who lost money. One such case (mentioned briefly earlier) involved a strange kind of money: virtual money. Bitcoin.

So what is Bitcoin? Judge Lassiter barely knew the answer to this question before a case was filed in her court involving an electronic Bitcoin trading platform that was mysteriously hacked, causing thousands of people to lose hundreds of thousands of Bitcoin.

Bitcoin is usually described as electronic money, cryptographic currency, or digital currency. To be specific, Bitcoin is a piece of digital property. It is like a digital bearer instrument. A string of numbers is sent over an email or text message in the simplest case. It is transferred from digital device to digital device, over the Internet, rather than by hand. The U.S. Internal Revenue Service has thus far defined it as property, not currency. There are many, lesser known crypto-currencies emerging. Most of the operations at which the currency is traded, stored, or "mined" are in remote places offshore or other unlikely places: Malta; Eastern Europe; North Korea.

Bitcoin was allegedly first "created" or "conceived" in the year 2008, supposedly by an anonymous person or group of persons using the name Satoshi Nakamoto. In 2009, the first Bitcoin started being "mined." To be more specific, Satoshi Nakamoto began communicating computer puzzles or algorithms to be solved, out over the Internet, and whomever solved them first earned (or "mined") a Bitcoin. It was essentially a worldwide math competition involving very complicated math problems, and it required very powerful computer systems (consuming huge amounts of power) to solve the problems. These computers became known as Bitcoin rigs or mining rigs. There was said to be a finite number of Bitcoin that would ever be issued: 21 million and the influx of it into commerce would be gradual. It became a gold rush of sorts, with people—some in college dorm rooms, some in open-air warehouses in Siberia and subarctic areas of Canada (where the powerful Bitcoin rigs could stay cool), some in Washington state (where excess power capacity was cheap), and some eventually in the Silicon Valley—buying large quantities of the Bitcoin rigs, some eventually financed by private equity, to increase their computer power and speed, so as to solve the algorithms and mine more Bitcoin.

Eventually, there were a lot of Bitcoins in existence, creating the next question of how to get Bitcoin into the stream of commerce and make Bitcoin usable. Websites or "Bitcoin exchanges" were created in this nascent market, where people could go to the website, create an account, and then, once registered, users could trade Bitcoin online (for "fiat" currency—that is government backed currency, such as U.S. Dollars or Euros or Yen) using what was supposed to be a secure online trading platform. People could also store Bitcoin in a virtual vault for safekeeping or electronic wallets (a wallet is a Bitcoin address or set of addresses than can be used to store or transfer user Bitcoins). How does this all work? Allegedly, only the owner of the asset can send it, only the intended recipient can receive it, the asset can only exist in one place at one time, and everyone can validate transactions and ownership of assets anytime they want. This is done on the Internet-wide distributed ledger called the "Block Chain" (*i.e.,* the so-called public record of all Bitcoin transactions, which is a computer technology that creates a public, tamper-proof and anonymous digital ledger). One buys into the ledger by purchasing one of a fixed number of slots, either with cash, or by selling a good or service for Bitcoin. One sells out of the ledger by trading his Bitcoin to someone else who wants to buy into the ledger. There are very low or sometimes no fees. The coins themselves are merely slots in the ledger.

Although it has been hyped as having less potential for fraud than credit card usage, in the bitcoin case in Avery's court, one of the world's largest Bitcoin exchange sites had hundreds of thousands of Bitcoins go missing, then collectively valued at hundreds of millions of U.S. dollars. The missing Bitcoin prompted the company to file a bankruptcy case in France—the center of its main interests. Hacking was suspected by former management. There were many tens of thousands of customers in more than 100 countries with balances on the Bitcoin exchange that had lost Bitcoin. Eventually a Russian national was arrested in Europe for the alleged hacking. But still not all of the missing Bitcoin had been recovered. Several U.S. law enforcement agencies and various foreign law enforcement agencies were "all over the place" trying to find the missing Bitcoin as well as missing fiat currency. A massive money laundering scheme was suspected. It was a bizarre entrepreneurial saga, to say the least. Judge Lassiter presided over the bitcoin exchange's U.S. Chapter 15 ancillary bankruptcy proceedings. There were few answers as to how investors in the company were ever going to be repaid lost fortunes. There were a lot of angry people—from young college student geeks to Wall Street investors. Was one of these angry people a geeky fan of *The Hitchhiker's Guide to the Galaxy* and also the letter writer? Many folks in the investigation loop thought the theory might have legs. The trading price of Bitcoin dropped significantly while the case involving Bitcoin was pending in Judge Lassiter's court. Maybe someone held her accountable? Judge Lassiter asked many times in court for someone to explain to her how Bitcoin could be so fascinating to people as an investment vehicle or medium of exchange, when it had no intrinsic value, was not supported by the full faith and credit of any government, nor any physical asset. She even asked was Billionaire Warren Buffet right, that it was "rat poison squared." She received dozens of angry letters from investors after she was reported to have said this. Meanwhile, the founder of the company was currently in a Singapore prison. There were those that held him responsible and wanted Avery "to do something about it." There were others who wanted Avery "to somehow put an end to this, order a bankruptcy trustee to find the real hacker, and let the founder get back to running the platform."

And then there was the precious metals coin minting company known as Rand Mint, tucked into a sparsely populated part of the Texas Hill Country—actually not too far away from the Waco, Texas compound where the infamous cult leader David Koresh had notoriously died in flames with his Branch Davidian followers back in 1993. Rand Mint was formed and owned by two charming handsome brothers, Charles and Daniel Rand (identical twins who were in their thirties and had spent a couple of years of their life at the Koresh compound). One brother was college educated; the other was a high school dropout who once conducted self-help motivational seminars. Their good looks and charm had apparently been effectively used to convince people to invest millions of dollars in their minting business. The customers of the minting business included community groups who distrusted the U.S. dollar and were preparing for a financial apocalypse by investing in silver and gold coins that would serve as an alternative form of currency when needed. Similar to the Bitcoin case, this case involved millions of dollars' worth of missing commodities: in this case actual precious metals and coins rather than virtual money. Among the cast of characters who had invested in the company were various wealthy individuals who distrusted the federal government, and now they were unwittingly and ironically forced to seek vindication and justice in the federal courts. The Rand brothers had allegedly fled to Bangladesh early during the case, and allegedly were getting a fresh start in the same business abroad, where they were already making new enemies in other countries.

Did someone think the collapse of these companies, and the loss of the investors' fortunes, was all Avery's fault? Avery didn't think so. But who knew, anymore.

As Avery sat in her chambers late one afternoon pondering these two cases and wondering if the FBI was focusing on them at all, her court reporter Sheila entered the room. Sheila looked rather shaken. Sheila had been cleaning out the courtroom as she often did, walking through the back rows of pews, seeing if there were stray papers or books or anything else that the lawyers or parties may have inadvertently left recently. Lawyers were always forgetting things. On the back row of the courtroom, Sheila had found a yellow legal pad and a paperback copy of the book *Hitchhiker's Guide to the Galaxy*. On the front page of the yellow legal pad, the following was handwritten in block letters with blue ink:

"I PITY YOU, JUDGE LASSITER. YOUR LIFE EXPECTANCY IS NOT VERY FUCKING LONG."

There were rudimentary drawings all over the page of eye balls.

As usual, the Deputy Marshals were summoned into chambers to report this latest discovery. As usual, silence followed.

Chapter 21:

Two Missing New Jersey Judges— Coincidence or Not?

Avery, like all judges, had invaluable, indispensable law clerks, interns, and externs to help her in her daily work. The law clerks were bright, idealistic young lawyers, who deferred higher paying jobs at large prestigious law firms (Big Law) to work at the elbow of a federal judge and see the inner workings of the court—the "sausage making" of the law—as Avery sometimes would say. The interns and externs were usually third-year law students at one of the Texas law schools who rotated in and out after each semester. Avery usually chose these student interns and externs carefully, and it was one of her favorite parts of her job—getting to interact with bright, energetic, and inquisitive future lawyers who had ambition and a heart for the law.

During the time frame that Avery received her death threats, she employed an intern named Matt Smith, who had earned an undergraduate degree from Princeton University and was currently on leave from The University of Texas School of Law. Matt Smith had grown up in central New Jersey—somewhat close to where Avery had family. This had been a common thread that drew her interest to the intellectually curious young law student, in addition to his great credentials and sweet personality. Matt Smith was invaluable in not just performing careful, thorough legal research and otherwise helping around chambers; he was actually unbelievably helpful in putting together clues and "persons of interest" that the FBI and Deputy

Marshals might want to consider as the possible threat maker. Matt put together lists of people that had difficult cases and showed particular anger when adverse rulings were issued. He put together lists of persons he perceived had nerdy, quirky personality traits. He even went back and listened to audio recordings and reviewed transcripts for situations in which Avery had mentioned "42" or made veiled references to the *Hitchhiker's Guide to the Galaxy*. Matt Smith always made sure that the Deputy Marshals knew ahead of time when Avery was making a last-minute schedule change and might need to leave the office early for a professional function, meeting, or just to run errands. Matt monitored the news, websites, blogs, and all kinds of internet sources to see if anything appeared that might remotely seem relevant to what was going on in Avery's life. In fact, Matt Smith was so diligent and perfect, that Avery's staff found him rather annoying. "Brown noser" is what Avery's career law clerk, Millicent, sometimes good-naturedly grimaced. "I am pretty sure he is gunning for my job, no holds barred," Millicent joked.

"Millicent, don't be so negative. He is just like you were at that stage. Eager to please. What's wrong with that? You know that you both are indispensable around here!"

"I know. It's just that I feel like he is constantly competing with me. He has this superficial charm that he switches on immediately when you are around. And he has this vaunted estimation of his own self-worth, but he is pretty glib and shallow if you ask me."

"Ouch! Millicent, that is so harsh. Do you really mean what you are saying? Am I going to have to separate you two for the rest of his internship?"

"No. I'm sorry. I probably sound insecure. He and I just aren't getting along lately. He works insanely long hours—always trying to one-up me it seems. Make me look like a slacker or something."

"Millicent, I certainly do not think you are a slacker. But you do sound a little insecure. Matt is just trying to make a good impression, so that he will get a good reference from me. That is really an admirable thing, don't you think? Try to appreciate all the work he is helping us with—it is making both of our lives easier."

"I know. I'm sorry."

"You know, back in the days when I was a young summer associate at Madison, Spencer & Collins, I remember a young male summer associate who used to drive me crazy trying to create the impression that he worked harder than anyone else. Back then, there were human receptionists who answered the phones 24-hours-a-day. During off-business hours, when someone received a phone call, the receptionists would page that person over the loud speaker intercom, so that the person's name would go blaring through the law firm. The young male summer associate that I remember would call up to the office after hours and ask the receptionist to page him, so that the partners still at the office would assume he was there at all hours, hard at work. A real poser. Is that what you think Matt is, Millicent? A poser?"

"Oh, he is a poser, alright. A parasitic poser who constantly peppers me with questions, sucks knowledge out of my brain, and then uses that knowledge to impress you—pretending like my ideas are his ideas! But unlike the guy in your story from Madison, Spencer & Collins, Matt is really here at all hours. I mean all hours. I wouldn't be surprised if he is spending the night in the office some nights. And when he is not doing case work, he told me he is composing a musical or operetta based on the book *Crime and Punishment*. How weird is that?"

"Uh, that's kind of weird, alright."

"He is hoping it will be selected for 'Assault and Flattery' at UT Law School next year. Or maybe the Dallas Bar's 'Bar None' follies."

"Oh, good God. Well, Millicent, be nice. Maybe I will talk to Matt about collegiality and teamwork. But please. I think you should work on these things, too, Millicent!"

The next morning after her conversation with Millicent about Matt, when Avery arrived in her chambers at 7:30 am, Matt Smith was already there hard at work, listening to Verdi's *La Traviata* playing softly on a Bose speaker as he furiously typed on his laptop. He appeared startled when Avery walked in on him and looked as though he had been up half the night. Maybe Millicent was right about him spending the night at the office. Matt, indeed, always seemed to be around—no matter what time Avery arrived. Matt had brought his pet cat Ghost with him to work that day. It was a Friday. Avery, being the animal lover that she was, was flexible most of the time if her staff wanted to "take turns" bringing their pets to work on Fridays—as long as they were quiet and inconspicuous while there. Ghost was a white and gray Maine Coon cat that was polydactyl (that is, a cat with extra toes), similar to the ones that inhabit the Hemingway House and Museum at Key West, Florida. Matt had recently adopted Ghost, shortly before he began clerking for Avery.

Anyway, Avery was going to talk to Matt about trying to coexist with Millicent better, but Matt had some sobering news upon Avery's arrival at the office that took higher priority. "Good morning.

172

Judge Lassiter, have you heard about the two federal judges in New Jersey?"

"No. What do you mean?"

"There are two federal judges in Camden, New Jersey who are missing under suspicious circumstances. A federal district judge and a federal bankruptcy judge."

"Oh, no! Who? I know some of the judges up there. And what do you mean suspicious circumstances?"

"District Judge Ronald Murphy and Bankruptcy Judge Helen Lupinaci. They both haven't been seen or heard from in a couple of weeks. At first, apparently no one was too worried—they were supposed to be on a 13-day cruise together. But now, it has officially been described as a case of two missing persons and possibly foul play. Apparently, they never got on the cruise ship that everyone thought they were on."

"Oh my God. I know both of them, Matt."

"No kidding? All of you judges seem to know each other. How do you know them?"

"Well, I see them at judges conferences every now and then. But years ago, when I was a very young lawyer, I worked on a Chapter 11 bankruptcy case of an Atlantic City, New Jersey hotel and casino— The Regent Hotel & Casino. I represented the hotel and casino, and we put together a sale of the property during the bankruptcy case to Chinese-American billionaire Karl Lee. Judge Lupinaci was the bankruptcy judge who presided over the Chapter 11 case, and Judge Murphy was the district judge who handled numerous appeals of orders from the bankruptcy judge and other ancillary matters. I must have been in their courts over 100 times back in the late 1990's. This is very troubling. What else do you know about it? Can you send me whatever articles you have seen about this?"

"Sure. But there aren't many news articles just yet. I just happened to hear about it last night when my brother and I were Skyping with an old Princeton buddy of ours in New Jersey, who happens to clerk for a judge—I think the judge's name is Judge Belzer—in the same Camden, New Jersey court house."

"You have a brother? How did I not know that about you, Matt?"

"I haven't mentioned him? I'm surprised. Yes, my brother is named Marcus. He is a portfolio manager for a hedge fund—Toro Capital—which is based in Boston, but he travels all the time. He manages collateralized loan obligations—CLOs—or some Wall Street complicated securitization stuff that I don't understand. He's crazy smart. But I'm smarter. Much smarter. I'm sorry. I shouldn't be making jokes at a time like this."

"Well, if you hear anything further from your friend or on the news, please let me know. I'm going to call Deputy Marshal Mark Eason and see what he knows from talking to others in the Marshals Service. I hope this is just a horrible misunderstanding about their whereabouts and not something tragic. Did your friend say if Judges Murphy or Lupinaci had received any threats or had any crazy high-profile cases going on or anything like that?"

"Nope. I really don't know. I told you everything I learned from my friend."

Avery walked out of her office and down the hall to visit her colleague, Judge David Hall. Judge Hall was always in the office very early, reading the daily advance sheets and case updates. He was also always in tune to all of the judge and lawyer gossip that was out on the streets, so to speak. Avery wanted to know if he had, by chance, heard anything about Judges Lupinaci and Murphy. Judge Hall tended to know everything. Not because he was a gossip himself, but simply because he had so many friends and people felt comfortable confiding in him. Not this time. Judge Hall had heard nothing and was shocked and worried like Avery. Judge Lupinaci had been one of his instructors at "baby judge school" (that is, the basic training that all new federal judges go to through the Federal Judicial Center, once they are appointed). He would make some phone calls today and see what he might learn.

Chapter 22:

The New Jersey Connection.

Judge Lassiter had to go into court on that Friday morning for a 9:30 a.m. docket. It was probably going to last awhile. But Avery asked Annalise to call Deputy Marshal Mark Eason and see if he would come talk to Avery after court about the two New Jersey judges. She also asked Annalise to call her former law partner at Madison, Spencer & Collins, Ward Scott, who was now semi-retired, to see if he was in town or up at his lake house in South Carolina. Avery wanted to try and schedule a lunch with Ward if he was in town. She and Ward Scott had worked on The Regent Hotel & Casino bankruptcy case together (which had lasted over two years), and Ward would be very interested to hear about this strange situation involving Judges Lupinaci and Murphy.

"Tell Ward I'll meet him for lunch anywhere but the Fossil Club," Avery shouted to Annalise before darting into the courtroom. Avery knew that the Fossil Club was one of Ward's go-to lunch spots. Avery had unpleasant memories of the Fossil Club, which was a private club in a downtown Dallas skyscraper that was the domain of the city's oil industry elite—where big deals had been cut and fortunes won and lost since Spindletop and the 1930s East Texas oil boom. Avery's unpleasant memories stemmed from Avery's early days practicing law, when women had not been allowed to join or even eat in the main dining room at the club (there had been a separate room for women to dine). It made it awkward, to say the least, when male clients wanted to meet their lawyers there to discuss business.

Perhaps it was unfair of her to harbor these negative feelings still. Things had changed a lot there in the last two decades. But some wounds heal slowly, and Avery still perceived that the club was full of Scotch-drinking J.R. Ewing wannabes. She still felt awkward, every time she stepped into the dark-paneled, chandelier-filled, red velvet decorated institution. Ward Scott was a smooth and respected lawyer who could always walk into the grand dining room there, full of larger-than-life Texas oil barons, from old wildcatters to modern day frackers, and know every man in the room—having represented all of them at one time or another. But Avery still felt uncomfortable going there.

Judge Avery had a brutal 9:30 a.m. docket involving a large department store chain, Tex-Lots, that had filed bankruptcy. She called today "slip and fall" day. The department store chain was in bankruptcy because of overwhelming bank debt and landlord problems and dropping in-store sales. Another victim of the Internet's and Amazon's slow takeover of the retail world with online sales— Millicent gloomily said. But today, there was a parade of "slip and fall" personal injury lawyers in Avery's courtroom who were especially angry that Tex-Lots did not have enough liability insurance in place to pay the potentially large claims of their clients—people who had slipped and fell while shopping in various Tex-Lots department stores around the state.

The courtroom was full of people in neck braces, knee braces, wheelchairs, crutches, casts, and even one guy with an eye patch (it was as though all of their injuries had just occurred yesterday—even though some of the alleged incidents were quite old). This is a sample of what life is like, for businesses who cater to the public. No matter how careful and cautious retailers and other businesses think they are about maintaining a safe environment, people stumble and fall, and a personal injury lawyer is nearby, it seems, to hand out business cards and convince folks that this was, ironically, their "lucky day"—he could hopefully convince a judge or jury that it was all the fault of the store. On the other hand, in fairness, these lawyers play an important role in the system. Sometimes businesses are careless, even reckless. Someone needs to be vigilantly out there, to keep them honest and rectify the wrongs when they happen.

As Judge Lassiter saw the sea of purportedly injured people, and listened to their lawyers drone on about how she should implement creative measures to insure that nobody in the bankruptcy case got paid a dime before the "slip and fall" victims got their day in court, she thought back to The Regent Hotel & Casino case from the late 1990's. She remembered some similar hearings before Judge Lupinaci involving tort plaintiffs, and she was filled with great sadness about what may have happened to Judge Lupinaci and Judge Murphy.

In The Regent Hotel & Casino case, there had been a very large number of "slip and fall" plaintiffs that were suing the hotel and casino. Casinos such as The Regent are open to the public 24 hours a day, seven days a week, and have a constant stream of people—many of whom are tipsy from drinking and tired from too many hours of gambling or partying. Judge Lassiter remembered dealing with hundreds of those "slip and fall" plaintiffs who were angry during that case. They would stand up and scream at her in court, "How could a casino 'go broke' and file for bankruptcy? How could a casino possibly ever run out of money? They are flush with cash, right? How could there be hundreds of millions of dollars of unpaid bond debt and bank debt and vendor debt? Where did all the money go? They are hiding the money! This is a scam!" As strange as it sounds, casinos frequently file Chapter 11 bankruptcy cases—and it's not usually because of anything illegal and fraudulent that has transpired. These types of properties are very expensive to run. Their capital expenditures are immense. Their security infrastructure and administrative overhead are enormous. The regulatory and legal compliance procedures they must follow are complex and costly. There is stiff competition and a fickle public that easily tires of one casino's slot machines and tables and wanders on to the next property on the boardwalk or strip—in the hopes of getting more free drinks, food, and other "comps." The "slip and fall" plaintiffs in The Regent Hotel & Casino case did not accept any of this as a suitable explanation. Of all of the many tort plaintiffs in The Regent Hotel & Casino case, the one that stood out the most to Avery was a "dram shop" liability case.

Dram shop liability is a legal concept in the United States that pertains to a bar, tavern, or other business establishment at which alcoholic beverages are sold. "Dram shop" laws are named after establishments in 18th century England that sold gin by the spoonful (called a "dram"). The concept refers to the body of law that governs the liability of business establishments that serve alcohol. The laws vary from state to state, but, generally, an establishment may face lawsuits and, ultimately, have to pay damages if they serve alcohol to a customer whom they knew or should have known was intoxicated, or if they serve alcohol to a minor, and that intoxicated person or minor subsequently causes an injury or death to third parties as a result of an alcohol-related car crash or other accident. This liability is usually enforced through civil lawsuits and, if a plaintiff wins a suit against both an intoxicated driver and the business establishment at which he was served, damages are apportioned between the two defendants. While the earliest dram shop laws date back to the 18th century, modern day lobbying groups such as "Mothers Against Drunk

Drivers" have successfully pushed for enactment and enforcement of stricter dram shop laws.

In The Regent Hotel & Casino case, there had been a dram shop claim made against the casino pertaining to a teenaged female that had allegedly been served alcohol at the casino one balmy Sunday night a few months before the casino filed its Chapter 11 bankruptcy case. The 16-year-old female left the casino drunk, in a beat-up car, late that night and, approximately 45 minutes later, swerved into oncoming traffic, crashing head-on into a car being driven by a father of three children who had just gotten off work from his job as a custodian at a large pharmaceutical company's headquarters. Both the 16-year-old girl and the father she struck were killed. The surviving spouse of the man, on behalf of herself and his three children, was seeking millions of dollars of damages from The Regent Hotel & Casino, due to the accident. The case was not at all clear-cut. Proving fault of an alcohol vendor can be a difficult task. It is easier in the case of a minor (whom should never have been served alcohol at all) than in the case of an adult who may be served until intoxicated, but whose intoxication might be hard to gauge. But in this case involving the 16-year-old, there was no evidence that the 16-year-old had actually been sold or served alcohol by employees at The Regent. There were videos that showed the teenager at one time wandering around the labyrinth and mazes of the casino floor and picking up patrons' drink glasses— sneaking off with them and drinking from them. But there were also videos of casino floor personnel chasing her out of the gambling areas. There were also videos of her coming and going up the hotel elevators during the course of the evening and even mingling out by the swimming pool. The teenager appeared to not only be sneaking people's drinks, but perhaps pickpocketing and engaging in other types of petty, criminal activities. Perhaps she was part of an under-aged prostitution ring or a grifter of some sort. She had a fake ID on her at the time of the crash and was later discovered to be a runaway from Pittsburgh, with a father in prison and a mother who was in-and-out of drug rehab facilities. As difficult as it was, Avery's client, The Regent Hotel & Casino, and its insurer, had insisted that Avery fight liability in this dram shop liability case. And fight, Avery did. Avery knew how to fight in the courtroom. The Regent felt strongly that they had acted appropriately and that the 16-year-old female was essentially a juvenile criminal whom they had never actually served and, in fact, they had tried everything within their power to run her off of the property. The girl managed to craftily sneak past personnel a few times, but the casino employees were not at all negligent. And for all anyone knew, the teenaged girl may have been served alcohol somewhere else on the way home or had a fifth of whiskey in her car that she may have hurled out the window.

Avery was ultimately successful in obtaining a take-nothing verdict for her client in the dram shop liability case. Her client felt absolutely vindicated. Avery had been brilliant in defending the casino. Karl Lee, the new billionaire owner of the hotel and casino, was ecstatic that Avery had saved him potentially millions of dollars in connection with his new investment and gave Avery an all-expense paid trip to the Canyon Ranch Spa in Tucson, Arizona after it was all over, so Avery could "decompress in luxury." But, deep down, Avery felt a little sick about it all. She still remembered the plaintiff-mother with her three young boys standing in the courtroom after it was all over, just pitifully staring at her. Avery learned later that the mother committed suicide a short time after the trial, by swallowing a bottle of pills with Vodka, and Avery wondered whatever happened to the children.

Judge Lassiter was suddenly jolted from these old memories by the reality of the current moment in her own courtroom. One of the slip and fall plaintiffs in the Tex-Lots case had come forward and asked if he could take the witness stand and tell Judge Lassiter his story. This was "out of order," but Avery decided to let the fellow have his day in court and be heard. Every judge knows that sometimes people just need to have their chance to speak what is on their hearts and minds. The slip and fall plaintiff was named Mr. Ko. Mr. Ko looked perfectly fine, but he testified that, while in a Tex-Lots store in Wichita Falls, Texas, while carefully browsing through housewares one afternoon, he had tripped on a pallet of unpacked inventory of some sort and then stumbled onto some carelessly displayed lava lamps. Yes, lava lamps. Mr. Ko described the cluttered aisles of the Tex-Lots store, with all its allegedly negligently-created traps and hazards at every turn, but the most terrible hazard of all was the dozens of garish, jutting lava lamps into which he had stumbled. Any reasonably prudent person should know that lava lamps can present a great danger to the shopping public. When Mr. Ko stumbled into them, one particularly pointy coned-shaped lava lamp had plunged right into his left rib cage. He said his torso was basically impaled and severely injured. Then several months later, he was diagnosed with stomach cancer. And it had now spread to numerous internal organs. This was allegedly somehow all the fault of Tex-Lots and their negligent failure to maintain clean aisles and, of course, due to their careless displaying of lava lamps. Mr. Ko next started pulling out his shirt and unzipping his pants and said he wanted to show Judge Lassiter his hose. As Avery stood up and screamed "please, stop!" two Deputy U.S. Marshals charged into the courtroom, expecting the worst. But Mr. Ko had, in fact, only pulled up his shirt and pulled down his pants to show Judge Lassiter the plastic hose that was taped onto his abdomen and was apparently feeding chemotherapy into his system. Avery banged her gavel and stated that court was in recess.

When Avery went back into chambers, Annalise helped Avery take her robe off and handed her a bottled water. Annalise was so kind. Avery asked Annalise if she was listening in on the court proceedings from the chamber's speakers, and Annalise nodded affirmatively. "Do you think I got anything wrong this morning?" Annalise grinned. "You are sometimes wrong, Judge, but you are rarely clearly erroneous." Avery grinned back. "Yes, I suppose that's all that matters—at least to the appellate courts." Annalise brushed some lint off of Avery's robe and said almost in a whisper, "Why don't you take a 10-minute breather, then go back out to court and quickly wrap things up. By the way, I've tried reaching your old partner, Ward Scott, and I haven't gotten an answer. His secretary at Madison, Spencer & Collins says she thinks he is going to be working at his lake house in South Carolina this entire week.   And Deputy Marshal Eason said he is not at liberty to talk about Judge Lupinaci's and Judge Murphy's situations."

Avery sighed. "Of course, he's not at liberty to speak to me. See no evil, hear no evil, speak no evil. I am apparently on a need to know basis. I either get willfully obtuse answers or no answers at all."

Avery sat down in her chambers and put her head down on her large wooden partner desk. It was one of her favorite treasures in her office. It was a regal, beautifully carved hunk of blond oak that reminded her of the Resolute desk in the Oval Office—although it was currently covered in a sea of pens, post-it notes, paper clips, and legal treatises. The special antique desk had been handed down and used by many judges in the past before her. Avery wondered if any of those former judges had ever experienced what she was experiencing right now. She wished she could close her eyes and somehow channel their collective wisdom.

Chapter 23:

The Portugal Incident.

The year had swung surreally into June now. Seven months had passed since Judge Lassiter received her first death threats. If there was ever a time when Avery felt like she needed a relaxing vacation to decompress, it was now. Avery announced, much to the Deputy Marshals' consternation, that she was departing on an early summer vacation with her family to Portugal—one of her favorite places on the planet. If someone still wanted to kill Avery, they surely would not follow her all the way to the Iberian Peninsula—one of the remotest places on the European continent. And if they did kill her in Portugal, well fine—Avery would at least die at her favorite earthly spot (hopefully while baking in the sun). After much angst and argument, the U.S. Marshals Service acquiesced to Avery's plan—but announced that one of their personnel, Deputy Marshal Ginny Oliphante, would accompany the Lassiters to Portugal as a precaution. Ginny from the Block. Sending just one Deputy Marshal with Avery was a rather unusual move. Avery could live with that compromise. Ginny Oliphante, Avery's violet-colored Deputy, was so delightful. And Avery knew that Ginny was well traveled and would probably actually enjoy the trip—even if Ginny was technically on duty. Avery and the family enjoyed their respite from all of the craziness back home—until a terrifying, bizarre incident near the end of their journey.

The Lassiters and Ginny from the Block set off first to enjoy beautiful days of sightseeing in hilly Lisbon, Portugal, with its trolley cars, fog, and Old World feel. Avery talked nonstop with Ginny as she was packing up to leave. So did Julia.

"So why do you people like Portugal so much?" Ginny asked. "I've been reading about it. It sounds sunny and beautiful and rich in history and all that, but it doesn't seem to be one of the more popular tourist destinations in Europe for Americans."

"Well, it's probably less popular because of its location and somewhat difficult accessibility. But trust me, it's fabulous." Avery went on to explain that Portugal is a rectangular sliver of land, about 125 miles horizontally wide and 325 miles vertically long, approximately the size and shape of the U.S. state of Indiana, on the far western portion of Europe's Iberian Peninsula. Lisbon (also known as Lisboa), where they would spend the first half of their trip, is approximately in the middle of the country (that is, it is roughly midway between north and south), and is almost on the west coast. They would spend most of the other half of their trip on the Algarve Coast—the southern coast of Portugal, just a little west of the country of Spain's more touristy Costa del Sol. Avery says Lisbon reminds her of a cross between Madrid and San Francisco--with a little splash of Rome thrown in the mix. Lisbon is a port city and the river running through it is referred to as the Rio Tejo (Tagus River). The city has a huge suspension bridge that was built by the same company that built the San Francisco Golden Gate bridge and it looks very similar. It was originally called the Salazar Bridge (after a former dictator) but was renamed the "25th of April Bridge," as a reference to a Portuguese revolution in 1974. Lisbon also has a longer Calatrava-designed bridge that is 10.7 miles in length (the longest in Europe) and is called the Vasco da Gama Bridge, after the famous voyager.

Avery rattled on like a tour guide talking about her favorite subject, as Ginny from the Block pretended to be interested, all the while walking around the house, making sure windows were locked and cameras and other security equipment were fully charged and operational. "You know, both the Romans and the Moors originally populated Lisbon, so it has this cool Mediterranean feel. It was at one time one of Europe's richest cities, as a result of the Age of Discovery, until an earthquake in 1755—which leveled two-thirds of the city. Anyway, Lisbon has this more humble, traditional, working class feel than, say, Paris or London. It has this labyrinth of narrow cobblestone streets with two high areas—the Alfama and the Bairro Alto—and a lower area known as the Baixa. We will go see the Sao Jorge Castle, at the top of the Alfama area, which was originally an 11th century Moorish castle until the founder of Portugal, Afonso Henriques, conquered and eliminated the Moors from the country. Also, there is a 330-foot statue of Christ with outstretched arms, on a hill overlooking Lisbon, similar to the famous one in Rio de Janeiro, Brazil. We'll have to take a selfie there—can you imagine? You're Catholic, Ginny, so you have to do it! Oh, and, in the nearby Belem district, where sailors sometimes left for voyages, there is the spectacular 'Monastery of Jeronimos,' with attached church, where sailors might stay and pray before voyages. At Belem, there is a tall 'Belem Tower' that welcomed sailors home. And you and I should go to the Bairro Alto area of Lisbon one night. There is a fun, bustling night life there, and the famous 'Fado music' clubs and restaurants. 'Fado' is a form of music unique to Portugal that features sad and soulful vocalists backed up with three acoustic guitarists. Traditionally, women sang about their men lost or of unknown whereabouts on sea voyages. Ginny? Ginny! Are you even listening to me?"

Avery had shared these stories a million times, it seemed. Now, she was passionately sharing them with her Ginny—violet-tinged Ginny, as Avery referred to her. However, violet-tinged Ginny was not fully engaged and listening to Avery's spirited discussion. She seemed more concerned about whether the Lassiters' house would be safe and secure while everyone was gone. And, besides, violet-tinged Ginny had fully researched everything that there possibly was to know about Portugal in preparation for their trip. That's the kind of thing that the U.S. Marshals do. They are, after all, professionals.

Avery and Ginny from the Block and the family spent many fun days frolicking around Lisbon. They also ventured to the picturesque town of Sintra—via a short train ride from Lisbon. Sintra emanates a beautiful medieval-feel, with a national palace with white cone chimneys that can be seen for miles, and an abundance of shops selling one of Portugal's special art forms—colorful painted clay tiles (originally an art form brought from Spain and then copied by the Portuguese). Avery brought home several porcelain colorful roosters from Sintra and gave them out to friends and family as gifts. The rooster (the so-called "Galo de Barcelos")—supposedly symbolizes honesty, integrity, trust, and honor—and is based on a legend where a dead rooster arose from a banquet table to crow and prove an accused man's innocence, just as he was being hanged at the gallows. It is an unofficial symbol of Portugal. Avery liked that story and the symbolism and its significance to the law. Also, very high up on the hill in Sintra, there are remnants of a Moorish castle that was literally built into the stone of the mountain more than a thousand years ago. Sintra also has the famous "Palacio de Pena," which has been referred to as the Versailles of Portugal.

After their busy days in Lisbon and Sintra, the Lassiter family journeyed to the Algarve Coast. They rented a couple of Alfa Romeo

Giulietta sports cars in Lisbon to drive there. There is a somewhat fast, easy tollway that is often foggy and not well lit at night, but it is a convenient path from Lisbon to the Algarve.

The Lassiters relaxed several days at a secluded resort near the town of Albufiera (which is approximately at the half-way point along the roughly 100-mile sandy stretch of the Algarve Coast). The resort at which the Lassiters enjoyed staying is lush and green and tranquil—surrounded by umbrella pines with wide, flat canopies like the ones found primarily in Africa and in some of the warmer areas around the Mediterranean. In addition to umbrella pines, there are cypress trees, palm trees, orange trees, sage, and even some cacti. The resort has cobblestone paths and pretty, white stucco villas with red-tile roofs, fountains, and—last but not least—an extended family of friendly orange and white cats that are always sweetly meowing for guests' attention. There is also a beautiful shaded, boarded walking path to the pristine, uncrowded beach. The crowd at the Algarve Coast on that June vacation seemed entirely European except for the Lassiters and Ginny. Ginny was grateful for that. It made it easier to spot an American who might want to kill Avery or her family. The Algarve Coast of Portugal is overall very uncommercial, slow paced, and pleasant.

After an idyllic retreat, a bizarre incident occurred at the end of the trip. One night, Avery adventurously suggested that she and Ginny from the Block spend the next day driving one of the speedy Alfa Romeo rental cars to the town of Sagres, at the southwestern tip of Portugal, which is the western-most spot in all of mainland Europe. Before Christopher Columbus discovered the "New World," Europeans thought that Sagres was the end of the world. It has that feel. Officer Max and the kids had seen it all before, and they preferred to stay behind at the resort and lounge at the pool. So, the next day, Ginny and Avery drove west to visit the remnants of "Fort Sagres" by themselves, to see where the Portuguese defended their kingdom, hundreds of years ago, against the occasionally invading Moors from Northern Africa, and where there was a famous maritime school (founded in 1420 by "Prince Henry the Navigator," the quiet, scholarly, religious middle child of King John I of Portugal). This maritime school served as "mission control" for sailors who went on daring voyages in the so-called "Age of Discovery."

Avery twisted Ginny's arm into letting Avery drive the Alfa Romeo Giulietta down to Sagres that day. One of the hardest parts of the U.S. Marshal protection for Avery was not being able to drive herself anywhere anymore. The Deputy Marshals chauffeured her everywhere. Avery had not driven at this point in approximately seven months. She was getting a little fearful that she may have forgotten how to drive. Avery loved her fast, little Audi ragtop convertible sedan back home. She loved fast cars generally—the faster the better. One of Avery's favorite weekend past times was to go driving out in the country on sunny days with Baxter, out by the Texas Motor Speedway, with the Audi top down, with wind streaming through Baxter's chestnut wavy ears and Avery's tousled blond hair. Freedom! In fact, Officer Max would get quite upset if he knew how fast she sometimes went. Anyway, Avery was anxious to get behind the wheel of the little Alfa Romeo. Ginny from the Block was not easily convinced, but she figured that if Avery drove, Ginny could keep a sharp lookout for any trouble. Avery floored the little Alfa Romeo down the winding Algarve coast highway that day. She imagined herself on *Grand Tour*.

Once at their destination, Avery and Ginny parked the spunky Alfa Romeo at a spot about 100 yards from where a walking path begins, that leads to Fort Sagres. They walked together for about two hours and Avery talked and talked—she was more relaxed than she had been in months. Avery loved showing Ginny this place and sharing the history. There is not much left of the navigators' school (due to a 9.0 earthquake and tsunami that hit Portugal in the year 1755), but there is still a quite interesting 100-feet wide circle on the ground that is believed to have been a navigational compass or sun dial. Avery explained that, originally, the voyager expeditions from Sagres were focused around exploring the Muslim world and Africa. But Prince Henry the Navigator had pressed the often-scared sailors to go farther and farther. Almost every famous discoverer about whom school children learn had trained at Sagres: Columbus; Vasco da Gama (who found the sea route to India); Bartolomeu Dias (who was the first to go around Africa); Pedro Cabral (who discovered Brazil, after allegedly making a wrong turn right); and Ferdinand Magellan (who first circumvented the earth). It was often from Sagres that these and other discoverers set sail, establishing and controlling trade routes, and colonizing places along the African coast, places in India and China, and Brazil. Portugal accumulated huge wealth in those days of colonization, by bringing home treasures from the East, but Portugal is not so wealthy anymore. Perhaps the modern-day government has regrets about the loss of wealth resulting from their predecessors' inaction—not having granted Columbus's request for resources to sail into the unknown West (thus, Spain funded Columbus's expedition instead). Additionally, as earlier mentioned, the 1755 earthquake and tsunami caused enormous damage to the country.

Avery loved Sagres. To her, it was a place of charm and adventure. She felt like it was one of her own secret hideaways, with the added bonus of having rich historical significance. And she was so happy that day with Ginny—that she had managed to go there and escape some of the unpleasantness of the last few months. She was lost in thought as she and Ginny walked back from the top of Sagres toward their parked Alfa Romeo. The beaches and surf in Sagres are spectacular with huge cliffs, craggy rocky formations and caves, and enormous crashing waves. It's so gusty that tourists must be careful not to get too close to the edge of the cliffs. Ginny kept looking around, behind, beside and in front, as they walked back to the car, as if someone might jump out and push Avery off of one of the cliffs. Avery laughed about this. But as they walked closer to the Alfa Romeo, their laughter abruptly stopped. As they sauntered toward the end of the walking path, toward a large sign explaining the stone mariner's compass and how the enigmatic structures there at Sagres were unearthed, suddenly they both saw a message spray painted in red on the sign, spelling out in English:

"JUDGE L: HE WATCHES ALL YOUR PATHS."

And beneath the sign on the ground was a mannequin, like the kind that one would see in a department store window, with a blond wig and dressed in a black judicial robe, lying contorted in the sand, with some sort of crimson substance smeared on and around it, as though it was covered in blood. Avery looked at Ginny and gasped. Ginny turned pale as a ghost and said, "Shit just turned real. Get behind me, Judge."

Ginny did not have a gun because she was not permitted to carry a firearm into Portugal—regardless of her position and Avery's situation. There is not that type of reciprocity between Portugal and the United States. Every country is different in that regard. Avery wasn't sure what Ginny had in mind, but she cautiously followed her instructions and slipped behind her. As the two of them crept closer up the path toward the Alfa Romeo, suddenly a figure could be seen, leaning against the back of the Alfa Romeo, smoking a cigarette. He was a thin, white male with brown dreadlocks, wearing aviator sunglasses, jeans and a hoody sweat shirt, and with a backpack. Probably in his mid-twenties. Avery completely froze. Her heart was racing. They were approximately 20 yards away from the car by this point. Ginny immediately grabbed and pushed Avery toward the only thing close to a "safe spot" that was visible, the tiny Fort Sagres Museum (which was a small stone building, only about 800 square feet in size), where they entered and Ginny immediately began throwing shelves and racks as barricades against the door and looking for anything possible to use as a weapon—grabbing a fire extinguisher to presumably bash into the head of the culprit if necessary. While continuing to search for makeshift weapons, Ginny simultaneously began making phone calls to her supervisor, the U.S. Embassy, and others to report what was happening. Despite Ginny's shouting at her to stay away from the windows, Avery kept creeping toward them, to get a better look at the man by the Alfa Romeo. After a few moments, the man jumped into a red Renault Clio parked nearby, and sped away. The man was fairly ordinary in appearance (other than having dreadlocks), and mostly covered up, except for his forearms and hands, so it was going to be impossible to give a good description of the man. But Avery at one point had whipped out her smart phone and started clicking pictures frantically. Avery's hands trembled and shook—in a crisis one's fine motor skills are the first to fade—but she managed to take a pretty decent photograph of the Renault's car license plate.

As the man drove away, Avery turned to Ginny and asked, "What just happened? Did that really just happen? I can hardly process this!"

Ginny simply told Avery to stay in place; a car was being sent to take them to the Lisbon airport and a second car would be sent to the resort in Albufiera to pick up the rest of the Lassiters and take them to the airport.

"Why can't we at least drive ourselves back to the resort, Ginny, and let me pack up my things myself and ride to the airport with my family? I just want to be with my family right now! What if the guy in the Renault is going to them next?"

"Judge Lassiter, I am sorry, but you have got to calm down and trust me. We don't know what the guy may have done to our car. He may have placed a bomb in it. We have to just stay put and wait on the car that is being sent for us. The Portuguese authorities are going to take care of us. They will have guns and a full protective detail to escort us to the Lisbon airport."

"Good God! This cannot be happening!"

Part IV:

"Shit Just Turned Real."

Chapter 24:

Back to Reality—at Least the "New Normal."

The plane flight back home from Lisbon to Texas was stressful, to say the least. And not just because Avery was squeezed into a middle seat in coach, accompanied by Ginny from the Block, Officer Max, and two sullen teenagers who were annoyed about having their vacation cut short (first world problems). What were the odds that the person who was threatening Avery could fly almost 4,800 miles to Portugal and track her down to Fort Sagres—practically the remotest spot in Western Europe? How did the person even know where Avery had gone? Hardly anyone in Avery's life knew where she was. Only a very few family members, friends, her staff, a travel agent, and a few people with the FBI and Marshals Service knew of her travel itinerary. Was someone hacking computers or phones? Was Avery's house or office bugged? She didn't know what to think anymore.

Avery had managed to take several fairly decent pictures on her smart phone before and after the red Renault had sped away at Sagres. If there could be any doubt, Ginny said that the Marshals Service and FBI did not think there was any chance whatsoever that what had happened in Portugal was random and coincidental. Apparently, the FBI was "all over this," according to Ginny. It would not be that hard to track down the driver of the red Renault—although it was likely going to be a rental car. The FBI would also get the flight manifests of flights going into and out of Lisbon over the last several days and would cross reference passengers against people who had cases in Avery's court. But, once again, Avery would have to wait. Wait like a sitting duck.

Avery had seriously been considering putting an end to the judicial protection after the Portugal trip. It had been seven months now since the first death threat letter was sent to her house and chambers. The letter writer had never done anything except send bizarre (albeit threatening) communications. She had been convinced at this point that the anonymous letter writer (and voicemail sender) was a "howler" and not a "hunter." Sure, he may have been a troubled and warped "howler." But just a "howler." It was time to stop the nonsense and let the "howler" win. Fine. He had scared her. He had gotten everyone's attention. But life goes on. Everything had changed now with this Portugal incident. Now, Avery had to reconsider everything. If this idiot had actually gone all the way to Sagres, Portugal and stalked her on vacation, then he could not be dismissed as merely a crackpot "howler." He was now—at a minimum— orchestrating elaborate scare-tactics and no telling where he might want to take this all.

When the flight touched down, Avery called the office. Annalise reported that there were no court emergencies. Things were calm with her cases. Avery told Annalise that she would be back in the office mid-day tomorrow. Annalise seemed startled by the early return but did not ask any questions regarding why she had cut her trip slightly short. Avery asked if she could speak with Millicent but forgot that Millicent had gone out of town to take some continuing legal education training this week. Avery then asked for her intern Matt instead, and Annalise transferred the phone to Matt. Avery first asked Matt about some of the research projects she had assigned to him before she left town. Then she asked whether he knew anything new about Judges Murphy and Lupinaci. He did not. He said he had not heard from his friend in a few days and there had been nothing further in the news. Avery said she'd see him tomorrow.

"Tomorrow? Why are you back early, Judge?" Matt asked.

"I just decided to cut things short. You know how I am. Never can stay away too long."

"OK. See you tomorrow."

After ending her phone call, Avery asked Ginny if she knew anything about Judges Murphy and Lupinaci. Ginny smiled uneasily. "You know that if I did, I couldn't tell you."

Avery signed. "OK. I understand. I just am so concerned. I really admire both of those judges so much. I haven't seen or talked to them in years. But they are delightful human beings. It's just so strange that the two of them would both disappear when apparently together. I mean, it sounds like foul play for sure. As much as I hate my own situation, I think of the possibility that something has happened to them both, and I realize that their situation might be so much worse than mine. I mean, something has obviously happened to them, right?"

Ginny from the Block smiled an uncomfortable, awkward smile. "Judge Lassiter, you know I cannot divulge anything about an ongoing investigation. Really, I could get fired. Only people higher up in the food chain than me are allowed to communicate threat investigation updates."

"Don't call me Judge Lassiter, Ginny. For God's sake, you just spent two weeks with me and my family on vacation in Portugal. Call me Avery!"

"I can't do that Judge Lassiter."

"Fine."

"By the way, how does my hair look, Ginny from the Block, after walking in the gusty winds of Sagres several hours, then flying on a plane for another nine hours?"

"I am sorry, Judge, but it looks like Rod Stewart. Circa 1980."

"Thanks, violet Marshal girl. You are not looking so fresh yourself."

"What do you mean, Judge? Is my lovely violet shade fading or something?"

Ginny's smart phone suddenly rang, and it was clear that she was talking to someone from the Marshals Service. After a few abrupt "okays" she hung up and said, "Follow me. We have an escort that is going to take you and your family to a car, and I will get the family's luggage."

"What is it, Ginny? What was that phone call about?"

"Judge Lassiter, shit just turned real—I mean *real* now. There was no bomb or anything like that with our Alfa Romeo rental car. But there was a note left on the car windshield. The note was written on stationery from the same resort we were staying at in Albufiera. The note read:

> *'Honorless Lassiter: The time is*
> *drawing nigh. The first part of the*

trilogy in five parts is about to begin.
Very soon. You'll know it when you see
it.'

"There is a forensics team that came in and thoroughly dusted the Alfa Romeo for prints and combed the surrounding ground and also the spray-painted sign and the mannequin. And, of course, they are tracking down the red Renault. Among other things, the guy standing by the car was careless enough to throw down his cigarette butt, so we can probably collect DNA from that. And they are working on analyzing the pictures you took on your smart phone for any clues. Anyway, I want you to remain calm. Maybe this is going to be a big break in the case."

"Okay. Okay. I'm numb, Ginny, but I am okay." Avery's eyes welled up with tears. "Let's not tell the kids about the Sagres stalker. I don't want them to hear about this. I'm going to just tell them I had a work emergency and had to get back to court and hold some hearings. They'll believe that. It's the story of my life. I just don't want them to know about the stalker. Please."

Ginny from the Block gave Avery a long hug. Ginny's instincts told her something bad was going to happen soon. She just didn't know what.

Chapter 25:

The First of the Trilogy in Five Parts.

The next morning Avery slept in a bit, woke up and did laundry, and walked Baxter around the neighborhood a few times (with Marshals in tow, of course). Everyone was completely silent on the walk. It felt like an apocalyptic silence to Avery. Avery had always been a true believer in Thoreau's statement that an "early morning walk is a blessing for the whole day." But there was nothing relaxing about this morning's walk.

After the walk, Avery decided to swim a few laps in the pool, and then went into work midmorning. She, of course, didn't have any court hearings on her first day back from Portugal, since she was not even supposed to be home yet, but she felt she needed to get into the office and focus her mind on work and not the howler or hunter or whatever he was. Avery's stomach was in knots and she was still feeling a little jet lagged. Truthfully, Avery enjoyed being at the courthouse these days almost more than at home, because she felt both safe and somewhat private while at the courthouse. When she was at the courthouse, the Deputy Marshals on her protective detail simply walked her to her chambers and left her alone the rest of the day, since there was plenty of "normal" security in the courthouse while she was there. In other words, work felt normal. It was everywhere *else* that Deputy Marshals were near her side. She appreciated and respected their zealous vigilance. She just sometimes felt awkward and longed for solitude.

Montana Tom was back as the Deputy-in-Charge of Avery's protective detail when she returned from Portugal, so he would be driving her into work. That was nice. He was a calming influence. She needed a calming influence today. Avery said Montana Tom had a nice, green color emanation like Deputy Eason. Maybe he would tell Avery a story about fishing and being chased by a grizzly bear in 23 degrees below zero weather outside of Butte, Montana. He was always good for an amazing nature story. He was the former Secret Service Agent that sometimes worked her protective detail. If he didn't have a great nature story, he might have a story about one of his former gigs protecting Dick Cheney or Hillary Clinton.

As soon as Avery jumped into Montana Tom's black Suburban G-ride and they began the journey into downtown Dallas, Avery started in with her usual third-degree inquisition of the Deputy-in-Charge *de jure*. Did Montana Tom know about the events that had happened in Portugal? What did he know? The answer was that he already knew everything. Apparently, the Deputy Marshals all received a daily briefing about Avery's situation. Avery wished that she, too, received a daily briefing. Anyway, Montana Tom shared her amazement and confusion about what had happened. The odds of her death-threat culprit knowing about her trip to Portugal and tracking her down to a walking path at Sagres, seemed absolutely inconceivable. Even more disturbingly, it was now clear that the culprit was not just any old "howler." At the very least, he was also a stalker. An international stalker at that.

Montana Tom quizzed Avery: "Who all knew about your trip?" He thought someone must have had loose lips. The answer was that the only people who knew of Avery's plans were her closest family and a couple of friends, a few colleagues, her staff, a travel agent, the Marshals and the FBI. Montana Tom shook his head in frustration.

"Good God! Too many people, Judge! Someone could have said something casually on the elevator or in the courthouse hallway—no telling who might have overhead the details of your trip and repeated it. What about your court calendar? Was your court calendar posted online? Did it show you were out on vacation?"

"Yes, but, of course it did not show where I was going!" Avery sighed.

"Were you wearing a Fitbit or your Apple watch over there? I don't trust those things. I can't believe someone hasn't told you to stop wearing those by now."

Avery grabbed her wrist, as if to hide the Fitbit that Montana Tom obviously had observed she was wearing. She felt ashamed, as if the Marshals were disappointed in her or held her accountable somehow. She thought that she had been extremely cautious about sharing the details of her trip and regarding all of her habits, for that matter. Heath and Julia had learned to be extremely careful over the months. She had interrogated the kids and they swore that they did not tell any of their friends where the family was going on vacation. They were no longer allowed to use Facebook or any forms of social media. And, of course, everything in life was "top secret" with Officer Max.

As Montana Tom and Avery made their way into downtown and approached the area near the courthouse, they were both quiet. Avery kept thinking about the Portugal incident and whether she had been careless in sharing the details with too many people about her trip. She was ashamed because she thought Montana Tom thought she was careless, and she had disappointed him.

Avery and Montana Tom were stopped at a red light by the McDonald's fast food restaurant across from the courthouse, and

Avery was considering whether she wanted to ask Montana Tom to go through the drive-through at the McDonald's, so she could get a cup of coffee to get her through her lingering jet lag. She figured that her supply of Keurig coffee cups at work might be low—since she had been gone for a while. In the McDonald's parking lot, there was the usual group of homeless people gathered around. Avery eventually talked herself out of asking Montana Tom to pull in, thinking that he would not want to deal with the riff-raff of all the people standing around in the parking lot. As Avery and Montana Tom gazed around waiting for the red light to change, they both suddenly saw an unbelievable sight at the exact same time. A black, shiny, old-timey car, which they both recognized as an old Ford Prefect, was parked in the McDonald's parking lot. Its license plate: "HGG 42." As they looked at each other in shock—both processing what they were seeing—Montana Tom yelled, "Get down, Judge, now! Get down in the floor board right now!" He abruptly pushed Avery into the floor of his Suburban, grabbing the nearest thing he could find for a shield, Avery's briefcase, and putting it over her head.

What happened next was mostly a blur to Avery. Montana Tom slammed the Suburban in reverse, and accelerated at top speed, swerving his vehicle sharply toward the left, then jerking the car back into drive (making what, in law enforcement circles, is known as a J-turn). He turned on the red lights and siren in the vehicle, picked up his radio and shouted some sort of law enforcement codes into the mouth piece. He then began to speed away the wrong way down a one-way street—all the while motioning and yelling for people to back up or turn around and go the other way. As this was all happening, suddenly the black Ford Prefect exploded into a massive ball of fire and a dark plume of smoke erupted out of it, enveloping the McDonald's parking lot and surrounding areas. Avery felt and heard the deafeningly loud concussion from the blast and her ears were ringing. She could hear ghastly screaming and yelling and car alarms blaring. The next thing Avery remembered was being yanked out of the black Suburban and flung over Montana Tom's shoulders and carried away somewhere. She could smell and taste smoke, choking and blistering her throat. Avery deliriously whispered to Montana Tom, "What's happening? I can barely see or hear anything. Are we dying? I don't feel like dying today, Montana Tom. Tell me that today is not a good day to die. Isn't that what you always say?"

"You are not going to die on my watch, Judge. Stay with me. We are both okay."

Everything went black as midnight for Avery.

A few hours later, Avery awoke in a hotel room. It was nice—in fact it was luxurious. It looked like it might be The Mansion hotel in Dallas, but she could not see out of the windows. The drapes were drawn. Across the room, Officer Max sat in a chair, sending text messages furiously. He looked up and saw Avery staring at him. He put his phone down and walked toward Avery with a sanguine expression.

"Hey, Avery. You're awake? Can I get you something?"

"Where am I?"

"The Marshals took you to a safe house."

"A safe house? It looks like The Mansion hotel to me."

"Well, Avery, you certainly do know your 5-star hotels, don't you?"

"Hey, I worked at Big Law for 17 years. Damn right, I do. But who is paying for this and why am I here?"

"I don't know whose paying for it. We will probably get a huge bill at some point. And if we don't, I'm sure we will have to pay taxes on it or something. You want to order room service? May as well go big or go home."

"Seriously, what is going on? Why am I here, Max? And, by the way, why are you here and all greened up like you are about to go kick in the door of a drug house? You look like you are about to go into Rainbow 6 mode."

Officer Max was wearing camo clothes and had on his green bullet proof vest, duty belt, and a black knit cap. The only thing that was missing was black face grease and background music from *Apocalypse Now*.

"It's a long story. We both had an eventful day, Avery. Let's just leave it at that. My day is not important."

"No. Tell me. What was eventful about your day, other than this, I suppose?"

"Oh, another person died in Sam the Terrorist's custody. We pulled over a car on a traffic stop. It was a stolen car, but it looked like a woman was inside who didn't really fit the profile of a car thief. So we weren't geared up or expecting anything really. Just were wanting to find out how she happened to be driving a stolen car. Then as Sam started approaching the stolen car, and I was back in my car, the woman pulled out a can of lighter fluid, doused herself, flicked on a cigarette lighter, and caught herself on fire. She died right there in front of us before we knew what happened."

"Are you shitting me, Officer Max? How many people can self-immolate in one cop's career? Was she dressed like a fake Dick Cheney?"

"Nope."

"So why are you all greened up like that?"

"Don't ask. It's a long story. Things got more complicated after the woman doused herself in the lighter fluid and went up in flames. It was a Charlie Foxtrot situation like you would not believe. I'll explain tomorrow. I feel pretty terrible, actually. I didn't even get to check my personal phone and get the message about what was going on with you in downtown until a couple of hours after it all happened."

"It's okay." Avery paused for a long moment. "Well, I guess I have been asleep awhile. But kind of a weird coincidence, don't you think, that you were essentially dealing with an unusual car fire situation around the same time as the McDonald's episode?"

"Don't make a conspiracy out of it. Just another day in my life, as far as job stuff. My exploits today hardly compare to what you have been through. Avery, how much do you remember about McDonald's today?"

Avery looked at Max with a melancholic empty gaze. "I remember everything that happened. At least I think I do. Maybe not. There was a Ford Prefect at the McDonald's by the courthouse. I believe Montana Tom and I both realized what kind of car it was at the very same time. Then there was an explosion. Fire and smoke. Chaos. Blood. Lots of blood. Max, I know this sounds weird, but all I could see was people bleeding and screaming. It was like a war zone. And then it goes blank for me. I don't know if I passed out or just went into shock or what. Oh my God! Where's Montana Tom? I am pretty sure that man saved my life today. I have to talk to him."

"He's outside the room. I think he has a lot of paper work that he's required to do. Actually, the poor guy will probably be buried in a blizzard of paper work for the rest of his life, after what happened."

"How many people were hurt today? Where are the kids?" Suddenly the reality of what happened began settling over Avery.

"The kids are both with friends. Julia is staying at Dara's house. Heath went to stay at Ben's house. They are fine. Baba Jo and the pets are minding the home front. Please, just relax, Avery. Montana Tom or I will give you the full report about casualties at the McDonald's maybe tomorrow. Just try to relax for now. Here's the menu for room service if you are ready. And I'm sure you will want to see the over-priced wine list."

"Casualties? Oh my God!" Avery jumped off the bed and ran to the hotel room door and opened it. There were two Deputy Marshals standing there including Montana Tom. They both looked surprised and immediately grabbed and ushered Avery back inside the room.

"Montana Tom, please get in here. Please!!!"

Montana Tom sighed. He walked in the room. It was no use trying to argue with her.

"First, you saved my life today. I know you did. Don't deny it. Thank you." Avery gave Montana Tom a long, fervent embrace. He turned red and looked embarrassed.

"Montana Tom, I don't remember too much, but I do remember that you were driving like I would imagine they teach

Secret Service Agents to drive. I don't know how you processed everything so quickly and figured out that the Ford Prefect was going to explode. But I am grateful you did. How did you know?"

"Just instinct, Judge. That's a very unusual, unmistakable car. I think, from the look on your face as it was all happening, you pretty quickly realized what kind of car that was and put two and two together yourself, that something wasn't right. I didn't know for sure what was going to happen. Didn't know if a guy was going to pop out with a rifle or hand grenade or what, but I knew something was going to happen. I wouldn't be very good at my job if I wasn't smart enough to figure that one out."

"OK, second. Is The Mansion hotel the Marshals Service's idea of a 'safe house'? This is crazy. Nice, but crazy."

"It's just temporary, obviously. We just needed a quick, safe place to go. I couldn't take you to the courthouse or to home. The Marshals Service has some pretty good connections and options when we need them. I'm glad you approve. I'm guessing this is more like what you were accustomed to during your law firm days. Not so much the kind of place public servants usually get to go."

"OK, you know what I am going to ask you next. How many people were hurt? Killed? Was anyone arrested? Is this all over now? Please tell me! What was the damage?"

Montana Tom reluctantly glanced over at Officer Max. They both had blank expressions.

Chapter 26:

In Memoriam: Judge Helen Lupinaci and Judge Ronald Murphy.

It was a rainy, soggy July summer day in Princeton, New Jersey. Avery, with her Deputy Marshal escorts, was attending the funeral for Federal Bankruptcy Judge Helen Lupinaci. The day before, Avery had attended the funeral of Federal Senior District Judge Ronald Murphy in nearby Cherry Hill, New Jersey. Two weeks earlier, Judge Lupinaci and Judge Murphy had both been found dead, gagged and bound with ropes, in the trunk of the 1958 model black Ford Prefect that had exploded in the McDonald's parking lot adjacent to Avery's courthouse. Their bodies were charred and burned, and their identities could only accurately be determined with dental records. The actual cause of their deaths (burns, smoke inhalation, body trauma, or something else prior to the explosion) had not been publicly announced. Five homeless individuals, standing near the car, were also killed in the explosion, as was a young nurse and two college students standing at a bus stop a few feet away. There were ten total fatalities. A few other passers-by were badly burned. Several people inside the McDonald's were injured with shards of glass and debris when the blast blew through the restaurant's windows. The catastrophic blast destroyed several other cars in the parking lot. The bomb had been created with ammonium nitrate fertilizer, liquid nitromethane, Trenchrite, Seismogel, and Seismopac—something very similar to what was used in the Oklahoma City Federal Building bombing back in 1995, only it was made with far smaller quantities of ingredients and caused a thankfully smaller blast. There was nevertheless a large, deep crater in the McDonald's parking lot and yellow crime tape and investigators on the scene for weeks. There was no damage to the federal courthouse where Avery worked, but it was on lock down until further notice, as a normal precaution. It would likely be reopened to the public again sometime in August. The episode was obviously too close to the federal building for anyone's comfort. No one could be completely sure if the bomber thought he had a stronger bomb and had intended to also target the courthouse or not.

Suddenly, it appeared as though the tragic disappearance of Judges Lupinaci and Murphy, around the same time as Avery was dealing with her own death threats, was more than a strange, sad coincidence. Suddenly, the Marshals Service and FBI were working around the clock, trying to figure out what connection there was between these two federal judges in New Jersey and one in Texas, and who might want all three of them (if not more people) dead. What was the "trilogy in five parts"? Was Avery supposed to have been the third judge incinerated in the explosion? Was Montana Tom's quick driving the only thing that foiled the plan? The Marshals and FBI Agents were either dumbfounded, or simply not speaking to Avery about what they were deducing.

Judge Lupinaci had been a wonderful human being—a wife, mother and grandmother who served on the bench for almost 30 years and was 70-years-old. She was the daughter of Italian immigrants who had moved to America from Sicily, opened an Italian restaurant in Brooklyn, and toiled for a better life for their children. And she was the mother of both a renowned opera singer and a physician. She went to mass regularly. She taught commercial law classes at nearby

University of Pennsylvania Law School. She was everyone's favorite Camden judge. Judge Murphy was likewise wonderful. He was 92-years-old and still taking cases on senior status at the Camden courthouse. He was brilliant, still sharp as a tack, and was genuinely kind and gracious. He had been a hero in World War II in the Army, winning many medals including a Bronze Star and Purple Heart. He had been gravely injured in 1944 in combat, while involved in the liberation of France, when a mortar round landed behind him on the battlefield. Shrapnel had torn into his back, intestines, and leg. He had survived but spent several years in a hospital getting many surgeries and treatments. Many years later, he went to college, law school, became a respected federal prosecutor, and eventually a federal judge. He, like Judge Lupinaci, should have been recommended for sainthood.

What did Avery possibly have in common with these two New Jersey judges? And, assuming there was a common link, how could their killer be in Portugal leaving frightening messages at Sagres for Avery, just two days before planting a fertilizer bomb and cremating Judges Lupinaci and Murphy in an antique car across the street from Avery's courthouse in Texas? And how was the antique car—likely not drivable—transported with the bodies of Judges Lupinaci and Murphy inside of it—to the McDonald's parking lot? There were so many unanswered questions. Were there multiple culprits involved? Meanwhile, the FBI was apparently cross-referencing every case that the three judges had each been assigned over the years, to try to find some common link or common party (or parties) that might be angry at all of them. Avery did not have any recollection or knowledge of any overlap of their cases. When Avery asked if Judges Lupinaci and Murphy had received death threats, she was not given any answer.

The Lassiters had some extended family members in Princeton, so Avery stayed a few days after the funerals to visit with them. The Deputy Marshals would not allow Avery to stay at her relatives' house overnight. She had to stay at the Nassau Inn, surrounded by what seemed like an outrageous number of Deputy Marshals. Avery tried to make the most of it and distract her mind from the tragedy. She persuaded the Deputy Marshals take her to all of her favorite places with the New Jersey Lassiter clan. Her favorite pancake house across from Princeton University. Her favorite pizza place. Even the "hot wings" joint that, strangely, the infamous brothers Lyle and Erik Menendez (now incarcerated for killing their parents) once owned— the Deputy Marshals were mildly amused by that bit of trivia. But nothing felt right. Avery was naturally devastated by what had happened to Judges Lupinaci and Murphy. She was emotionally ravaged by the deaths of the innocent bystanders. And she had no idea why this had happened and whether she had been targeted to die that day, too.

Everywhere Avery went, she felt like she was being watched. Avery remembered the words in her original threat letter—that the letter writer *watched her always.* Avery felt like she was exposing those around her to unnecessary harm. Her relatives in New Jersey were not at all relaxed about all the hoopla. If the person who wanted Avery dead could track her down in Portugal, surely the middle of New Jersey was no obstacle. Nowhere seemed safe.

Avery and the Marshal entourage headed back home soon, and Avery returned to the office once the federal building was reopened. She was so sad and shaken that she could hardly imagine how she could keep going forward. She had to. But it was unbearable. She was strangely embarrassed—like she had done something to contribute to all of this. It was horrific. Anyway, the office continued to feel like the only place she really felt normal. There was so much security in the courthouse—especially after the McDonald's tragedy—that it felt like nothing could happen there. When she arrived back in the office early on the morning after her return to Texas, Matt Smith, her intern, was sitting at his desk—as usual he was the first one in the office. He looked a little frazzled.

"Matt, do you ever go home? And are you okay?"

Matt shrugged and frowned. "Actually, not really."

Matt explained that some Deputy Marshals had been in the office earlier and asked to photograph his hands. He complied—what choice did he have? But he now regretted it. He felt upset and sort of violated. He did not know what reason they would possibly have for doing something like that. They had not explained anything to him. Could Judge Lassiter find out?

Avery promised she would. But she was extremely concerned and confused herself. Matt handed her the perfectly organized bench memo he had prepared to update her for her morning docket. She grabbed a cup of coffee from the Keurig, slipped in her office, and began preparing for her day. She made a note to call Deputy Marshal Mark Eason after her morning docket and find out what the hand photography on her intern had been about.

Chapter 27:

Hand Forensics.

There is a professor of anatomy and forensics in Dundee, Scotland[5] who, in recent years, has begun helping law enforcement officials track down rapists and pedophiles who happen to video record their crimes. The professor does this by studying the veins, scars, and other markings on the backs (or dorsum) of a perpetrator's hands that happen to be shown when recording their hideous crimes. The professor first began using this technique as a tool to help government agencies identify disaster victims after mass tragedies occurred. Then the technique expanded to assisting in crime-solving, particularly in the case of filmed or recorded sex abuse. The Scottish professor has created a data base at the University of Dundee's Department of Anatomy and Forensic Anthropology that contains photographs of hands, divided into 24 parts, from the fingernails to the wrists, and checks for 27 distinctive qualities. In short, the veins on the back of a person's hand create a pattern that is unique, from person to person, even in identical twins. Apparently, when a body is growing inside a mother's womb, cells in the hand assemble spontaneously–rather than following a pre-established blueprint. This means that not only are the vein patterns as unique as fingertip whorls and palm prints, but they are enclosed by skin and cannot be altered (unlike fingerprints). Moreover, even things like unusual finger nail

[5] Dame Sue Black, Professor University of Dundee, Department of Anatomy and Forensic Anthropology.

qualities, pigmentation, freckling, knuckle creases, and scarring can provide identification means. Avery had read about this professor and the emerging technique and wondered if this might have anything to do with the Deputy Marshals photographing her intern Matt's hands. But why?

When Avery finished court that morning, she called Deputy Eason to talk about the hand photographs. "Why are you taking pictures of my intern's hands, for crying out loud?"

As Deputy Eason listened to Avery's questions, a long awkward pause followed. Deputy Eason apologetically stated that he could not discuss details, but that they had retrieved several fairly decent photographs from Avery's smart phone of the young man who stalked her and Ginny down in Sagres, Portugal and they had been able to zero in and expand the view of his hands. Now, the Deputy Marshals, at the request of the FBI, were essentially going around photographing the hands and forearms of virtually every male individual who had some kind of connection to Avery. They were also studying the video security camera recordings from many months' worth of court hearings in Avery's court and even studying certain lawyers' hand morphology. Finally, they also had some video tape that they were studying from the McDonald's parking lot where the Ford Prefect had exploded. Matt was just one of an extremely large number of men who were being asked to agree to get their hands photographed. Deputy Eason said that he had explained all of this to Matt, that the Deputy Marshals were basically needing to undertake this exercise with every male who was currently or recently in contact with Judge Lassiter—even Judge Hall, down at the other end of Avery's chambers, and Officer Max and their son Heath were going to have their hands and forearms photographed later. Deputy Eason wasn't sure why Matt would take things so personally.

"He clearly consented, Judge Lassiter!"

"I don't understand this, Mark. Not at all!" Avery bemoaned. "Matt and Judge Hall, for that matter, were here when I was in Portugal. Who suggested photographing their hands? And Max and Heath? Are you implying that my own husband and son are suspects? What is going on? I don't mean to insult your intelligence or the methods of the FBI, but sometimes I just don't understand how the FBI thinks and how they choose to expend resources and track down leads. What are they doing for Christ's sake?"

Avery pleaded and pleaded with Deputy Eason to tell her something more—anything—to help her understand the logic of what was going on and to make her feel like some sort of progress was being made in the investigation. If he couldn't tell her anything about her own death threat investigation, maybe he could tell her something about the assassination-investigation into Judges Murphy's and Lupinaci's murders. There had to be some connection—obviously since their assassinations were orchestrated right across the street from the Dallas courthouse—but what on earth might it be?

Deputy Eason (a.k.a. the Big Easy) was not so easy. He once again politely denied to offer any information. Avery had never had such difficulty getting people to crack as she did with the U.S. Marshals. They were kind, caring guardians to her. But they had mastered the skills of confidentiality and secrecy to a high art form.

Chapter 28:

Southern Road Trip and the Strange Disappearance of Billionaire Karl Lee.

It was deep summer, August, now. The digital clock in the Lassiters' kitchen had just marked 270 days since the U.S. Marshals first invaded their backyard. Avery guessed it really didn't matter much these days. She and Baxter didn't enjoy spending much time in the backyard in August anyway. August in Texas is a treacherous time, with its oppressive heat. The mercury in the outdoor thermometer shoots up above 100 degrees Fahrenheit most days. The blistering air is humid, still, and quiet—except for the occasional chirping of crickets and loud buzzing of cicadas. The glare of the white, hot sun hurts a person's eyes, and it sears the ground, causing the grass and flowers to turn crunchy brown, dry up, and wither. The cracked and scorched earth gets infested with fire ants. Avery worried about Baxter this time of year, since canines are incapable of perspiring like human beings. All they can do is pant and search for a spot of shade. Baxter's canine roots were in the cool, damp regions of the British Isles. Avery wondered if King Charles II of England ever could have imagined that the progeny of his royal lapdogs would wind up in such a strange, faraway place as Southlake, Texas.

In this third week of August, Avery was somewhat subdued. Her mind was in a different place than it had been for the past several months. She was home packing up her baby boy, Heath, to go away to college. Heath was excited, but Avery was suppressing her emotions—as she so often did in recent months. Things seemed unorganized and chaotic, because Heath had made a last-minute change of plans to go to school in Atlanta, Georgia at Emory University, rather than his earlier pick of Oklahoma State. A long road trip through the Deep South was in store for the Lassiters later in the week. They left the house at 6:00 a.m. on a Thursday morning. Even Baxter got to go on the family road trip. After dropping Heath off at college, Avery, Officer Max, Julia, and Baxter (accompanied by their Deputy Marshal escorts, of course) would spend a few days at the lake house of Avery's friend and former law partner from Madison, Spencer & Collins—Ward Scott—in Seneca, South Carolina. Avery joked that Baxter, in particular, loved these trips to the Scotts' lake house. They had visited there a few times. The Scotts owned a golden retriever, Lark, who was beautiful and intelligent like Baxter and was also a very fun companion with whom Baxter liked to run and play.

The drive from Southlake to Atlanta is pretty dull. It is basically an 800-mile straight shot east on Interstate Highway 20, through East Texas, Louisiana, Mississippi, Alabama, and Georgia. The scenery is utterly unchanging for 800 miles (tall thick trees lining both sides of the highway; lots of billboards advertising personal injury lawyers and casinos; and a Waffle House and Cracker Barrel about every five miles). Rain showers and light summer storms followed the Lassiters most of the trip. Julia asked after a while why there are so many Waffle Houses in the South. No one seemed to know the answer to that question.

On the drive to Emory, Avery heard a news story while listening to the car radio, just around the time that they were passing through Jackson, Mississippi. The story caused Avery great concern. It was a story about Karl Lee, the well-known Chinese-American billionaire businessman. Karl Lee had mysteriously vanished according to news reports, about two weeks earlier. Avery had met Karl Lee back in the late 1990's when she represented The Regent Hotel & Casino in its Chapter 11 bankruptcy case in Camden, New Jersey. Karl Lee was the "stalking horse" bidder who swooped in and had purchased The Regent Hotel & Casino out of bankruptcy and completely refurbished and re-themed it. Karl Lee was a veritable hero in both the Atlantic City community and with Wall Street investors, because not only had he brought back The Regent from almost certain demise—causing it to regain its prominence as the shining star of the Atlantic City Boardwalk—but he had brought back Atlantic City itself, from a crime ridden, fading destination of yesteryear to a new hot spot among tourists and the younger, "hipper" crowd. Atlantic City was now not only a huge generator of jobs and revenue for the State of New Jersey but was back in competition with the historically glitzier Las Vegas. And it was now taking back lost market share from the Native American reservation casinos. Karl Lee was a brilliant and creative entrepreneur whose investments now went well beyond the real estate and casino industry. He was a philanthropist and all around wonderful human being. Avery and her former colleague Ward Scott actually became rather well acquainted with Karl Lee during The Regent Hotel & Casino bankruptcy and resulting acquisition. They represented Lee on a couple of unrelated business ventures in subsequent years—specifically, forays investing in the oil and gas exploration and production business in Texas, and also in the acquisition of a Galveston hotel. Avery had lost touch with Karl Lee after going on the bench. She wasn't sure if Ward Scott maintained a business or social relationship with Lee anymore, but she was sure his disappearance would be a topic of discussion with Ward at the lake house—given their mutual past dealings with Lee. Apparently, Karl Lee had been in Macau recently, in connection with the grand opening of his new casino, there. That had been the last time

Lee was seen publicly. Mr. Lee had taken a commercial flight back to the U.S. He was accounted for up until the time he got off his plane at JFK Airport in New York City. Apparently, a private limousine service had picked him up at JFK airport and never made it to Lee's house in Short Hills, New Jersey. The limousine driver was missing as well.

The Marshal caravan made it to Atlanta around 8:00 p.m. on Thursday night. After a night of rest at a hotel in Midtown, the Lassiters and Deputy Marshals had breakfast at The Flying Biscuit the next morning, walked Baxter a bit in Piedmont Park, and then headed over to the Emory campus and helped Heath move into his freshman dormitory, just a stone's throw from the tall white hovering buildings of the Center for Disease Control (CDC) that are adjacent to the campus. Avery hugged and kissed Heath goodbye, told him good luck, to "make good choices," and not to worry about her. She said that she hoped that no virus-infected laboratory mice would escape from the CDC and make their way into Heath's dorm room. Baxter seemed to somehow understand that comment, because he appeared to be dutifully on the lookout for rodents the entire walk back to the car.

As Avery and the Deputy Marshals made their way back to their vehicles, Avery's face turned serious. She asked Montana Tom, who was part of the Marshal entourage, if he had heard of the businessman Karl Lee. Montana Tom replied that, of course, he had. Avery mentioned the story that she had heard on the radio driving to Atlanta, regarding Lee's mysterious disappearance that was naturally thought to be foul play at this point. Avery had a strange thought. It seemed unbelievably bizarre that she had worked on a case almost 20 years ago in which both Judges Lupinaci and Murphy were involved (those two judges had handled all the court hearings in the Chapter 11 bankruptcy case of The Regent Hotel & Casino) and they, of course, had disappeared and then were murdered across the street from Avery's courthouse. And now Karl Lee, who was involved in that very same case—eventually buying the hotel and casino and making such a splash in Atlantic City—had gone missing.

Montana Tom shook his head, looking into the distance, and calmly replied, "Bad things happen all the time, Judge. And coincidences happen all the time. Do you know how many people are probably hating Karl Lee right now for getting permission from the Chinese government to build that new casino in Macau? Some people in the casino industry in the U.S. hate him simply because he is a Chinese-American who essentially took over Atlantic City by storm. Now, people in China and Hong Kong hate him because they think of him as 'defecting' to America, and then coming back and making money off of the Chinese. And do you know how many people target billionaires for the simple reason that they are billionaires? There are so many possibilities for foul play with someone like Karl Lee. I highly doubt that a 20-year-old transaction in the New Jersey federal courts involving The Regent Hotel & Casino and Judges Lupinaci and Murphy is high on the list of what the law enforcement officials will be focusing on, in the investigation of the disappearance of Karl Lee."

Avery sighed, looking a little embarrassed. "I guess you are probably right, Montana Tom. I need to stop trying to play Sherlock Holmes, I guess. That's what those 12-year-old FBI Agents are for, right? Let's hit the road. You are going to love South Carolina—even if all you are going to do is stand around like a statue watching over us."

The Lassiters and Deputy Marshals then piled into the dark-tinted G-rides and headed up to Seneca, South Carolina to spend a few days with Ward and Caroline Scott (and, of course, their lovely golden

retriever Lark). Baxter napped along the hour-and-a-half drive, no
doubt dreaming of the Scotts' lakeside retreat and the adventures that
he would be having with Lark over the next few days. Lark was such
a beautiful and regal dog. Her breed, the golden retriever, has been the
most entered of all dog breeds in the Westminster Dog Show,
historically. It's no wonder why. They are exceptional canines.
Anyway, the place where Lark and the Scotts lived when they were
away from Texas was a 6,000 square foot, 3-story lake "mansion" on
picturesque Lake Keowee, just a few miles up the street from Clemson
University where Caroline Scott now taught. Most of the Scotts'
neighbors were celebrities, professional athletes, retired successful
lawyers, or titans of the investment banking world. Avery always
looked forward to spending time with her former senior partner from
her old law firm days, with whom she worked the most. Ward was
now semi-retired. Ward had been very much responsible for the arc of
Avery's career. Ward and Avery jokingly referred to themselves
sometimes as fellow combat veterans. They once survived a domestic
terror attack together at the Sacramento, California Capitol Building
late one night in February 2001, when Madison, Spencer & Collins
was hired to provide legal consultation to the California legislature
during a financial crisis facing the state government (the domestic
terror attack involved a government-hating irate tanker truck driver
who drove his big rig up the Capitol steps and rammed it into the
Senate chamber, just as legislative sessions had adjourned; Avery and
Ward often recounted the horrific story over evening drinks on the
Scotts' long, breezy porch overlooking Lake Keowee). Anyway,
Ward and Caroline had a beautiful property and were always such
generous, gracious hosts when the Lassiters visited. The outside of
their property was decorated with lush plants and colorful flowers,
multi-level decks, Koi and goldfish ponds, waterfalls, and a private
boat dock that housed a 27-foot $200,000 black Cobalt boat (with a

bathroom—as Avery was always quick to point out) and other expensive water toys. Every window of the Scotts' house had spectacular views of the lake, mountains, and Southern flora. Ward and Caroline were great conversationalists and could often be a little quirky, a bit like one of those Southern couples from a Tennessee Williams play, often squabbling about what wine to open, the indoor temperature, or when and what to serve for dinner (dinner is usually served at 10:00 p.m.--probably because Ward never could stop taking work phone calls from Madison, Spencer & Collins until then; also because the Scotts always spend about three hours collaborating in the kitchen, creating a gastronomic masterpiece for dinner, no matter what the occasion). Avery's favorite thing to do during all of this was to drink Chardonnay (picking out one of the finest labels from the Scotts' huge underground wine cellar) and wander around the Scotts' property with Baxter and Lark, stopping to feed the many Koi in the many massive ponds scattered around the back.

As the Lassiters and Deputy Marshals pulled into Seneca, they stopped to eat lunch at Diener's Diner (owned by a sweet Mennonite family), and Avery began calling the Scotts on her smart phone. There was no answer, but they had told her she could come on in to the house if no one was home. The Scotts might be running errands in nearby Greenville. Avery had the code to the large iron gate at the front of the Scotts' property, and also one to their house. So, after lunch, the Lassiter/Marshal caravan headed to the Scotts to begin a few days of rest and relaxation.

The 15-minute drive from the diner to the lake house was a trek over a winding road full of lush and mossy green trees. There were lots of places to buy peaches, boiled peanuts, bait, and gun ammunition. And plenty of signs praising the victories of the Clemson Tigers. As the Lassiter/Marshal entourage entered into the quiet cove in which the Scotts' lake house was situated, it was clear that the Scotts were not home yet. Avery told Montana Tom the code to the iron gate and the Marshal vehicles streamed onto the cobblestone path down to the lake house. Avery could hear Lark barking inside the house. Lark must have heard the sound of unfamiliar cars and became agitated.

As the Lassiters started to pile out of the vehicles, Montana Tom abruptly stopped them. He ordered them to stay in the vehicles while he searched the perimeter of the property. Avery rolled her eyes and snickered a little. "Isn't this a little extreme, Tom? Can't we just relax this one weekend?" Montana Tom reminded Avery of the episode last June in Sagres, Portugal, and also reminded her that Seneca, South Carolina was extremely easier to access than Western Europe. Of course, Montana Tom was right as usual.

As Montana Tom walked the property, Deputy Jason Fuentes (Avery's cerulean blue Marshal, "CB") shouted out from the vehicle behind them that Montana Tom should pay attention to a big plastic drum that was on the Scotts' porch. It didn't look like a normal thing to have on one's front porch.

At that moment all eyes focused on the Scotts' porch. There was, indeed, a large industrial drum positioned just past the steps of the front porch. No visible labeling appeared on it. It looked oddly out of place among the puffy white hydrangeas, crepe myrtles, and hibiscus gracing the Scotts' regal entry.

"You think we should open the drum?" Montana Tom replied. "How am I supposed to open that drum? And, for all I know, it is something the Scotts ordered and had delivered."

For a few moments Montana Tom and CB quibbled about whether they should call the ATF's bomb squad and the FBI's HazMat teams and, meanwhile, "back the Hell out of there as fast as they could" because of the drum. Before they made a determination, their discussion abated, because the Scotts came honking up the road in their Range Rover, waving friendly hands out of the window. They punched in the code to the iron gate and came flying down the cobblestone path. The Deputy Marshals began looking increasingly nervous, like they had a bad feeling about the 45-gallon drum sitting on the Scotts' porch.

Ward and Caroline stepped out of their vehicle and greetings were exchanged. They were an elegant, handsome couple. It was always odd to see Ward relaxed and not dressed in his usual Dormeuil Vanquish business suit and expensive Italian loafers. Today he had on a Tulane Law School sweat shirt, khaki shorts, and a baseball cap. Caroline looked stunning as always, dressed today in a tennis outfit from an early morning game she worked in at the nearby country club before the Scotts had headed over to Greenville to run errands. Caroline was a lovely Southern belle, who always looked like she had come straight from the beauty salon, even when sweating through tennis clothes and after hours of errands. After, the Deputy Marshals were introduced, Montana Tom nodded at Caroline and pointed to the porch. "Ma'am, we were a little curious about the big drum on the porch. Hate to be nosey, but can you tell me what that is?"

Ward and Caroline turned and looked toward the porch. They both looked at each other curiously. "Honey, what is that? Did you order something?" Caroline asked.

"No. I have no idea. It wasn't there when we left this morning."

The Scotts had simply made a quick trip to the dentist in Greenville and then picked up groceries. They had been gone, at most, three hours.

"Who has access to this property?" Montana Tom asked. "Yard man come today? Maid? Anyone?"

"No. Not today."

"I notice you have security cameras all around this place. Can you give us access to the video recordings?"

Ward quickly waved Montana Tom into the house to show him the computers where the cameras' video recordings were wirelessly sent and stored. Montana Tom stopped Ward and first insisted that the Deputy Marshals do a sweep of the interior of the Scotts' large house. As Montana Tom approached the house, he noticed that the lid of the drum was actually partially open. He could see liquid inside. He smelled a pungent odor emanating from the drum, like rotten eggs. This suggested to him that this was something other than a bomb, but he could not be sure.

The next three hours were a circus. Avery was horrified and embarrassed that the Scotts had been drawn into her topsy-turvy, turbulent world during what was supposed to be a relaxing weekend. The Deputy Marshals were not going to take any chances. They called in local law enforcement, the ATF's bomb squads, and federal hazardous materials experts from the Office of Homeland Security. They were going to study the camera recordings and likely eventually decide whether they would have to render the drum safe by blowing it up, or whether it was safe to simply remove it.

The Scotts and Lassiters (and, of course, Lark and Baxter) were at least given permission to go out on the Scotts' Cobalt black boat and spend some time far out on Lake Keowee. Deputy Jason Fuentes went out with them. He spent all of his time either looking through binoculars, texting on his phone, or talking to people on his walkie-talkie device. Finally, after they had explored every corner of the lake, Deputy Fuentes got the "all clear" signal that they could return to the Scotts' residence. When Avery asked what had happened, Deputy Fuentes shook his head and said, "Not for me to tell you, Ma'am." Avery could not help but be extremely nervous. She was remembering the voicemail that was left on her chambers' phone last April. There had been a reference to leaving human remains in a drum of sulfuric acid. But the drum could be anything, right? Caroline always had various gardening and other do-it-yourself projects planned or in the works. Perhaps she had forgotten about ordering something or a neighbor had brought her something that she thought Caroline could use. The Scott's garage was full of similar odds and ends.

When they all returned to the lake house and docked and exited the Cobalt boat, the plastic drum and all the extra law enforcement personnel (except for a couple of Deputy Marshals) were gone. Apparently, after reviewing videos and the 45-gallon drum, the law enforcement personnel had collectively decided that there were no explosives in the drum, and it was safe to remove it. A Haz-Mat team had confiscated the drum and taken it to a lab somewhere to study its contents. They would hopefully get a report soon.

Meanwhile, everyone decided to relax a bit. Avery showered, then wandered through the Scotts' wine cellar and picked out an interesting looking Sangiovese-based red blend wine with which she was unfamiliar—she'd ask Ward to tell her about it later. Baxter enjoyed a nice long nap next to Lark on the Scotts' back porch. Ward and Caroline debated what they would prepare for dinner (usually something Italian), with Ward stopping every few moments to take phone calls from the legions of young lawyers toiling away for him at Madison, Spencer & Collins. It was a Friday evening, but that meant nothing in the world of Big Law. Ward Scott's loyal, young lieutenants would stay at the office and keep billing until the project was done. Officer Max kept watch on the back porch with Montana Tom and Deputy Fuentes and nervously paced and paced. Avery always wondered if Mad Max knew much more about the FBI and Marshal investigations than she did. Professional courtesy, and all. Maybe Montana Tom and Deputy Fuentes felt more comfortable or obligated to confide in a fellow law man about everything that was happening.

At around 10:00 p.m., as everyone was finally settling down for the late-night Rigatoni Bolognese that the Scotts had just placed on the dining room table, Montana Tom stepped inside from the back porch with a grim look on his face. Suddenly the whole atmosphere in the house darkened. It was obvious from Montana Tom's face that there was some sort of bad report he was about to share. "Everyone, we are going to need to head out of here at 0-600 tomorrow morning. Judge Lassiter, you and I and Deputy Fuentes are driving up to Charlotte and taking the first plane direct to DFW Airport. The rest of the family will drive back to Southlake with the other Marshal escorts. I am sorry to cut your visit here short. But this is on orders from headquarters."

"What's going on? It's the drum, right? What was in the drum?" Avery forcefully asked.

"Well, I have been given permission to tell you that the drum was full of sulfuric acid and lye and sludge that could possibly contain human remains. Whose remains are not yet known. And it is unclear if there will be enough DNA derived from it to identify the human victim or even corroborate that there was a human in there. It will likely be a few weeks, frankly, before we have thorough test results. We have also studied the video cameras. Apparently, around 11:00 a.m., a U-Haul truck pulled up to the Scotts' gate, and the driver must have somehow known the Scotts' gate code. Two white males unloaded the drum from the U-Haul truck and put it on the porch and quickly left. Not much of their faces showed. They had knit hats fully covering their heads and sunglasses. Probably going to be difficult to get any identifying information from the video. But, of course, the FBI will likely be able to track down who rented the U-Haul truck and where. And they will probably be analyzing their hands—if I know the FBI. But there was a note in the Scotts' mailbox that we found just a few minutes ago." Montana Tom pointed to a zip lock back in his hands that contained a white envelope inside. Montana Tom continued, "And one of the two delivery guys in the U-Haul truck, indeed, put something in the mailbox. Here, put on these gloves. I am going to take it out and let you read it."

Montana Tom's hands were strong and steady, but Avery's were not. Avery fumbled to put on the thin blue gloves that Montana Tom gave her and reached for the envelope. On the front it read, "*Honorless Judge Lassiter and Mr. Scott.*" Inside the envelope, the note read:

> *"Enjoy your weekend. Consider this to*
> *be the second part of the trilogy in five*
> *parts. Somewhere you made a choice.*
> *All followed to this. The accounting is*
> *scrupulous. The shape is drawn. No*
> *line can be erased."*

Montana Tom added, "Obviously the envelope and note will be sent to Quantico to be analyzed. I'm guessing these rantings in the note are more cryptic references to that weird *Hitchhiker* book?"

"No, actually, they're quotes from the author Cormac McCarthy's book, *No Country for Old Men*," Avery and Ward said almost in unison. Sometimes it was as though they shared the same brain—after 17 years of working on legal cases together. And Avery says that working in Big Law is like "dog years"—7 times 17 years, equals 119 years.

Montana Tom said, "How do you people know this kind of shit? I guess I should ask if you have any ideas on why this psycho is apparently quoting a different book now?"

Avery walked over to the Scotts' granite kitchen counter and grabbed her brief case. She reached in and pulled out a paperback copy of the novel *No Country for Old Men*—one of the two books she had brought along on her trip to read. "Coincidence?"

Caroline Scott passed out.

Chapter 29:

In Memoriam: Lee Dongfeng ("Karl Lee") . . . Maybe.

Three weeks passed. It was now September. The beginning of high school football season in Texas had the community of Southlake caught up in its usual frenzy. Signs emblazed with "DRAGON NATION...PROTECT THE TRADITION!" had popped up in the usual spots all over town.

Avery also had a new extern from SMU Law School, Gabriella, and her trusty intern Matt Smith had gone back to Austin, Texas to finish his last year of law school. Avery would miss that sweet kid. She felt bad for all the drama he had to witness these past few months. It had, no doubt, sort of tainted the internship experience for him. Avery remembered how humiliated he seemed on that day that the Deputy Marshals came to photograph his hands and forearms. Hopefully Matt wouldn't go back to campus and tarnish Avery's reputation at the law school, telling people "you don't want to work for that crazy judge—too much drama" and such. Avery depended on a good steady flow of talented law interns and externs to help her in her daily tasks. Gabriella seemed like a terrific young woman who would be up for the task. Avery told her all about the death threat situation that had been going on when she interviewed Gabriella, and Gabriella did not seem the least bit bothered. In time, Gabriella would prove as invaluable as Matt. The law schools kept producing a reliable stream of very talented, enthusiastic young lawyers, to be sure.

Avery tried to go on with life as usual and enjoy the change in seasons and all the fun rituals that Fall brought. But the national news reports made that impossible. On September 15, the Associated Press reported that Chinese-American billionaire businessman Lee Dongfeng (more popularly known as Karl Lee)—now missing for over three weeks—was now feared to have been kidnapped and murdered. However, the exact circumstances were still unknown and under intense investigation. Several million dollars had been wired out of one of Lee's Hong Kong bank accounts into a series of offshore bank accounts, in the Cayman Islands, then Guernsey, with the trail of monetary transfers finally going cold in the Cook Islands. And a mysterious letter had been received at Karl Lee's Short Hills, New Jersey home, stating that Lee was dead—that he had been tortured violently—and that his remains had been left to dissolve in a drum of sulfuric acid, placed in "a remote area of South Carolina." The story was being discussed and analyzed 24 hours a day on cable news - "tragedy TV," as Avery referred to it.

Only a handful of people knew the exact circumstances. The real story was that the drum—now thought to have contained Lee's remains—had been left at Avery's former law partner's lake house in Seneca, South Carolina, with a note left in the mailbox quoting Cormac McCarthy and stating that this was "the second part of the trilogy in five parts," whatever that meant. And the other part of the story that few people knew was that the mixture of sludge and sulfuric acid in the drum was unidentifiable. Not a trace of human DNA was found. With no body or positive proof of death, the family of Karl Lee could not probate his estate—his family's lives were currently in shambles because of this legal technicality. And Lee's business empire seemed to be collapsing almost overnight. The stock price of his casino companies had lost half of their value since the first news of

Lee's disappearance. Lee's other businesses were suffering as well. Lee was thought to have single-handedly run all his companies and was wholly responsible for creating their successful brand. His grown children were now fighting amongst each other and did not have the respect of the companies' employees, the Wall Street banks, or the private equity funds that backed Lee's companies. And, if this were not all bad enough, a strange cyber breach incident had recently occurred at The Regent, in which hackers had shut down the hotel's key card management system, locking guests outside of their rooms until a large ransom was paid. The Lee family had succumbed to the hackers' demands to transfer a large sum of Bitcoin to a cryptocurrency exchange site based in Malta.

Par for the course, Avery had not been allowed to tell anyone why she abruptly returned from the Scotts' lake house in late August, by plane without her family. She had simply told her staff that she needed to catch up on work and felt guilty staying away (the usual excuse). The Scotts were now back in Texas, too. They currently had 24-hour-a-day protection themselves. Avery was not sure why this extra step had been implemented. The Scotts were innocent bystanders who had been dragged into this nightmare in the worst sort of way. Sure, the envelope left at the Scotts' house mentioned Ward Scott in its "greeting." But surely the Scotts' lives were not in any kind of special danger. Caroline Scott had even been forced to go on "sabbatical" from her teaching position at Clemson indefinitely.

Avery could not extract herself from all of the TV news coverage about Karl Lee. His life seemed so charmed and he had accomplished such great things. He was reportedly worth more than $40 billion in U.S. dollars. He had holdings in manufacturing, pharmaceuticals, and energy, in addition to his better-known extensive holdings in the casino industry. He had given hundreds of millions of dollars to charity during his 64-year lifetime. He left behind a wife, three grown children and eight grandchildren. Karl Lee's vanishing, and the alleged gruesome details of his murder and disposal of his remains, was fast becoming the crime story of the century.

Avery decided to skip Friday Night Lights on this particular September evening, and told Officer Max to go on to the Southlake-Carroll Dragons football game without her. Julia wouldn't mind if Avery missed her playing her clarinet in the school band half-time show this one time, but Julia would be devastated if both her parents missed the game. Besides, the opponents this week were a terrible team from West Texas (a rarity) and the game would be uncharacteristically boring. Avery would enjoy a good book out by the swimming pool, turn on some Sting music, and try to turn her mind off from all of the Karl Lee TV coverage.

Later that evening, Deputy Marshal Ginny Oliphante came out of the RV command post that was still, after 10 months, parked in the Lassiters' backyard and walked up to Avery, who had now retired to her hammock on the back porch. She asked if Avery was doing okay, picking Baxter up and tickling his belly as she looked down at Avery.

"Ginny, I know we all know by now that my death threats and the deaths of Karl Lee and Judges Lupinaci and Murphy are somehow connected, but I cannot help but think this all ties back to something that happened 20 years ago in the Chapter 11 bankruptcy case of The Regent Hotel & Casino. Am I being ego-centric or losing my mind? I mean *obviously* there is a connection here that we are all trying to decipher. It feels like this would be obvious to anyone at this point. Yet no one with the FBI or Marshals Service will even entertain a conversation with me about it. It is like they are blowing me off, as though I have manufactured something ridiculous—like no one would suddenly decide to lash out about something that happened almost 20 years ago. I know that it may seem a little farfetched at first blush, but The Regent case is the only thing that binds all four of us together—or all *five* of us, for that matter, if Ward Scott is now part of this unhappy club that is being targeted. I mean no one will even tell me for sure if they think Ward is at risk—or if he and Caroline were just unlucky enough to be my friends who invited me and my family to visit."

"Judge, are you actually thinking that some New Jersey senior citizen gambler, or a laid off employee from the casino, or some angry Atlantic City resident might really be holding a grudge after 20 years over something like a bankrupt casino? Think about that objectively. That just doesn't compute."

"Ginny, you know that there has been a notorious history in the distant past of mafia types being involved in the casino industry. Maybe, unbeknownst to any of us, there were some mafiosos secretly behind the scenes at The Regent who were angry about our legal strategies and the results in that case. We employed a business strategy through the legal process of a Chapter 11 bankruptcy case to allow a Chinese-American to take over that casino and ultimately revamp the entire casino industry in Atlantic City. Maybe that caused the mafiosos to lose lots of money, not to mention power."

"Mafiosi."

"Huh?"

"It's 'mafiosi' not 'mafiosos.' I should know. I am part Italian. Mostly Puerto Rican, but my grandma was Italian." Ginny said. "Anyway, when you put it that way, Judge Lassiter, it actually sounds somewhat plausible. Have you shared this theory with Mark Eason or any of the other Deputies-in-Charge?"

"Yes, but they won't really react. They say that this is just one of a great number of theories that the FBI is exploring and that they are not at liberty to say any more."

Ginny giggled, "So you think the Gambino crime family is sending a Texas judge death threats? You think that a little-known fact about the Gambino crime family is that they are geeky fans of *The Hitchhiker's Guide to the Galaxy*? Sorry, Judge, but the more I think about it, there are just too many anomalies here that just don't seem to connect."

Avery frowned. "I feel like no one is taking me seriously anymore, Ginny. Not even you. Not even my Ginny from the Block."

Avery stormed in the house, shut off all TVs, and went to bed— Ruger revolver beside her on her nightstand. After dozing for a while, she bolted up, grabbed her smart phone and texted Ward Scott, asking if he would meet her for breakfast Saturday morning at Café Brazil near his and Caroline's local townhome. She wanted to brainstorm a bit with him regarding something. Ward quickly replied that he would meet her at 9:00 a.m. at Café Brazil.

"Bring Lark. Remember Café Brazil is dog-friendly. I'll bring Baxter."

"OK, I will. Lucky dogs."

Chapter 30:

Past is Prologue . . . Maybe?

"And by that destiny, to perform an act

Whereof what's past is prologue;

What to come,

In yours and my discharge"[6]

Avery, Baxter, and their Deputy Marshal escorts *de jure* arrived at Café Brazil at shortly after 9:00 a.m. Ward was already seated at a table in a back corner of the cafe, with his own hulky private bodyguards sitting conspicuously at the table next to him, pretending to read their smart phones, as they carefully scrutinized everyone who walked through the door. Similar to Avery's Marshal guardians, they were not that good at blending—in this case, in a café full of mostly soccer moms and students and professors from the nearby SMU college campus. Ward's security detail looked like retired cops, and they probably were. Ward was typing on an iPad, talking into a cell phone, and reading a stack of papers all at the same time. Ward never slowed down, not even on a Saturday morning. Ward was always "Mach 2, hair on fire," as the young lawyers at Madison, Spencer & Collins used to joke.

---

[6] William Shakespeare, The Tempest, Act 2, Scene 1.

Avery went immediately to the coffee bar and poured herself a cup of Bourbon Pecan Praline flavored coffee and then sat down next to Ward. Avery's Deputy Marshals kept a pleasant distance—probably because of Ward's nearby bodyguards. One Deputy Marshal stood outside the door and one just inside the entrance. At first Avery did not see Lark and was temporarily crestfallen for Baxter that she had not come along with Ward. But as Baxter started sniffing to find a suitable place under Avery's and Ward's table, he was overjoyed to see Lark, waking up from a nap. The dogs cozied up next to each other.

"Good God, what flavor of coffee did you get today, Avery?" Ward said with his brow furrowed, as though he was wincing in pain from the aroma. "I always cringe at the flavors people put together, to ruin a good cup of coffee."

Avery smiled. "Not all of us were indoctrinated into adulthood with dark black coffee in a metal cup in the jungles of Vietnam."

"OK. I don't mean to rush you, but I have to be quick this morning. I promised to go out and visit with the folks at Maverick Energy today about a pretty bad well accident that you may have read about happening last week in the Eagle Ford shale play. It's terrible. The death toll is rising as we speak. More than a dozen workers are dead and there is pretty bad contamination of some nearby areas. The company is weighing its options—if you know what I mean."

"OK. Got it. I, of course, heard about it. It sounds just horrible, and I feel bad taking up your time right now with that tragedy requiring your attention. This won't take long. I am going to ask you to think way back to our past, circa 1998. I want to brainstorm with you about when we were working on The Regent Hotel & Casino case in Camden, New Jersey."

"Yeah? Well that's going pretty far back in the past, alright. But, not surprisingly, I have been thinking about that case a great deal in the last few weeks. Judges Lupinaci and Murphy. Karl Lee. You. Me. We all worked on that case. And we all five now seem to be in the crosshairs of a mad man. I mean... I guess we have all been in the same guy's crosshairs. Nobody is telling us shit about what they know about Murphy's and Lupinaci's murders or whether they received threats like you. And we don't even know for sure whether Karl Lee is dead or if this is all some big hoax."

"A hoax? Why on earth would you think the Karl Lee thing is a hoax?"

"There are all kinds of rumors swirling around in the business world right now that maybe he is not really dead."

"OK. Well that surprises me. I don't know what to think about that at all. Anyway, Ward, I am starting to wonder if this could be the mafia. New Jersey mafia. Think about it. I mean, we certainly never heard about any mafia connections to The Regent. But it certainly wouldn't be irrational to speculate that the mafia may have had their grips on some aspect of the casino. We both know that it was extremely controversial when Karl Lee came in and made his successful play to take over the property. He changed up everything. Brought in new management. New security. New vendors. He even put pressure on the New Jersey politicos to replace the existing members of the New Jersey Casino Control Commission to get some fresh and more progressive faces in there to bring things into the twenty-first century. And, of course, he eventually took over other properties and transformed Atlantic City. If there were any remaining vestiges of the old school mafia in Atlantic City in year 1998, they had to have been obliterated after the Karl Lee era got underway. And when you add to all of those facts the horror of dissolving a body in a drum of sulfuric acid, the way someone supposedly did with Karl Lee—everyone knows that's a favorite technique of the mafia and drug cartels."

"Ok, but wait, Sherlock Holmes. There are at least a couple of problems with your theory. First, the mafia doesn't wait 20 or so years to do its dirty work. Second, the mafia doesn't send some minion on vacation to creep on their target in a foreign country and do nothing while he is there except leave macabre artwork to intimidate her. The mafia does swift, quiet hits. Third, how do you explain all the Ford Prefect and *Hitchhiker's Guide* lunacy? I mean your theory isn't insane, Avery. It's just almost insane. Have you shared this theory with the FBI or Marshals?"

"Yes. I have brought it up with them multiple times. First, after the McDonald's tragedy. Then repeatedly after the Karl Lee news hit the airwaves. I have told you before and I will tell you again. They don't share anything with me, Ward. I talk to them and they politely appear to listen, but they don't really react at all or say 'hey that makes sense' or 'hey, we will run that down.' They are too busy doing things like photographing and studying people's hands."

"Huh?"

"Never mind. You probably wouldn't believe it if I told you."

"What about the leads that they were supposedly going to track down on the U-Haul truck at my lake house? Did they track down where it was rented and by whom?"

"It was rented in Trenton, New Jersey, but whomever rented it used a fake ID. So far, that has been a dead end. Apparently, whomever rented and was driving that U-Haul truck is still a mystery—they left no bread crumbs whatsoever. Anyway, Ward, I just have no idea what leads are being aggressively pursued at this point. So, here is what I wanted to talk with you about. What if we hire our own private detective to do some snooping around in Atlantic City and see what they can learn about mafia figures that may have been secretly connected to The Regent back in the 1990's and may have been hurt financially when Karl Lee came in?"

Ward leaned back in his chair and tapped his spoon on the table nervously. Actually, Ward never seemed nervous; just frustrated frequently. "Avery, let me just sleep on this. I don't know if it is a good idea to be running our own off-the-books investigation. For all you know, the FBI and Marshals are tracking down this very theory and just won't tell you. Besides, I'm just not sure it really makes sense. I mean, the Ford Prefect and *Hitchhiker Guide* and geek side of all of this are what tanks the mafia theory, if you ask me."

Ward paused a few moments. "How about this? Let's think about every detail of The Regent case. It went on for over two years. There was so much litigation that spawned out of that bankruptcy case. Think about it. Remember that crazy card counter class action lawsuit—that group of professional gamblers that was arguing that they were owed a billion dollars because the casino would kick them out of the property whenever they suspected them of card counting? Those guys were scary nuts, as I recall. Remember the WARN act claims and the angry laid off employees? And all the personal injury claimants? I mean, there were bankers who lost their jobs when the casino couldn't pay off all their debt. There were pissed off hedge funds. There were literally hundreds of parties that were financially hurt. Maybe there is somehow a tie there to your death threats, to Judges Murphy's and Lupinaci's murders, and to Karl Lee that connects back to The Regent bankruptcy case and Karl's takeover of it—I'll give you that. But even that connection feels like a bit of a stretch—let alone bringing in a mafia connection."

Avery glared at Ward in weary exasperation. "I am so tired of everyone thinking my theories are crazy. Maybe whomever is behind this all has been in prison for 20 years and that's why he is just now lashing out. Just because The Regent case was far back in the past does not mean that someone might not still have a long festering grudge. Ward, think outside the box—as you always used to say to me when I was a young associate! I truly think that the FBI is convinced that some lawyer or party who has been in my court recently, and also had cases in Judges Murphy's and Lupinaci's courts, is the one behind this all. I don't think that they believe Karl Lee's situation is in anyway related to any of this. I don't think they are considering for one moment that The Regent case could possibly be the common link in all of this. But I feel in my gut that they are wrong. We need to drill down and think about whether there was something in The Regent case that involved a Ford Prefect or the number 42 or *The Hitchhiker's Guide*. Remember how the casino was always cycling new slot machines and games in and out? Did one of them have a *Hitchhiker* theme? Or was "42" somehow significant in some popular game?"

"Let me think on this, Avery. I promise I'll call you in a few days."

Avery got up and stormed out of the café, pulling Baxter abruptly to her side. The Deputy Marshals startled to attention and accompanied Avery out of the café, flanking her on both sides.

Chapter 31:

Case Break—Mystery Solved on the Ford Prefect.

Finally, in early October, the FBI and U.S. Marshals asked to meet with Avery and Ward Scott together, regarding a possible break in the case. Apparently, they had a promising theory they wanted to reveal and explore with them. It had something to do with a Ford Prefect, but they needed to brainstorm with both Avery and Ward. Avery was shocked and cautiously excited. For once, she felt like she was finally being appropriately consulted on a theory. It had to be something pretty solid.

Everyone showed up in Avery's chambers at noon, the day after Columbus Day. Avery was feeling a little sluggish that day—the Texas-OU "Red River Rivalry" football game had been played the preceding Saturday at the Cotton Bowl in Dallas and she had attended with friends (and the Marshal entourage, of course). It was a great victory for the Longhorns, but Avery had enjoyed one too many fried food delicacies during her stroll around the State Fair after the game. She was slow to recuperate. Baxter was with Avery that day—Avery had brought him along to work with her. He was suffering from one of his recurring ear infections, and Avery wanted to keep an eye on him and doctor his ears herself several times a day. He would be napping all day by the fish tank in Avery's chambers. Avery thought he liked Avery's big fish tank and the gurgling peaceful sound of the water inside it.

The FBI started the meeting by asking Avery and Ward what they knew about the Ford Prefect automobile and did they remember any litigation in The Regent bankruptcy case involving this kind of car?

Avery sighed. "Gentlemen, with respect, don't you think I would have mentioned that by now if I did?" I have been urging you to consider whether that case is somehow a relevant common link among at least me and Judges Murphy and Lupinaci."

The truth was that Avery's memory was very good. But federal bankruptcy judges such as Avery handle several thousand cases per year. And the Regent case was, of course, many years before she even became a judge. Anyway, Ward Scott had a mind like a steel trap, and he did not remember anything involving a Ford Prefect either.

One of the baby-faced FBI Agents then went into a discussion of the automobile generally. The Ford Prefect was a line of British cars which Ford Motor Co.—United Kingdom Division produced from 1938 to 1961. It was a boxy, upright car. Certain of the models looked like something that one would see in a Hollywood depression era movie. There were not many places or years that one could buy them directly in the United States ever. There was a place in Jersey City, New Jersey that sold them for a while.

FBI Agent Navarrez continued, "Anyway, Judge Lassiter, do you remember in The Regent case handling a lawsuit filed by a widow against the casino involving Dram Shop liability? Apparently, the widow's late husband had been in a car crash with a female teenaged drunk driver who had been at the casino shortly before the car crash and the widow's lawyer argued that the teenager had wrongfully been served alcohol by the casino and the casino should pay the widow and her children millions of dollars of damages?"

"Sure, I remember that very well," Avery calmly replied.

"Well, it turns out that the husband was driving a 1958 Ford Prefect. Actually, the very same kind that exploded across the street with Judges Lupinaci's and Murphy's bodies in it."

"Wow. I didn't remember that detail. Did you, Ward?"

"No. I guess during that case we were so focused on other details—focusing on the videos of the teenager walking around the hotel and casino property, and whether she had actually been served alcohol and what not, that we really were not focusing on the car models and the details of the actual crash. The details of the crash were not at issue at all. It was all about the casino's possible negligence and liability."

"Are you all starting to think that my threat, and Judges Murphy's and Lupinaci's murders—and I guess Karl Lee's possible murder—have something to do with that Dram Shop lawsuit?"

"Well, think about it. This is an extremely rare car. And you and Ward defended The Regent against this multimillion-dollar lawsuit. Judge Lupinaci was the judge who handled all the pretrial matters in the lawsuit and Judge Murphy handled the ultimate jury trial. And Karl Lee was the ultimate beneficiary of your success in the lawsuit, so to speak, since he ended up acquiring the hotel and being relieved from having to pay out that multimillion-dollar claim."

"Well, further connect the dots for me. If someone is lashing out at us all regarding that lawsuit, who do you think it is? The wife committed suicide. There were three small boys. Do you think this is some crazy 20-year vendetta that the children are now pursuing?"

"Actually, yes, that is a working theory now. But we have not been able to track down the children. After the mother committed suicide, they went to live, first, with a very elderly grandfather who—get this—had been a mechanic at the Jersey City dealership which sold Ford Prefects for a few years. The children's father that was killed by the teen driver (the old man's son) probably got the car from him. But then the grandfather died from asbestosis or Mesothelioma, without a will, fairly soon after the boys went to live with him, and there appear to have been no relatives who wanted to take the kids after that. The kids went into a Catholic-run orphanage in Woodbridge, New Jersey for a while after the grandfather's death and were apparently split up and fostered out eventually. There are also some records of the boys being altar boys at a now-notorious Catholic parish in South New Jersey, where a pedophile priest was accused of sexually abusing dozens of young boys—and the Catholic Diocese there eventually filed a bankruptcy case under the weight of massive molestation claims. The boys likely had a double dose of horrible luck of not just being orphaned, but then being victims of that priest, Father Ignatius, since his bad acts were first discovered in 2002 and the trail runs cold on the boys somehow after the year 2002. It's as if they vanished around that time. It is unclear if they ran away or what."

Avery and Ward looked at each other, both searching their memories. Avery finally spoke up. "The boys' last name was Braden. I remember that. Are you telling me that you have searched every data base in New Jersey and otherwise and you cannot track these Braden kids down?"

"Actually, one of the Braden boys apparently died of a freak staph infection while in foster care. There is a death certificate for a Richard Braden from 2002. But that is the last public record we can find on any of these boys. The other two boys were twins."

"What about the Department of Motor Vehicle records for the Ford Prefect that was carrying Judges Lupinaci and Murphy?"

"The tag was a fake. And the VIN was obliterated. Obviously intentional. And we still aren't sure how a car like that could have made it from New Jersey to Texas with the judges in it. The car was positioned in a spot at the McDonald's parking lot where no video camera happened to catch it. Don't know if the car was towed there or what at this point."

"So where do we stand?"

"Well, we are trying to track down the two unaccounted for Braden twin boys. We are also continuing to keep our minds open to other possibilities. Because this still all feels pretty farfetched. If you will recall, the letter communications strongly implied the letter writer had spent time in your courtroom—the references to approaching your bench and the morbid references to blood and all. We are still, among other things, trying to find overlaps between cases that you and the other two judges handled. And, remember, Karl Lee even had some business ventures that you and Mr. Scott handled for him in Texas. You have told us about a couple of gas fields that you helped him purchase several years ago. And a hotel down in Galveston. We also have found that, with Karl Lee's many business dealings in the State of New Jersey, he has had other litigation in front of both Judges Murphy and Lupinaci over the years besides The Regent. For example, some securities litigation and several lawsuits against his pharmaceutical company. We can't let our guard down and think the Braden boys (wherever they are) are the only possibility."

With that, the conversation ended. Annalise ushered the serious FBI and Marshal personnel from the office. Agent Navarrez reminded Avery and Ward that their conversations were confidential and "nothing leaves this room."

"I know, I know. I am a rock. I absorb nothing. I say nothing. And nothing breaks me. At least I think I am correctly paraphrasing the lecture that you gave me several months ago when this all started."

"Uh, yes. Thank you, Ma'am."

Avery turned to Ward once the FBI and Marshal personnel had left the office. "Could it be that 'all things truly wicked start from innocence?'" she said.

"What?" Ward replied.

"It's a quote from Hemingway. Seems fitting right now. Could those innocent little boys, that I can still picture standing there next to their widowed mother after that Dram Shop liability trial, actually be the ones behind all of this?"

"You know, I would have believed your mafia theory sooner than I would have believed this."

Chapter 32:

Austin City Limits.

It was now November; a week before Thanksgiving. Avery could not believe that she was soon approaching the one year "anniversary" of being under Marshal protection. She also could not believe that there had been more than a month of silence from both the FBI and the death threat culprit. She had heard nothing at all since the meeting October 13 in her chambers with Ward, the FBI, and the Marshals. Avery was once again wondering if the FBI was at a stalemate or did they know something that they were not telling her. How could these elite federal investigative agencies not have tracked down the Braden twins by now, to have either ascertained their likely involvement or eliminated them as suspects? If they could track down people like the Una-bomber and Whitey Bulger, what could be so hard about these two boys from New Jersey?

Avery was packing up a bag in her bedroom at home on an especially nice warm Wednesday in November. She would be driving down to Austin with Ward Scott and the Deputy Marshals mid-morning. She and Ward were going to be making a presentation at a bankruptcy law conference in Austin. She and Ward would be speaking to 300 or so lawyers and other professionals in the restructuring and insolvency community regarding oil and gas law issues. "A riveting subject, to be sure," Avery joked.

The Deputy Marshals hated it when Avery engaged in public speaking, but she didn't really care. She did a lot of it—it is expected of judges. Avery went down to this particular law conference in Austin every November. She had an old law professor from her University of Texas Law School days that she always enjoyed seeing. She also always took the opportunity to visit with some of her former law clerks, interns, and externs who were still in the Austin area or who otherwise traveled to the conference for continuing legal education. And, best of all, she seized the opportunity to stay a couple of days at the Four Seasons Hotel and Spa on Lady Bird Lake and visit some of her old law school haunts on nearby Sixth Street in downtown Austin.

As Avery packed, she stopped to listen to the latest daily cable news coverage about Karl Lee. There was still no proof of his death, and the legal and family drama engulfing the Lee empire had now reached an absolute crisis level. The quarreling among Lee's wife and his grown children was more rancorous than ever. They had all taken to Twitter on an almost hourly basis, publicly airing their disputes in a very distasteful and embarrassing way. The boards of directors at all of Lee's corporations were bickering as well. Meanwhile, certain extremely aggressive hedge funds were starting to buy up blocking positions in the shares of his companies, as well as debt all over the capital structure of the Lee empire—an obvious sign that they smelled opportunity. Hedge funds are drawn to distressed companies like sharks are drawn to blood. The Regent Hotel & Casino was particularly hard hit. Bondholders of the casino were starting to form ad hoc committees consisting of the largest holders of the debt and would soon be conducting "beauty contests"—that is, interviewing legal counsel and financial advisors for a possible out-of-court restructuring and likely Chapter 11 bankruptcy case. It barely made any sense to Avery. Lee disappeared three months ago, and it was as though all of his companies fell off of a financial cliff. How could one man be so indispensable to his companies? Avery guessed it was really true, that companies needed to have succession plans for this type of thing and Lee's companies—as well run as they were—did not have any. Avery wondered how Judges Lupinaci and Murphy would feel if one of their most high profile and successful corporate restructuring cases ended up being a "Chapter 22" (lawyer-lexicon for a second Chapter 11 case; 11 times 2).

Avery imagined that the lawyers at the conference in Austin would be gossiping nonstop about the possibility of another Regent bankruptcy case and other possible Lee companies that might need to be run through the cleansing bath of bankruptcy. Lawyers in the corporate restructuring field can be like vultures, waiting to swoop onto the carcass of a dying company. A variation of "barbarians at the gate," as some have called it. They are in the misery business for sure. Ward sometimes grumpily called them "the lowest common denominator" in the lawyer food chain. Avery always chastised him that this was not entirely fair. Actually, the lawyers in the corporate restructuring field tended to be creative problem solvers who were great at cleaning up financial messes. They were the "fixers." They were often brilliant—having chosen an area of law practice that was far more complex than something like tort law or criminal law. One had to be both a financial wizard and legal wizard to be successful in the field. Still, Avery hated how the lawyers in this field loved to gossip about tragedy. The only thing that this group of lawyers loved to do more than gossip about corporate calamity was talk about how busy they were and how many billable hours they racked up in the preceding month. Toxic chest pounding. It was Avery's personal belief that lawyers tended to lie spectacularly to one another about how many hours they billed. Just like the cliché of the fisherman who lies about the size of the fish he catches daily.

Avery was jolted from her negative thoughts by violet Ginny. "Come on, Judge Lassiter. Time to hit the road if you want to get to Austin in time to go to Iron Works for a barbeque lunch. Remember you promised to meet some of your former externs there today."

"I'm coming."

Chapter 33:

The Short-Selling Brother.

The Marshal caravan transporting Avery and Ward Scott arrived in Austin at 12:30 p.m. It was good that they would miss the noon rush at the barbeque restaurant. Ward asked to be dropped off at the Four Seasons first—he wasn't in the mood for socializing with a bunch of "snot nosed millennials" and, besides, he had a conference call starting in a few minutes (a frequent excuse for him). Ward could be so harsh.

After dropping Ward off at the hotel, Avery and her Deputy Marshal escorts headed to the Iron Works. As they made their way through traffic, cyclists, and joggers, Avery's smartphone rang, and the Caller ID showed it was FBI Special Agent Navarrez. That was a surprise. He never called. Avery wished he would call with information, but he never did. Avery answered anxiously.

"Judge Lassiter, this is Special Agent Navarrez. How are you? I hear you are in Austin today for a legal conference?"

"Yes, what's up? I was just heading over to a barbeque restaurant to have lunch with some of my former externs and interns."

"Is Matt Smith going to be there?"

"I don't know for sure. He was invited, but he said he might not be able to attend. Why do you ask?"

"We have turned up something potentially significant about his twin brother. Did you know Matt has a twin brother?"

"A twin? I knew Matt had a brother. He's mentioned him. He's a financial type—works for a Boston-based hedge fund, I think. But he never said that he was a twin."

"A financial type? Uh, no. Where'd you get that idea? His twin brother was, until recently, a janitor at the federal court house in Camden, New Jersey."

"What? Are you sure you have all this right? Matt told me his brother went to Princeton, same as Matt, and was a portfolio manager—a real Wall Street wizard. I think he said he worked for Toro Capital—a very prestigious hedge fund. I think he said his name is Marcus."

"Yes, his name is Marcus. Why do you think Matt would lie about Marcus's job?"

"I don't know. That's crazy. I'm just at a loss. I hope he is not ashamed of his brother or something like that. Is this the information that you called 'significant'? I mean, I am certainly troubled that Matt would be dishonest regarding his brother. I have to process that one. He is such a good kid. It's shocking to me he would lie to me like that—or think he needed to be ashamed about that. But how is that 'significant' to your investigation?"

"Well the fact that he is a janitor and that Matt lied about it is not the significant part. The significant part is that we have discovered that Marcus *short sold* a bunch of stock in various Karl Lee companies early last August—shortly before Karl Lee went missing. Do you know what a short sale of stock is?"

"Are you asking me if I know what a short sale is? Really? Kid, what is it that you think that I do for a living?"

Avery immediately felt bad for calling Special Agent Navarrez a kid. But for this millennial FBI Agent to really wonder if a federal bankruptcy judge who formerly practiced at Big Law in the corporate restructuring arena knew what a short sale was seemed rather demeaning.

"Agent Navarrez, I am sorry. But, yes, I know what a short sale is. It's a rather risky investment strategy in which one tries to make money by betting that a company's stock will drop precipitously in value. There are different ways one can do it actually. How did Marcus supposedly do it and when exactly?"

"Well, Karl Lee went missing the third week of August. On August 6, Marcus Smith went online and filled out forms to borrow $40,000 from his 401K account. Then he took some of the money and went to a broker and used it as collateral (for a margin requirement) and borrowed 1,000 shares of the ultimate parent company of The Regent Hotel & Casino. The stock was at that time trading at $80 per share—so he "borrowed" stock worth $80,000. The transaction was set up where he was required to actually purchase the "borrowed" 1,000 shares of stock from the broker in 90 days, and the purchase price for the stock would be whatever the market value was for the stock at that 90-day point in time. So, then Marcus, of course, sells the borrowed stock, and makes $80,000 on that sale. And then two weeks later, Karl Lee goes missing. Within a few weeks later, when Lee is believed to have been kidnapped and likely murdered, his corporate empire falls into shambles. The Regent stock price takes a nose dive, eventually dropping to $10 per share. Marcus Smith then goes in and closes out on his short sale, when the price of the Regent's parent company's stock is trading at $10 per share. So he only had to pay the broker $10,000 at that point to close out the purchase of the earlier-borrowed stock. He made a quick, tidy $70,000 profit. And he, of course, gets back the entire margin requirement that he had to put up from the money from his 401K, since he didn't end up losing any money on the transaction. Now, how do you think a 28-year-old janitor from Camden, New Jersey has the great instincts to do a short sell of Regent stock in early August, two weeks before its patriarch goes missing and the stock plummets? Hell, maybe Matt was right. Maybe Marcus is a wizard of Wall Street. We are also looking into some other short sales that happened in connection with Karl Lee's pharmaceutical company. There could even be more here that Marcus did that we are going to stumble upon. We found some postings he made on a website called Seeking Alpha which short sellers frequently log into for investment tips. Marcus was trashing The Regent—saying negative things about the casino and how Lee's empire wouldn't survive without Lee in the picture. It was an outright assault against the Lee empire, to be honest. The stock seemed to dip a little more with each of his postings.

"This is crazy. Do you know if Marcus is a day trader or something like that? I mean, does he do this kind of stuff often? And do you have any reason to think Matt knows or even participated in it all?"

"We are looking into all of that. We think the answer is 'no' to all of those questions, but we want you to watch out for Matt if you see him today."

Avery was dumbfounded. "Watch out" for him? What exactly did that mean? She didn't know how she was going to greet Matt if he showed up at the lunch.

Luckily Matt did not show up at lunch. Avery tried to enjoy her visit with some of her favorite old interns and externs. After lunch, she headed to the Four Seasons and spent the rest of the day in her hotel room, preparing for her and Ward's presentation the next morning. She felt like room service would be fine for dinner. She had a nice room with a terrace overlooking Lady Bird Lake and the Congress Avenue Bridge. She was looking forward to sundown, when she could see Austin's famous bat colony flying out from under the bridge.

Chapter 34:

Streaker at Nine O'Clock.

Avery woke up early the next morning and texted Ward asking him what time he would like to meet downstairs for last minute preparations for their presentation. They decided to meet at 9:00 a.m. Their presentation was scheduled for 9:45 a.m. Avery thought about jogging on the trails around Lady Bird Lake before she showered. It was a typically beautiful, sunny Austin day. The Longhorn rowing team was down on the lake, as were a few fishermen. Joggers were everywhere. Avery felt like taking the jogging path up to Congress Avenue and then heading North toward the Capitol Building and maybe getting some coffee and breakfast tacos near the University of Texas campus. She talked herself out of it. The Deputy Marshals wouldn't like it at all, and she didn't want to get them out of sorts with her. They were already annoyed enough as it was, with her public speaking engagement.

When Avery went downstairs and arrived in the foyer outside the ballroom where the conference was being held, she saw her former University of Texas law professor, Professor Ross Milken, who was the chairperson of the conference. They exchanged greetings and he introduced her to a few of his students who had come over to attend some of the conference sessions. She asked Professor Milken if he knew if Matt Smith would be coming over this morning. Professor Milken had been one of Matt Smith's references when Matt had first applied for the internship for Avery. Professor Milken said he wasn't sure—that he actually had not seen Matt in quite a long while. Just as

Professor Milken was starting to tell Avery something else, Matt Smith came walking around the corner with a large smile on his face. He came up to Avery and Professor Milken. "Good morning, Judge Lassiter. I brought you your favorite Starbucks drink!"

Avery smiled back cautiously. "How thoughtful of you, Matt. It is wonderful to see you today. I wondered if you'd make it over." Avery awkwardly hugged Matt. As she did, she saw Professor Milken looking cautiously at Matt, then at Avery. Avery also noticed her Deputy Marshal guardians across the foyer uncomfortably scrutinizing her every move. "Are you going to listen to my presentation today, Matt?"

"Yes. I am looking forward to it. Judge Lassiter, could you introduce me to Mr. Scott? I have heard you mention him like 42 times, but I never was so lucky to meet him. He's a bit of a legend in the legal world. I'd be honored to meet him."

"Sure. Professor Milken, if you could excuse me for a moment, I am going to go grab Ward. I see him at the coffee bar over there."

Avery and Matt walked over to speak to Ward. The foyer was crowded with lawyers and financial advisors by this point. There were four Deputy Marshals in the foyer, two standing at each end, occasionally speaking into their sleeves. Avery stopped along the way to say hello to various friends and colleagues. Matt asked Avery along the way if she still had all of her bodyguards.

"You mean the Deputy U.S. Marshals? Don't call them bodyguards. That's rude. Yes, they are still with me—as you probably observed. They try hard, but they don't blend that well at these events."

"Are they making any progress on their investigation at all? I feel like I gave them so much information to work with."

"First, as you will recall, it is mainly the FBI who does all the investigation, not the Marshals. Second, I am on a 'need to know basis' with them. They don't tell me much. And I cannot share what I know. Sorry. I know you care, and I know you did a lot to help when you were working as my intern. Really. Your help was absolutely invaluable, Matt."

Avery and Matt had by this point caught up to Ward at the coffee bar. "Ward, I'd like to introduce you to one of my former interns, Matt Smith. He just finished interning for me in August. He actually had an externship for school credit, and then stayed on as an intern for a few extra months last school year and summer. He is now finishing up his last year at UT Law."

"Nice to meet you." They shook hands and exchanged small talk a bit.

"Judge Lassiter, could you and Mr. Scott use any help today? I know how uncomfortable you get with operating Power Points and audio-visual equipment generally. Would you like me to operate your Power Point or hand out materials or anything like that?"

"Actually, that would be great, Matt." Avery reached in her Coach bag and pulled out a thumb drive and handed it to Matt. "Here is my Power Point. It is the file called 'Troubles in the Oil Patch.' Professor Milken or his assistant can direct you to the laptop and other equipment at the front of the room. I'm going to run into the ladies' room really quick. Ward, I'll meet you up at the presenters' table in five minutes."

Avery headed over to the ladies' room, stopping several times along the way to say hello to different colleagues. She was feeling guilty and torn about the suspicions that had been raised in her mind after talking with FBI Special Agent Navarrez yesterday. She acknowledged that the story about Matt's brother's short selling of The Regent's stock in early August was somewhat troubling. And she was extremely bothered that Matt would lie to her about his twin brother being a financial manager rather than a janitor. But maybe Matt was just insecure and thought that a blue-collar brother would be a stain on his image. Avery hated that, if this was the case. She was not that superficial, and she tended to believe that most people weren't. As Avery approached the ladies' room, Ginny Oliphante, the violet Deputy Marshal, rushed up to her and whispered in her ear. "Judge, do you know about the FBI's latest theory involving Matt Smith's twin brother?"

"Yes. I mean, I know the FBI recently discovered that Matt's brother—apparently a twin brother—short-sold some Regent stock in August and made a quick $70,000 profit. They implied, without saying, that this made them concerned—like maybe he knew Karl Lee was about to go missing and the stock would tank in value. But I am not clear that they have a working theory that he killed Karl Lee or Judges Lupinaci and Murphy or anything like that."

"Yeah, well, personally I sort of thought your New Jersey mafia theory made more sense. For all anyone knows, Marcus Smith might be a day trader who, being from New Jersey, knows that traffic slows down in the casino business as summer winds down to an end. I mean, I wonder if the FBI even checked to see if he had done this sort of thing before. Maybe he just got extremely lucky this time because of the unfortunate circumstances involving Karl Lee. Anyway, just be careful around Matt, OK. We are watching all your paths here, Judge.

And we are watching his as well. We will be out here in the foyer while you are speaking and a couple of us will be in the ball room as well."

"Ginny, this all seems pretty farfetched. But thanks."

Avery started into the ladies' room. Ginny said she would be right outside the ladies' room door.

"Are you sure you don't want to come in with me and check under the bathroom stalls?" Avery grinned and snickered. "Oh, I'm sorry. Thanks, Ginny from the Block, for all you do."

Avery lingered a bit in the ladies' room. She actually was feeling a little nauseous and dizzy. It wasn't like her to get nervous or anxious before a speech. Maybe it was the residual effect of too much barbeque and beer yesterday at lunch with her former externs and interns. As Avery straightened up her hair a bit and refreshed her lipstick, she suddenly heard a loud commotion in the foyer outside. She heard men shouting and people screaming and even some odd laughter. She might have been scared, but the commotion did not sound like people screaming in terror. Again, there was shouting, then screams mixed with laughter. Avery texted both Ginny and Montana Tom and asked what was going on out in the foyer. She didn't get an answer. She then texted Ward. Again, no answer. After a few moments, a female lawyer walked into the ladies' room, shaking her head and smiling.

"What's going on out there?" Avery asked.

"You missed it? Some naked man with dreadlocks ran through the foyer screaming something incomprehensible. It was quite a surreal scene. He was probably high on something. Some Austin weirdo, I suppose. The security guards were drawing guns and yelling for him to stop, then they tackled him. He is out there on the ground now in cuffs."

Avery bolted from the ladies' room. She saw Ginny from the Block and a hotel security guard holding down a naked man in the center of the foyer. He was white, had long brown dreadlocks, a long scruffy beard, and his torso was covered in tattoos.

Montana Tom rushed over to Avery. "Judge, we are assessing this, but we want you to go ahead and enter the ballroom and give your speech. We are ushering everyone into the ballroom and asking them not to come out here for the next half hour or so. The guy has no ID on him. This is probably just some weird Austin grad student or a homeless guy, hyped up on drugs. Probably sleeping on a bench or something outside by the lake and wandered up to the hotel property. You know, 'Keep Austin Weird' and all that nonsense. But it could be a ruse of some sort. Maybe he was sent in to be a distraction to the Deputy Marshals while someone more dangerous is here in our midst."

"Ok, well I thought streaking fell out of favor in the 1970's. You probably don't even understand that reference, Montana Tom. Anyway, I'll go give my geeky talk about trouble in the oil patch as you deal with this naked guy."

Suddenly Avery paused. "Montana Tom, that naked guy has brown dreadlocks. The stalker guy in Portugal had brown dreadlocks just like that. He was about that same age and size, too. He was wearing a long-sleeved sweat shirt in Portugal, so I don't know if he had those same tattoos."

Montana Tom looked concerned. "Judge, let me walk with you into the ballroom."

272

As Avery walked to the front of the ballroom, Montana Tom walked with her and announced to the room that he needed everyone to stay in the room for the next 30 minutes or so, while they dealt with the streaker out in the foyer. He apologized for the inconvenience. There would be a Deputy Marshal standing at the doors to ensure people would comply.

As Avery sat down, she winked at Ward. "I'm guessing this is a first. Have you ever had a naked tattooed guy run out and scream at your audience right before your presentation?"

"Can't say that I have. You were in the ladies' room, so you missed the real fun. He was quite a looker. You would have been impressed."

"Uh, I saw him cuffed down on the floor. That was enough for me, thank you. Poor Deputy Ginny from the Block. She was holding him down. She looked pretty disgusted."

Avery was feeling a wave of dizziness again. "Oh great."

"What's wrong?"

"Nothing. I'm just feeling a little dizzy and nauseous this morning. Probably the barbeque and beer yesterday. I'll be fine. Matt, are you ready on the Power Point?"

"Yes, ma'am. Ready when you and Mr. Scott are."

Chapter 35:

Part Three of the Trilogy in Five Parts.

Avery started off her and Ward's oil and gas law presentation by making some ice breaker jokes about the naked guy. "We will resort to anything to try to spice up a presentation about distress in the oil and gas industry. Pay attention. Wait until you see how we top that."

Avery launched into the presentation. Her dizziness had increased. Now her head was suddenly pounding. Her vision was blurred. Ward could see that she was not feeling well. He stepped in and started taking the lead more and more, to try to help Avery through it.

Avery looked up at the Power Point presentation to help her focus and get back on track. But when she looked up on the screen, she realized that something more was going on than just her nausea and dizziness. Avery now saw what appeared to be blood on the big screen. It was as though every slide had some special effect, giving the illusion of blood oozing from the top down. Was she hallucinating? Avery did not know what was happening and why her mind would be playing tricks on her this way. With each succeeding slide, the effects became more pronounced. There was the illusion of tangled tree branches behind the words on the Power Point presentation with blood dripping from them. Then the illusion of crucifixes dripping with blood. Ward started looking at Avery strangely and whispered, "What the hell, Avery? What's this weird shit on the Power Point about? Even your sense of humor is not this warped!"

People in the audience were now starting to squirm and look very uncomfortable. Avery had joked at the beginning of the presentation that they would do anything to make an oil and gas law presentation interesting—referring to the naked man with dreadlocks and implying there might be more fun gimmicks to come. Was this what she meant? If it was, it was not going over well at all.

Suddenly Avery looked over at Matt who was in control of the Power Point. He had a bewildering smirk on his face. She looked at her Starbucks coffee cup that was now almost empty. She had a horrible feeling. Had Matt perhaps drugged her coffee? Were the images up on the screen real or was she imagining all of this? Her dizziness and head throbbing were now almost unbearable. It was as though something sharp was slicing through her head. She now saw Matt standing up and taking his jacket off. As Avery started to wobble in her chair, finally slipping down onto the floor, she saw that Matt appeared to have what looked like a suicide belt tied around his waist. The belt had several bulky cylinders with ball bearings, nails, screws, bolts, and other objects that would serve as shrapnel. Matt was holding in his hand an activation device attached by a wire to the belt with a fail-deadly "dead man's switch" that Matt was holding down. If he released the switch, the bomb would be activated.

As Avery was groggily trying to process all of this, she saw Ginny from the Block at the back door of the room talking into her sleeve frantically and pulling her gun out of her holster. Ginny was processing everything herself. She realized that Matt was holding a "dead man switch." She could not take a headshot, because if she did, Matt's hand would be released from the switch and the bomb would detonate. As the confused crowd started squirming and rumbling, Matt began screaming toward Avery and Ward. "Part three of the trilogy in five parts is about to begin. Wake up, Judge Lassiter. You have to see this. This is all for you!"

Avery was trying the pull herself up off the floor, but her legs were like jello and her head was spinning. She was weak and disoriented and breathing heavily. The audience sat in their seats frozen and stunned. What was happening? This wasn't just some sort of unconventional presentation.

Ward Scott suddenly dropped to the floor to assist Avery. She was breathing erratically. Her pulse was elevated. She was slipping in and out of consciousness, it seemed. "Someone call 911! Everybody run! Get out of here!" Ward shouted.

"But, remember, the Marshal told us not to leave the room!" Matt Smith yelled out in response to Ward. As he shouted this, Matt Smith yanked into his back pack and pulled out what appeared to be 6-liter pressure cooker and some sort of circuit board. Ward Scott—a former Air Force officer, long before he was a lawyer, and a regular consumer of military magazines—recognized that the pressure cooker was jerry-rigged to be an improvised explosive device. A crude bomb. Matt was double armed. He had a backup plan if the suicide belt did not work,

Matt Smith screamed, "Judge Lassiter and Mr. Scott. You are the last part of the trilogy in five parts. Part one, Judges Murphy and Lupinaci. Part two, Karl Lee. Now part three, the two of you. Five deaths in three parts. You were all part of the problem. And, it all started with you and Mr. Scott, Judge Lassiter. It all started with you back in Camden. You ruined my life and my family's lives back in Camden. You have to die now. The day of reckoning is finally here.

And all of you people—you pathetic people who play your greedy legal games and destroy peoples' lives—you will die, too. Casualties of war. Casualties of *my* war against the corrupt legal system. I win. You lose. Game over."

As the confused audience of almost 300 people watched in horror, frozen in their seats, not knowing what to do, Matt Smith ran to the middle of the ballroom. Ginny from the Block began screaming at people to get out of the ballroom. Ginny began trying to engage Matt in a dialogue, telling him it was all over, and to come with her. Matt just laughed. He wouldn't budge. After a few seconds, Matt looked over at Avery and Ward and started walking back toward them.

Ginny realized that she was going to have no choice but to take a headshot. She did so with military precision, striking Matt right between the eyes with her Glock. As Matt fell to the ground, his belt detonated. Shards of metal, nails, and ball bearings exploded into the middle of the ballroom. Matt's body was obliterated and his head, from the wave of the explosion, was separated and blown clear of his body. A strange acidic smell also pervaded the room. There were bleeding people everywhere. It was Matt Smith's own carnival of blood. Some people were lying motionless and others were still running for the doors. People were crying out for help and others were assisting people in need. Montana Tom and two other Deputies and several Austin Police Department Officers suddenly burst into the room. They quickly rushed up to Avery and Ward Scott. They were covered in blood and unconscious. It did not look good.

"The Judge is down. Get the EMT, stat! The Judge is down!"

Avery could faintly hear Ginny from the Block screaming. She was not sure what had just happened.

Chapter 36:

Aftermath.

Avery woke up in a hospital bed. The sun was shining brightly into the windows. There were bouquets of flowers everywhere—especially bouquets of yellow roses and her favorite flower, rubrum lilies, making the room smell heavenly. There was a pile of envelopes on the bed stand next to her and balloons—some that read "Get Well" and others that read "Happy Birthday."

Avery could see the pinkish brown granite of the Texas Capitol Building in the distance, with the Goddess of Liberty statue on top of the rotunda gleaming radiantly, so she realized that she was still in Austin. She looked down and realized that she had gauze and bandages on her arms and legs. Suddenly she felt burning sensations in numerous places all over her body. She looked up and saw that Officer Max and Julia were in the room.

"She's awake, Dad!" Julia yelled as she ran to her mother's bedside. Avery realized at that point that Baxter was also there, in his travel kennel across the room. Yes, the hospital personnel agreed to let Avery's favorite furry creature into the hospital room. The nurses all thought that "cute little Baxter," as the nurses called him, would be the perfect medicine for all of Avery's burns and lacerations.

"Hey, Avery. How do you feel? It's your birthday, November 19." Officer Max whispered approaching her bedside and gently picking up her hand.

Avery looked at him, unable to think clearly. "November 19? Already? I am in the hospital? In Austin?"

"Yeah. Do you remember what happened?"

Avery was quiet for a few moments. "Yeah. I remember. I mean, sort of. I passed out during my and Ward's presentation at The Four Seasons. Matt—my former intern from last school year, I don't know if you ever met him—was saying all kinds of weird and horrible stuff. Talking about the trilogy in five parts, like in the letters. He was saying that we all had to die. He had this contraption of cylinders around his body and a wire detonator of some sort. Then Ginny shot him. Then there was a loud blast and screams and I felt sharp things searing into my body. It was a bomb, wasn't it? How long have I been here?"

"Five days. That was November 14. But they have had you sedated—actually, you have been in a medically induced coma. They just decided to let you wake up today. And yes, it was a bomb. It was a crudely put together suicide vest that Matt had. An improvised explosive device with nails, ball bearings, BBs, and metal and glass shards. He also had a pressure cooker bomb with him that was something like the Boston bombers and lots of other terrorists have used. Matt probably read how to put one together on the internet. I don't think they are teaching that sort of thing in law school these days. Ginny shot him before he set off the pressure cooker bomb, but the suicide vest still went off. There was no way she could have stopped that."

"How's Ward? Is he okay? And what about Professor Milken?"

"Professor Milken made it through unscathed. He was standing in the very back of the ballroom when it happened. Ward is in pretty bad shape. But he should make it. He's former military, for God's sake. He's probably been through worse. He's down the hall. Caroline is here, of course. Ward's burns and lacerations were significantly worse than yours. He had about 20 pellets of metal taken out of him. You only had about six. Ward was a hero for sure. He covered your body as soon as he realized what was happening. The irony is that Matt Smith apparently foiled his own plot to kill you two, by moving toward the middle of the ballroom for dramatic effect, or whatever. The explosion of materials was farther away from you and Ward than if he had just stayed at the front of the room. I guess he wanted to take down not just you and Ward but more people in the room. So much for Matt and Marcus Smith's 'trilogy in five parts.' It didn't work. Both you and Ward are going to make it. Matt, of course, didn't make it. He was blown to smithereens. So were some other people. But honestly, it could have been so much worse. The people at the Four Seasons—their security personnel, the Austin Police, the Marshals—they were all fabulous. They were just amazing. They saved so many people. We really owe them a debt of gratitude like you would not believe."

"Oh my God. This is unbearable, Max. Were people at the conference killed? How many people were hurt? Tell me, Max."

"You don't want to know, Avery. I'll tell you in a few days. Let's just say this was worse than their McDonald's fertilizer bomb, as far as level of destruction. You need to rest."

"Max, is this over? You said 'so much for Matt and Marcus Smith's trilogy in five parts'? And 'their McDonald's fertilizer bomb'? Have the FBI and Marshals pieced this all together for certain? Were the twins working together? They killed Judges Murphy and Lupinaci? Karl Lee? They were behind my death threats, too? Why? Why did they do it? Please tell me?"

"Avery, you need to rest. I'm sure your favorite millennial FBI Agents will come in and share all the details with you in the next couple of days. But the doctors want to watch your vital signs for a few hours after bringing you out of the coma. Just decompress awhile—as you love to say."

Avery's ears were ringing a bit. Perhaps a little residual tinnitus. "Did Matt try to poison me with the Starbucks coffee? Or did he just drug me, so I couldn't be alert when he was executing his plan? Am I fighting two things right now, Max? Poisoning and injuries from the bomb, too?"

"It wasn't poison. Just a drug to make you groggy enough not to function but to still sort of know what was happening. He probably knew that you were packing heat in your purse and that you might just whip out your little 38 revolver and kill his ass if you were alert enough to realize what was happening."

"Good God. I can't believe this. Why did Matt do this? What on earth made him and his brother do this? Matt was a wonderful, sweet intern!"

"Rest, Avery. Rest."

"OK. I'll try. Will you turn on the TV, so I can take my mind off of all of this, like you have instructed me to."

"Can't do that. This is all over the news, not surprisingly."

Avery looked over at Baxter in the kennel. She looked back and forth at Julia and Max. She began sobbing uncontrollably.

Chapter 37:

The Explanation—Every Saint has a Past and Every Sinner Has a Future.[7]

On November 20, FBI Special Agents Handley and Navarrez came to visit Avery in the hospital. Baxter was there, roaming the room by now. They gave him a treat. As a precautionary measure, one of the Deputy Marshals on the canine team was stationed outside of Avery's hospital door with Polly, a white lab, who was an expert in sniffing out explosives. Apparently, the FBI Agents had gotten one of Polly's treats from her handler and decided to give it to Baxter. Very sweet of them, Avery thought. Maybe she had been too harsh in her judgments of these young FBI Agents for all these months.

The FBI Agents were there to give Avery a report on what their investigation had revealed. It seems that Matt and Marcus Smith's real names were Matt and Marcus Braden. Their father had been the New Jersey man who, back in the late 1990's, while driving a 1958 Ford Prefect late one Sunday night, had been struck and killed by an intoxicated teenaged girl. Their mother, for herself and as the Braden boys' next friend, had sued The Regent Hotel & Casino for $42 million. The trial team of Avery Lassiter and Ward Scott had vigorously and successfully defended The Regent in that lawsuit. The Regent won a "take nothing" verdict. Judge Lupinaci had handled pretrial matters. Judge Murphy presided over the jury trial and

---

[7] Oscar Wilde, *A Woman of No Importance* (1894).

rendered the judgment on the jury's verdict. Karl Lee, the new owner of The Regent by the time of the jury trial, had reaped the benefits of that hard-fought court victory and praised his trial team—Avery and Ward. Mrs. Braden never appealed. She, instead, took a bottle of pills with Vodka and killed herself a few weeks later.

The Braden boys had thereafter been bounced around from their grandfather's care, and then to orphanages and foster care for years thereafter, after the grandfather died of Mesothelioma. The boys spent years at Our Lady of Perpetual Help, learning the moral and religious teachings of the Catholic Church under the pastoral care of the now-vanished Father Ignatius—who, unfortunately, betrayed the Holy Church and all of humanity—by molesting innocent children (likely, including the Braden children). The youngest of the Braden boys had died of Staph infection while being shuffled between the orphanage and foster care. The twins had been separated and adopted by different families eventually. Their names were changed to that of their adoptive parents. But then at some point, as young adults, the twins re-connected and both decided to go by the name of "Smith"— their mother's maiden name.

"We are double checking our research, but we think the boys may have been plaintiffs in the litigation against the Catholic Diocese in New Jersey that went bankrupt under the weight of all of the abuse claims—there were so many claimants, and not much insurance, such that each victim did not recover much in the bankruptcy case. And guess which judges presided over those cases?

"Judges Lupinaci and Murphy?"

"You got it. Maybe these boys had all kinds of reasons to be mad at the legal system."

"Geez."

"And that's not even everything. The boys' grandfather who died of Mesothelioma had filed a lawsuit against the company Johns Manville—a manufacturer of asbestos-containing products—back in the early 1980's, claiming he had acquired his disease after working many years as a boiler maker, repairing and building boilermakers in numerous plants, where he was exposed to pipe insulation manufactured by Johns Manville, containing asbestos. When Johns Manville filed bankruptcy in 1982, the grandfather somehow missed a deadline to file a claim and spent years after the fact, trying to get a share of the Manville Personal Injury Settlement Trust that was eventually set up, but he for some reason was not successful getting any settlement. He died practically penniless."

"Good God. This is unbelievable. So they and their mother lose in court when they sue The Regent for Dram Shop liability after their father was killed in his car wreck. Then they go to live with their grandfather, who dies penniless from Mesothelioma shortly thereafter—after unsuccessfully trying to recover some damages from the Johns Manville Trust. Then the boys go into an orphanage and get abused by a Catholic Priest, and the Diocese files bankruptcy in response to the victims' abuse claims. I assume they didn't get much of a recovery in that matter either."

"Yep, that's pretty much a summary of their lives up to adulthood."

Apparently, Marcus Braden had been a troublemaker for his entire life. Special Agent Navarrez explained, "He was slow intellectually, is believed to have never finished high school, and had lots of bad influences along the way. He also suffered from multiple forms of mental illness. He spent a few months in prison in his early twenties for forgery and identity theft. He seemed to straighten up and, a few years ago, got the job working for the janitor service that had the contract to clean the Camden Federal Courthouse. But he stopped showing up at work around the same time that Judges Lupinaci and Murphy disappeared and never came back. The FBI's investigation of flight manifests found that Marcus flew from JFK Airport to Madrid, Spain, during June, then managed to take a train into Portugal, over to the Algarve Coast. He must have been the one that left the spray paint message and mannequin at Sagres. Apparently, he got the details about your trip and the locations that you would be staying while there from his brother. We think he might have been planning something worse while there but lost his nerve or couldn't pull it off or something. I don't know if you remember, but you called into the office the day before you went on your walking tour to Sagres and spoke to Annalise and Matt about a research project and also about your plans to go to Sagres the next day—Annalise later confirmed that to us—and we assume that Matt relayed the information to his brother."

"Anyway, we are hopefully going to be able to put together a good case against Marcus based on both the circumstantial evidence and as a result of warrants we have gotten that allow us to retrieve data from both the brothers' cell phones and their computers. We have agents executing a search warrant at Matt's house right now, here in Austin."

"Where did Matt live?"

"On Pluto Street in East Austin. Not a very nice place for a UT law student. Small wooden rat trap of a house."

"You are shitting me!"

"Huh?"

"Remember the second letter that I was sent? Remember what the letter writer wrote: the universe is in the safe hands of a simple man living on a remote planet in a wooden shack with his cat.' Get it? Matt lived on *Pluto*. In a wooden ratty shack. And, Matt had a cat— Ghost. He used to bring Ghost to chambers sometimes!"

"God, what a weirdo. Anyway, we have agents searching the place now."

"And what about Marcus? Are Ward and I still in danger? Is that why Marshals and canines are here at the hospital outside the door?"

"You're not going to believe this, but Marcus was the naked runner at The Four Seasons. Apparently, his naked streaking was a ploy to distract the Marshals. The Marshals and hotel security were busy dealing with the naked guy, while Matt was doing his deadly business in the ballroom."

"Oh my God! I told Montana Tom, right before going into the ballroom that day, that the streaker sort of looked like the guy we saw in Portugal. They both had brown dreadlocks."

"Yep. It just all happened so fast. And he looked like any number of strange characters hanging out in any given place in Austin, Texas on any particular day."

"So, your working theory is that Matt and Marcus planned this whole thing together. God, it is so hard to believe that a kid like Matt would be capable of this. He went to Princeton and graduated with Honors. He was at University of Texas Law School and made the Law Review. He had his whole future in front of him. He was, frankly, one of the best interns I ever had. And he seemed so caring and kind. My instincts have never been so wrong about someone. Maybe Millicent was the only one who got accurate vibes from Matt. But she just thought he was a self-promoting brown noser."

"Well, who knows about Matt. Maybe he had mental illness like his brother. Matt was, apparently, highly intelligent, unlike the case with his brother, but they were identical twins—so perhaps he suffered from some of the same mental demons. We have snooped around a little and found out that the State Bar of Texas was slow-walking Matt's application to be admitted into the Bar, even before he had taken the Bar Exam. Apparently, the fact that there is this large gap of unaccounted for time, between 2002 and when Matt started Princeton, has been presenting a problem. Matt was 28 years old, and he actually started Princeton at age 22, not the usual 18-year-old right out of high school. Similar to how the FBI had problems tracking down any records for the Braden Brothers (a.k.a. the Smith brothers) once they began bouncing around between orphanages and foster homes, apparently the State Bar of Texas was running into the same problems in doing their background investigation, and Matt was not being very forthcoming with them about the details of his life. The State Bar could not even get Matt to disclose where he graduated from high school or produce a diploma or GRE certificate. Maybe he would have eventually given them the information, but he wouldn't for some reason."

Special Agent Navarrez continued, "Frankly, we are still wondering what else Matt may have been hiding. Anyway, maybe part of the reason that Matt decided to do something atypical and intern for you for almost a full year was because he was in no rush to graduate—because of the problems he was having with the State Bar. We don't even know if he and his brother concocted their elaborate deadly plans before or after Matt went to work for you. In other words, did he seek out the internship with you to be in a position to kill you? Or did he somehow realize after going to work for you that you had been the lawyer who deprived him and his mother and brothers of the $42 million judgment that they wanted against The Regent way back when he was a child? Frankly, as strangely coincidental as it seems, I tend to think that Matt only realized *after* he began working for you that you had been The Regent's lawyer back in New Jersey way-back-when, and it just sort of set him off—at the same time as he was agitated because he was encountering problems with the State Bar of Texas. Maybe Matt was starting to see the writing on the wall—that the State Bar of Texas was going to find something troubling in his past that was going to keep him from being a lawyer, and that spun him into some sort of psychotic episode that made him want to lash out and kill you and everyone he blamed for his troubled life."

"Why did Matt do it the way he did? He could have just killed me in chambers quickly and easily—without bringing so many other people into this? He had close access to me frequently!"

"Well, for one thing, as you know it's not that easy to get a weapon into the courthouse—even for an intern. Second, it's pretty well known that you carry. Matt had to know that you always have a weapon on your person, even when you are on the bench. So you were not the easiest target for him. It probably excited him that you presented a challenge to kill. Third, Matt probably got some kind of perverted pleasure from dragging this out and watching you be fearful and vulnerable while dealing with the death threats for all those months. He probably felt like he was in control of your emotions. We have concluded that he was even sending the Marshals and FBI on some wild goose chases frequently, by sending us false leads about litigants from your court who might have been mad enough to want to kill you. He is one of the reasons that this all took so long to figure out—because he bombarded us with names of litigants that allegedly should be considered suspects. Finally, more important than any of that, Matt wanted to do things in a blaze of glory. Maximum attention and maximum carnage. And his anger at the legal system was widespread—not just anger towards you."

"Sounds like the guys and gals at Quantico have Matt all figured out. Who actually killed Judges Lupinaci and Murphy? I assume Marcus, since he was the one up there in New Jersey?"

"We assume it had to be. As you know, Matt was here in Texas the whole time. But this is going to be hell to prove. There was no forensic evidence for the Lupinaci and Murphy murders. Just charred bodies with no DNA or other clues to even know the exact cause of their deaths. No videos from their house cameras or the court house. No witnesses to anything. Just email and text discussions on the two brothers' phones and computers that is arguably vague—if the right defense lawyer gets it. Karl Lee's body has never been found. So what we know happened and what the U.S. Attorney can prove happened are two very different things potentially. In theory, Marcus Braden, a.k.a. Smith should be charged at least with three counts of murder for the two judges and Karl Lee; two counts of conspiracy to commit murder as to you and Ward Scott; conspiracy to commit terroristic acts; maybe felony murders for all of the other people who died in the McDonald's and Four Seasons incidents; and of course, disorderly conduct for streaking through the Four Seasons hotel naked.

"Where is Marcus now?"

"He was sitting in an Austin jail for 72 hours, but there was only enough evidence at this point to charge him with disorderly conduct. At his initial appearance before a local judge here, a court appointed public defender made the argument that Marcus Smith was just here in town from New Jersey visiting his brother, and he had caught a ride with Matt to the hotel where he was allegedly going to just walk around downtown Austin a bit waiting on his brother. The attorney also represented that Marcus was high on bath salts that day (a drug which makes you feel hot). Marcus allegedly decided to walk back over to the hotel and find his brother, and once inside, he eventually stripped down and ran naked, simply trying to cool off from the effects of the bath salts. Marcus was about to be released from jail—as there was nothing concrete to hold him on any further—but then the district attorney convinced the judge to let the Austin Police Department take him to a mental health hospital for a psychiatric evaluation. He is sitting in a psych hospital right now, as we speak—a place called Green Acres. But, unless the prosecutors come up with something soon, he may be back out on the street any minute."

"Good God. I can't believe that would happen."

"We got pictures of Marcus's hands while he was in custody at the Austin jail and we are going to compare them to your smart phone photos that you took of the guy in Portugal. Remember, you actually got some pretty decent pictures there that we were able to retrieve and blow up, zeroing in on the hands. And we have some cigarette butts from Portugal that we will DNA-test against Marcus's DNA. We, of course, also have proof of Marcus short selling the Karl Lee companies' stock at a suspicious time—but of course we have the old *corpus delicti* problem with Karl Lee that may present an obstacle."

"So, basically, if the hand pictures and DNA all matches up to Marcus, he will be charged with stalking a federal judge and maybe nothing else? That gets him a ten-year sentence in a federal prison. Great."

"We are going to piece this together, Judge. Don't you worry. The U.S. Attorney will have a case to present to the federal grand jury before this is all over. I promise you that."

Avery paused for a few moments. Now tell me, Agent Navarrez. How many people were hurt or killed in the blast in the ballroom?"

"42 hurt. 28 killed."

"You cannot be serious."

Chapter 38:

5808 Pluto Street.

At 5808 Pluto Street in East Austin, Texas, FBI Agents were swarming the property, looking in every corner and cranny for clues to make their case against Marcus Braden, a.k.a. Marcus Smith—hopefully before he was released from the psychiatric hospital to which he had been sent for evaluation. It had been a slow process. The house could have been booby trapped, so they first had to make a thorough check of the property with dogs and the bomb squad personnel, before launching into their full-scale search. Now that the search for clues was underway, it was looking promising.

There were signs that Marcus had apparently been living at the house with Matt for at least a few weeks. The dilapidated abode was furnished quite nicely, despite its deteriorated outside appearance and humble neighborhood surroundings. There was a 60-inch TV screen and other fancy electronic gadgets and appliances. A Green Egg Grill was on the porch. A Colnago road bike was in the garage. Lots of booze. Perhaps these were all purchased with the proceeds of Marcus's miraculously successful short selling of Regent stock right before Karl Lee went missing and the stock tanked in value.

The house was a two-bedroom structure. In one of the back bedrooms, the FBI Agents hit the jackpot. On the wall of the bedroom was a startling sight. A huge canvas had been erected on the wall—approximately eight by ten feet—that was a reproduction of Michelangelo's *Il Giudozio Universale* (*The Last Judgement*)—the fresco that famously covers the altar wall of the Sistine Chapel at the Vatican. The fresco is, of course, a depiction of the second coming of Christ and the final judgment by God of all humanity. In the famous fresco, the souls of humans can be seen rising and descending to their fates (Heaven or Hell), as judged by Christ, in the center, who is surrounded by various saints. But in this version of *The Last Judgement*, on the Braden a.k.a. Smith brothers' wall, someone had essentially both marked over and "photo shopped" the canvas with their own unique modifications. First, in the section of the fresco below Christ, where the dead are being awakened by angels' trumpets and the Archangel Michael is reading from the book of souls to be saved, and there is a larger book to his right, listing the names of the damned souls destined for Hell, someone had written onto the book of damned souls the names Avery Lassiter, Ward Scott, Karl Lee, Helen Lupinaci, and Ronald Murphy. And immediately to the right of this scene, where the famous "Damned Man" is portrayed in the fresco, who is portrayed covering his left eye in fear of his fate, with demons and devils from the underworld grasping and biting at his body, the face of Karl Lee was photo shopped onto the "Damned Man's" face. Then in the lower part of the fresco, on the bottom right, where Michelangelo's famous fresco shows many damned souls being ferried into Hell by "Charon the Boatman," the face of Matt Smith was photo shopped onto the face of "Charon the Boatman" and the faces of Ward Scott and Judges Lassiter, Lupinaci, and Murphy were photo shopped onto the faces of some of the damned souls on the boat. Finally, the character Minos—the character from Greek mythology that was the son of Zeus and Europa who became one of the three judges of the underworld—had been altered. This is the figure that is depicted near the very bottom right of the fresco with ass ears and is grotesquely wrapped in a serpent that is biting at Minos's genitals. This Minos figure had the photo shopped face of Father Ignatius, the Catholic priest pedophile from the Braden boys' parish in New Jersey, placed over the face of Minos.

But there was more. In a desk drawer in this same back bedroom were pictures and newspaper clippings that mapped out the "trilogy in five parts" in spectacular fashion. There were old newspaper articles about the Braden father's car crash and death, the subsequent unsuccessful Dram Shop lawsuit against The Regent, and the obituary for the boys' mother. There were newspaper articles about Father Ignatius and Our Lady of Perpetual Hope, and the Catholic Diocese bankruptcy in New Jersey. There were all kinds of articles about the dozens of Catholic Diocese bankruptcy cases around the country and claims of sexual abuse of victims going unaddressed. There were newspaper articles about the Johns Manville bankruptcy case and the asbestos settlement trust. There were pictures of Judges Lupinaci and Murphy with "DEAD" written in black Sharpie marker across their pictures. There were pictures of Karl Lee, in all of his various international endeavors throughout the years. And finally pictures of Avery and pictures of Ward Scott from the Texas Lawyer, Martindale Hubbell entries, and on the cover of certain legal journals.

FBI Special Agent Handley made a quick phone call to the U.S. Attorney to explain what they had found on Pluto Street. He hung up and turned to one of the Deputy Marshals on the scene. Get over to the Green Acres psychiatric hospital and pick up Marcus Smith before he is released. We have enough to hold him."

The FBI Agents high-fived for a few minutes. Then they finished the process of gathering up the evidence.

Chapter 39:

Green Acres.

At 2:00 p.m. on November 20, six members of the U.S. Marshals Western District of Texas fugitive task force pulled up in their G-rides at the Green Acres psychiatric hospital. Almost a dozen Austin Police Department cars were there as well, surrounding the perimeter of the property. Unbeknownst to them, 15 minutes earlier, Marcus Smith, a.k.a. Marcus Braden had just finished up his discharge paperwork. He had been determined "not to be a threat to himself or others"—the magic words requiring release. He was deemed to have served his time for disorderly conduct for the naked streaking episode at The Four Seasons Hotel. He had been given by the nice folks at Green Acres some clean clothes and a few dollars for bus fair and a meal. He had been given an address and directions to a local Austin homeless shelter.

On his way out, Marcus Smith had asked the discharge receptionist if he could have a sheet a paper, so he could leave a note for anyone who might come by wanting to see him after he left. The receptionist cooperated, handing him a pen and paper. He wrote on the paper, "THIS AIN'T OVER" and folded the paper in half and handed it to her. "Thanks. Anyone who comes in looking for me— just give this to them." He walked out the door and slipped into a nearby wooded area.

The U.S. Marshals fugitive task force and police officers were all "greened up," as they like to say. Bullet proof vests, helmets, shields, and all the rest of their tactical raid gear. Some with rifles and some with hand guns. When the first two Deputy Marshals entered inside of Green Acres, they went to the receptionist and asked where they could find Marcus Smith.

The receptionist at the front desk replied, "He was just discharged, maybe 10 or 15 minutes ago. He asked me to give this note to anyone who might come in looking for him." She handed the Deputy Marshals the hand-written folded note which they quickly unfolded and read.

"Shit!!!!!!"

"Did I do something wrong?"

Chapter 40:

All-Points Bulletin: Oh Brother, Where Art Thou?

Over the next few days, an all-points bulletin was issued for Marcus Smith, a.k.a. Marcus Braden. His picture was plastered everywhere. He was near the top of the FBI and U.S. Marshals' "Most Wanted" lists.

Slow-witted Marcus Smith, remarkably, without the aid of his more intelligent twin brother, was apparently clever enough to anticipate all of this. Before the Deputy Marshals had even realized that he had slipped out of Green Acres, he had made his way to a nearby CVS Pharmacy, shoplifted scissors, a razor, and blond hair dye, then went to a nearby gas station bathroom and shaved, cut off his dreadlocks, and colored his remaining hair bright blond.

Law enforcement officials were camped out on Pluto Street, naturally assuming that Marcus might eventually make his way back there. And there was concern that he might try to reach Avery and Ward at the hospital. TV news stations were still broadcasting updates daily about the victims of the Four Seasons bomb attack, and the news reporters were typically standing in front of the downtown Austin hospital that was caring for Avery, Ward, and the other victims. So Marcus Smith could easily learn of Avery's and Ward's whereabouts and seek them out there.

But Marcus Smith was nowhere to be found it seemed. In fact, he was in plain sight. For days, Marcus Smith was encamped in plain sight under Austin's popular Congress Avenue bridge, blending with nature and the local homeless crowd. He paced there with a backpack on his back that he had buried on November 14 in the wooded grounds surrounding Lady Bird Lake, right before disrobing and running up naked into The Four Seasons conference room area. His court appointed public defender had presented a total fabrication to the local judge presiding over Marcus Smith's initial appearance hearing. Marcus Smith had not been high on bath salts, as his public defender had stated. He had not randomly entered into the Four Seasons hotel looking for his brother that morning of the suicide bomb. He had not disrobed to cool down from his high. He was, of course, part of the conspiracy to throw off the Deputy U.S. Marshals and distract them from protecting Avery and Ward from Matt's murderous plot.

Under the Congress Avenue bridge, Marcus occasionally pulled out a burner phone from his backpack and made phone calls and sent texts. He was transferring funds—all now anonymously and safely converted into Bitcoin and other cryptocurrency in offshore exchanges. All of the Feds thought Marcus Smith was dimwitted. But he was a Jesus of the Blockchain and a short selling genius. The Feds figure he was probably a hacker too—probably carried out the hack of the Regent's keycard system a while back and collected the ransom extorted from that fiasco. The homeless crowd looked at Marcus strangely, occasionally asking what was in his backpack and what he was doing there. He had a few marijuana joints in his back pack that he would hand out periodically, that would keep the homeless crowd out of his business. He also had a Beretta handgun that he would flash if anyone got too close.

Meanwhile, back on Pluto Street, a young FBI Agent spent hours on a desk top computer back in the bedroom where the canvas and other evidence had been found. The Deputy U.S. Marshals that were encamped at the Pluto Street house would occasionally ask if the Agent was playing on the internet or finding useful information. He quietly focused on the screen without speaking. After a while, he turned around and said, "Wonder if Karl Lee is really dead? His pictures in the drawer did not have "DEAD" written across them like Judges Lupinaci's and Murphy's. No DNA was ever extracted from the sludge in the 45-gallon drum. And get this, the day before everything happened at The Four Seasons, Marcus or Matt Smith, using an account in Marcus's name—the same account in which he shorted The Regent stock in August—bought a long position in The Regent stock. What if they just kidnapped Karl Lee and planned on releasing him eventually or something?"

"What do you mean?" one of the Deputy Marshals asked. "I don't follow."

"On November 12, it appears that Marcus Smith went long on an option contract, pursuant to which he has the right to buy 50,000 shares of The Regent stock at $10 per share on December 1. Right now, the stock is trading at $2 per share and The Regent has recently filed a Form 8K with the Securities and Exchange Commission indicating that "the Regent's going concern value is in question and that it is considering filing a Chapter 11 bankruptcy case." Most people would consider 'going long' on The Regent stock to be an utterly stupid investment strategy right now. But if the stock shoots up to, say, $20 per share, as of December 1, then Marcus can exercise his long option and purchase the 50,000 shares for $10 per share ($500,000) and it will be worth $20 per share ($1 million)."

"Shit! Get the canines back in here!" screamed one of the Deputy Marshals.

"Why?"

"I've got a strange feeling in my gut. Do you remember how the canines kept hovering near the closet in this room? We searched it again and again and never found anything. Let's bring them in now that the closet is emptied out. Let's see what the dogs do."

A few moments later, the Deputy Marshal canines, Polly and Brewster, were brought into the house and taken to the back bedroom. The dogs both immediately went to the empty closet, skidding across the slick hardwood floors as they approached. The dogs were actually trained to sniff out bombs, so their behavior was hard to decipher. They didn't make the usual signal to their handlers that they made when they identified explosive materials. But the dogs whimpered and acted agitated and kept sniffing at the floor boards in the closet. Earlier their behavior was harder to gauge than now. There had originally been a big trunk at the bottom of the closet. But now that trunk was gone, and the dogs anxiously and curiously clawed at the floor boards.

One of the Deputy Marshals had an idea. He began looking for loose planks. He found one. "Does someone have a crow bar or something similar?" Of course, someone had a crow bar. The Deputy Marshals have every tool imaginable in their G-rides. They are professionals. Moments later, expletives flew from several Deputy Marshals' mouths, as they crowded around the closet. A basement-like 8-by-8 covert room was underneath the ramshackle house. Bound and gagged and tied to a chair in the underground room was Karl Lee. He was passed out, but he did not look or smell dead.

Chapter 41:

The Fugitive.

Part of the reality that the United States Marshals Service must occasionally face is that they are not always going to catch their guy. It is an unpleasant fact of life for them. They don't like to lose a fugitive, but they sometimes do—at least for a while. Such is the case now with Marcus Smith, a.k.a. Marcus Braden.

Marcus Smith has never been tracked down. But the hunt for him will continue. The "Most Wanted" signs will go up on billboards and in U.S. Post Offices and with Interpol. There will be cooperation among law enforcement agencies nationwide and even worldwide. There will be surreptitious monitoring on occasion (the details of which are "classified"). Sooner or later, a great number of fugitives turn up—they eventually accidentally leave a trail of bread crumbs whether they realize it or not.

Karl Lee survived. When Karl Lee was found in late November in the small dilapidated house on Pluto Street, he was dehydrated, malnourished, and very weak. Perhaps Marcus Smith thought he would fairly expeditiously make it home to Pluto Street, in only a few hours or days after the Four Seasons episode, and he would keep Lee safe and sound a bit longer, until he was ready to take his next step with Lee—whatever that would be. But, as it turned out, Karl Lee was down in the Pluto Street underground prison, neglected for several days, until the Marshal/FBI hunch that led to his discovery (actually, the Marshal canines, Polly and Brewster, were the heroes that deserved all the credit).

As news broke that Karl Lee had been found by Deputy U.S. Marshals in Austin, Texas, after being missing for three-and-a-half months, and that he appeared to be in relatively good health, the stock price of The Regent soared, as did the stock prices of the other companies in the Karl Lee empire. Wall Street apparently expected that Lee would "right the ship" of his enterprise and soon the companies would bounce back to their former selves. Somewhere out there, Marcus Smith was once again enjoying a handsome profit based upon his amazing ability to "predict" the downward and upward cycles of the stock of Karl Lee's companies. Maybe he was not as slow witted as FBI Special Agent Navarrez had told Avery.

The FBI and U.S. Marshals continued to wonder whether it was a fluke that Marcus Smith had survived any harm from The Four Seasons episode, while Matt Smith perished. Was Matt Smith always intending to be a martyr that day at the Four Seasons or not? Did Matt Smith's plan change at the last minute? Did Matt originally envision that perhaps he would detonate only the pressure cooker bomb and bolt out wearing the suicide vest, and both he and Marcus would survive and somehow escape? Or was the master plan for Marcus to survive as a wealthy man all alone, without his twin brother? There were still a lot of unanswered questions. Among them, the FBI still wondered how the bodies of Judges Lupinaci and Murphy in the Ford Prefect somehow managed to wind-up in the McDonald's parking lot in Dallas, Texas last June, when Marcus had been in Portugal stalking Avery and her family during that time frame, and Matt had been at work every day in Dallas for that same time frame.

The U.S. Marshals' current "working theory" is that Marcus Smith is somewhere on a beach in Mexico. Mexico is not too far or difficult of an escape from Austin, Texas. And Marcus, of course, accumulated a nice nest egg created from his going short and long on The Regent stock. There was probably more money than the Feds had even been able to track down because, besides the money that Marcus Smith made maneuvering his buys and sells of The Regent stock, there was the millions of dollars wired out of one of Karl Lee's Hong Kong bank accounts into offshore accounts around the time that he went missing last August. This money was ultimately traced to an account in the Cook Islands, before the trail of money transfers went cold. Marcus likely had much more money (and Bitcoin) stashed away than anyone could imagine at this point.

Anyway, Avery said that she thought that the Marshals' "working theories" tended to be more reliable than those of the FBI. She also said that she bet that they would find Marcus Smith one day in Mexico. The U.S. Marshals had the best capture rate of any law enforcement agency in the world. They would be relentless in their pursuit of Marcus Smith. As Ginny from the Block would say, "he better be sleeping with one eye open. Kind of like Baxter does."

Avery didn't worry very much anymore. She would be more careful than ever about doing background checks for future interns, externs, and law clerks. She and her family would be extra cautious when retrieving and opening the daily mail. She said that she would forever grieve for the lost lives. She would never live a day without thinking of those lost lives and praying for their souls. But she would opt not to have U.S. Marshal protection anymore. The time for that was over. The Marshals had other things to do. Other sheep to protect. Important missions. Baxter had Avery back to himself finally. And he had his backyard back, too.

Chapter 42:

"It Ain't Over."

The note that Marcus Smith had left with the receptionist at the Green Acres Psychiatric Hospital in Austin, Texas, back on November 20, before he disappeared off the grid, had read: "It Ain't Over." And maybe it wasn't over after all. Marcus was, of course, believed to have slipped off to a Mexican beach somewhere. No one really knew for sure. The U.S Marshals and FBI continued to look for him.

On November 19, exactly two years after Judge Lassiter's original death threat letter (and on her 44th birthday), a package arrived in her chambers during the lunch hour. The return address was:

"Richard Braden, 42 Triq Birkirk, St Julian's, Malta STJ1217."

Annalise was out of the office on sick leave that day. Avery's newest intern, Lauren from SMU Law School, was opening the mail that day. She took a letter opener and broke open the seal. She pulled out the contents of the package. Inside was a book: *The Hitchhiker's Guide to the Galaxy*. Strange, Lauren thought. She left the day's mail, including the book, in Judge Lassiter's inbox on her desk that was designated for incoming mail.

Avery returned from lunch about 1:00 p.m. Ward Scott had taken her to lunch for her birthday at a new Stephen Pyles restaurant. As she put down her things, and sat down at her desk, she reached for the daily mail. A bar dues statement, legal periodicals, colorful holiday party invitations—the usual stuff. Suddenly she saw the book. Avery froze in startled terror in her chair.

Avery wasn't sure what to do. She needed to pause and collect her thoughts. She was tempted to phone the Marshals office immediately—as she knew she should—but she just couldn't bring herself to do it.

She eventually grabbed for some latex gloves that she kept handy in a desk drawer. Avery would forever have ingrained in her consciousness some of the precautionary measures that the Marshals had taught her during the Matt and Marcus Smith experience— namely, don't ever touch a suspicious package with your bare hands. She reached for the book. She cracked open the cover and inside there was a handwritten note on the front page:

"Hi, Judge Lassiter. Happy Birthday! You thought I was dead I bet—what with that nasty case of staph that I got as a little boy. I bet you didn't realize that the State of New Jersey does a rather shitty job of keeping up with its juveniles and does an even shittier job at protecting its computers from manipulation by hackers. Anyway, as Marcus said, 'It Ain't Over.' I am watching all your paths. I'll see you in 42 ... 42 minutes, 42 hours, 42 days, 42 weeks, 42 months ... well sometime. Fondly, Richard Braden (you know—the other brother)"

Epilogue: He Watches All My Paths—Avery's Post Note: A Tribute to the U.S. Marshals and Law Enforcement Everywhere.

"Honor never grows old. . . [H]onor is, finally, about defending those noble and worthy things that deserve defending, even if it comes at a high cost. . . that may mean social disapproval, public scorn, hardship, persecution, or as always, even death itself. The question remains: What is worth defending? What is worth dying for? What is worth living for?"

William J. Bennett, in a lecture to the United States Naval Academy, November 24, 1997.

There are many examples of unsung heroes in this world. And some heroes at least receive fifteen minutes of fame. But the United States Marshals Service definitely constitutes some of the unnoticed glue that holds our society together. They quietly protect the judiciary, the court family, and—most importantly—the public at large from untold harm. They are warriors and guardians. They are noble and honorable. They do not seek any glory. They avoid self-aggrandizement. They have nerves of steel. They stay in the shadows and keep us safe. To them, it is a matter of defending law and order— whatever the costs. They choose to do the hard things and they will die if they need to, because it is not about them and their comfort. Sacrifice is something that comes naturally for them. But the public at large usually does not see their work or ever know their names. They are largely quiet, anonymous heroes.

Guardians. Guardianship. All of us in life have a "higher calling" to be guardians to someone or something in this world. It is the highest privilege that we all have in our lives. Service (as well as honor) never grows old. A late, great judge in the Dallas federal courthouse used to greet his colleagues frequently with the following question: "What have you done for your country lately?"[8] The guardians always have done a lot for their country, on any given day. The guardians are like sheepdogs—hearty, good, and loyal—protecting their flock of sheep from danger, such as the wolves who, on the contrary, are predators and want to harm or kill the flock. Left to their own devices, the wolves will wreak carnage on the sheep without mercy.

Sometimes Officer Max talks about the terrible, sad things that he sees while doing his job. The streets where Officer Max serves can be so mean. He laments on some days that the world is an absolute cesspool. But still, it seems that most of humanity is kind and decent—productive people who care about other people, and would never intentionally harm anyone, and desire to make the world good. These are the sheep; the precious lambs. But the sheep and lambs need to have sheepdogs. They need warriors who are willing to walk into the heart of darkness, into the cesspool, and be fearless against the predators—and hopefully come out unscathed.

God gave everyone gifts—and life can be a challenge to discover and use those gifts. It seems as though God gave some people the gift of aggression, combined with a desire to use that aggression to help people. These are the warriors. There is nothing morally superior about being a sheepdog. It's just that the sheepdogs somehow can manage to survive and thrive in situations where others—the lambs and the more gentle humans—are paralyzed with

---

[8] The late great District Judge Barefoot Sanders, Northern District of Texas.

fear. And the sheepdogs—the guardians—choose to take on this role. They sniff out the perimeters. They stick their face into the wind. They bark at things that go bump in the night. They dutifully follow the danger to save others. As Lieutenant Colonel Dave Grossman has said,[9] they wait and yearn for the righteous battle. The sheepdogs think very differently from the sheep that they are protecting. The sheep in this world sometimes pretend or hold onto a fleeting hope that the wolves are not out there. Or they hope that they can change the nature of the wolves with time, effort, and patience. But the sheepdogs know better. They are counter-predators. They recognize that, unfortunately, sometimes they must resort to violence to counteract violence.

After a broadly publicized successful rescue mission by the U.S. Navy SEALs of a sea freighter off the Horn of Africa one Easter morning in the year 2009 (specifically, the freighter navigated by Captain Richard Phillips—later played by the actor Tom Hanks, in a movie), one of the heroic Navy SEALs (Ryan Job) who participated in that mission, killing Somali pirates in the process, was asked by a news reporter if he thought using Navy SEALs against Somali pirates was perhaps overkill. Mr. Job's response was, "despite what your mamma told you, violence does solve problems." This was the response of a sheepdog. A warrior. A guardian. A hero. But a lot of people simply do not understand. Maybe they just don't know what they don't know. Maybe they are lucky enough or blessed to have never stared into the face of evil during their lives. Maybe their family has never been threatened or harmed by one of these mad men.

---

[9] Dave Grossman, *On Combat: The Psychology and Physiology of Deadly Conflict in War and in Peace* (Warrior Science Group Inc. 2004).

Avery has realized more and more after her experience, and watching Officer Max, how duty-bound and self-sacrificing this subset of humanity is—the guardians. Lieutenant Colonel Grossman poses the question: Are we each genetically pre-disposed to be sheep, wolves or sheepdogs? Avery doesn't know. But, to the extent that she has a choice, she will never be like a head-in-the-grass lamb again.

Avery is grateful for her sheepdogs; her warriors. Her own husband is one of those sheepdogs. But she will never live her life depending on having a sheepdog nearby to guard her again. She will be a warrior herself. May God bless all the warriors.

"He keeps close watch on all my paths.

. . .

For God does speak—now one way, now another—though man may not perceive it.

In a dream, in a vision of the night, when deep sleep falls on men as they slumber in their beds.

He may speak in their ears and terrify them with warnings, to turn man from wrongdoing and keep him from pride.

To preserve his soul from the pit, his life from perishing by the sword.

. . .

He redeemed my soul from going down to the pit, and I will live to enjoy the light.

Job 33; 11-28.

My Cavalier King Charles Spaniel "Baxter"

If you enjoyed reading "He Watches All My Paths" please leave a review for my novel on Amazon or Good Reads. And if you would like to be notified on the release of the sequel, please follow my Author Page or follow me on Twitter @JudgeLassiter.

Made in the USA
Las Vegas, NV
07 February 2023

67093785R00184